Abject Authority

Clay Warrior Stories
Book #19

J. Clifton Slater

ii

Abject Authority is a work of fiction. Any resemblance to persons living or dead is purely coincidental. I am not an historian although, I do extensive research. This book is set in the time of the levied, seasonal Legion of the mid-Republic and not the fulltime Imperial Legion. There are huge differences.

The large events in this tale are taken from history, while the dialogue and close action sequences are my inventions. Some of the elements in the story are from reverse engineering mid-Republic era techniques and procedures. No matter how many sources I consult, history always has holes between events. Hopefully, you will see the logic in my methods of filling in the blanks.

The manuscript for *Abject Authority* has been stirred, mixed, shaken, and strained to remove double speak and dead-end plots by Hollis Jones. With each correction and red penned note, she has removed extra verbiage and tweaked the story. Her editing notes are the reason the tale makes sense and flows. I am grateful for her work and guidance.

All rights reserved by J. Clifton Slater

If you have comments, please e-mail me.

E-mail: GalacticCouncilRealm@gmail.com

To get the latest information about my books, visit my website. There you can sign up for my newsletter and read blogs about ancient history.

Website: www.JCliftonSlater.com

Thank you for being a part of Alerio's stories.

Euge! Bravo!

iv

Abject Authority

Act 1

The Latin tribes grew the Republic by force, if necessary, or intimidation when possible. Using their Legions, the Republic expanded the territory under their control. This included the northeast coast of Sicily, the Italian peninsula along both coasts, and northward through Tuscany.

Once subjugated, the allied tribes received the benefit of laws that assured property and personal rights. They inherited a currency where the value of the coins was consistent and acknowledged by training partners both within and outside their tribal lands. Further, the Republic embraced local Gods and Goddesses and added them to the pantheon of deities for worship.

And to manage the nominal yearly tribute for Rome and the number of auxiliary troops sent to the Legions, the Senate assigned Governors to the regions. Each a former Consul of Rome, the chief magistrates were either given the title of Praetor or Proconsul. Overall, the tribes thrived under the system. And Rome grew in resources and political sway.

Conversely, the people under the boots of Rome had the fabric of their society changed. Their currency was depressed to nothingness and their wealth stripped away by the new coins. Often Roman citizens purchased choice parcels of captured land. And while the locals had rights, they didn't have a vote or representation in the Senate.

And by placing the local Gods and Goddesses in with a multitude of deities, the peoples' once important objects of worship became entangled in a host of almost indistinguishable idols.

Adding to the dissatisfaction, the young men sent off to the Legion didn't always come home. But when they did, some brought home resentment. And the Governors, meant to hold the regions together, owed their allegiance to Rome and not to their district and the locals.

Despite the drawbacks, many communities lived with the reality. In settled regions, a Praetor served as the chief magistrate. He dealt with legal disputes and kept the peace. Although politically powerful, the Senate limited the Praetor to calling out a militia in response to riots, pirates, and bandits.

In unsettled regions, such as Sicilia and the northern borders of the Republic, the Governors held the title of Proconsul. Beyond the normal administrative work, these magistrates needed license to halt an invading army. To this end, the Senate authorized the Proconsuls to mobilize Legions, and to lead them against invaders.

Both types of magistrates, the Praetors and Proconsuls, had secretaries, enforcers, and investigators. The system of assistants allowed the chief magistrates to focus on the big picture. For the dirty details such as bodyguarding, crowd control, bringing in the accused, and investigating infractions, each magistrate had between eight and eleven Lictors.

Charged with managing the day-to-day issues of governing, Lictors needed to be tough and physically fit. These civil servants fell into two categories. Former Centurions doing a last assignment before fully retiring from the Legion. Or they were men starting on a political career by serving as Lictors.

Welcome to 251 B.C.

Chapter 1 – Do Something, Anything

Rasce strutted ahead of his brothers, Vesia and Cilnia. Although the footing on the steep trail made the trek difficult, as the eldest of the three, he felt it was his place to set the pace.

"Slow it up, Rasce," Vesia called from the back. "The horn and meat are heavy."

As the middle brother, Vesia assumed the role of mediator. He glanced back to check on the youngest. The inattention cost him. He tripped and sprawled face down on the hill. The giant horn from the wild mountain goat slid off his shoulder and tumbled away.

"Hold up," Cilnia shouted to Rasce. He stooped over his sibling and inquired. "Is anything broken?"

"Just my pride, little brother," Vesia assured him.

Cilnia moved forward, bent, and put two hands on the curved, five-foot long ibex horn. With a grunt, he lifted the huge bone to his shoulder.

"Do I need to come up there and carry both horns?" Rasce sneered. He easily bounced the other horn from one shoulder to the other. "Maybe I should carry you both."

"Shut up," Vesia said while adjusting the sack of ibex meat slung under his arm. "I tripped, get over it."

Rasce snorted, spun around, and strutted down the overgrown path.

"He's full of himself today," Cilnia noted. "You go ahead. The Nera River is at the foot of the hill, and I need to relieve myself. Make sure Rasce stops until I catch up."

"Want me to take the horn?" Vesia asked. "You already have the hide."

"No. It's my turn," the youngest replied.

Cilnia moved off the trail to do his business and Vesia rushed to catch up with Rasce. As he moved, he swung both hands to part the branches. With every swing, fall leaves fell around him in flashes of color. Free of the weight of the horn, he laughed and enjoyed the experience. At the top of the final slope, with the sounds of the Nera River splashing over rocks, he yelled.

"Rasce, hold up and wait for…" Vesia reached the top of the embankment, parted the last tree limbs, and froze.

His older brother knelt on the river stones. To his front were Legion spears and javelins while on Rasce's flanks Republic archers stood with arrows notched on their bows. When Vesia appeared through the trees, five arrowheads shifted to target him.

***

"Get down here and get on your knees," Optio Montem directed. "Where is the Bronze Man?"

At the mention of the highwayman, the fingers of the inexperienced archers twinged, and the shafts held by the newly trained light infantrymen wobbled. Their eyes roamed from the two men on their knees to the wall of foliage at the top of the bank, and back to the men on the river stones. Searching, they feared an attack from the forest by the Bronze Man.

At the height of their tension, the younger brother plunged into the tense situation.

"Look out below," Cilnia teased, "here comes the horn of justice."

Realizing that in his zeal, his younger sibling was charging into the patrol, Vesia jumped to his feet.

"It's only my…"

In that moment, Cilnia broke through the trees. Holding the wicked looking horn out front, he appeared to be assaulting the detachment.

***

The arc from aiming at the man who jumped to his feet to the bandit charging down the embankment took less than a heartbeat. Three arrows plucked Cilnia off his feet. While the youth died, the prized horn slid down the hill.

Vesia spun and ran with the intention of helping his little brother.

"Don't let that one get away," Optio Montem ordered.

Two arrows in his side took the middle brother to his knees. And a well thrown javelin drove the body of Vesia face first into the river stones. Seeing his siblings slaughtered, Rasce pulled his skinning knife and jumped at the closest Legionary.

But Montem had watched the big man closely. When Rasce leaped, the Optio slipped in front of his Legionaries. With an upper thrust, he propelled his gladius blade into the man's chest.

"What now, Sergeant?" a squad leader inquired.

Montem studied the three corpses while cleaning his blade. Slabs of meat and a fresh ibex hide stuck out from slings scattered beside the bodies. Along with a pair of giant mountain goat horns, he realized his patrol had killed a trio of hunters. Because the ibexes lived high in the mountains, the three couldn't have been involved in yesterday's robbery.

"Assign body bearers for the dead and others to carry the meat," the Optio instructed. "We'll take them back to the stockade and let the Centurion sort it out."

"What about the horns?" an archer questioned.

"I suppose the metalworker can use them to make knife handles," Montem considered. "We might as well take them. Let's go people, I want to be back at the fort before dark."

***

Two days later, at the cooperative's depot in Rieti, Grantian Suasus tossed a bundle of cotton sacks into his wagon. The material covered the lead pipes that occupied most of the cart's bed.

"I'll send word when we get in the rope," the shopkeeper promised. "Are you sure you won't stay and have a cup of vino?"

"No, the child and I need to get home," the Roman farmer replied. He rested a hand on his son's head. "His mother will have a fit if I keep him out after dark."

Pollio Suasus wanted to move out from under his father's possessive hand. As all seven-year-olds do, he balked at being called a child. Plus, being reminded his mother still controlled his life, irked the boy. But he remained in place, allowing the senior Suasus to ruffle his hair.

"Come on lad," Grantian urged, "let's get the supplies back to the farm."

With his father's help, Pollio mounted a horse. Once Grantian was seated on his horse, a servant snapped the reins, and a team of mules set the full cart in motion. They moved away from the depot, traveling slowly through the streets of Rieti. Being late in the day, little traffic delayed their passage. And despite the mules' gait and the heavy load, they soon left the town behind.

Once on the Viale Emilio Maraini, Grantian Suasus sat straighter and perused the landscape.

"This was once a lake and a marsh," Grantian explained. He waved his arm to indicate a wide stretch of the valley. Fields under cultivation and the estates of Roman citizens dotted the former lakebed. "Twenty-two years ago, Consul Manius Dentatus defeated the Sabine Tribes and claimed the territory for the Republic."

The boy got excited and started hopping up and down in the saddle.

"The General was a giant and used his hands to push the land upward," Pollio offered. "Then he tipped it over and poured the Velino River into the Nera."

Grantian laughed at the tale. He had heard and repeated it when he was a schoolboy.

"Dentatus was a great General and a wise Consul, but he was hardly a giant," Grantian clarified. "During the early days of his administration, leaders from the Sabine Tribe came to him with a problem. The center of the Rieti Valley was a lake surrounded by swamps. Anyone living near the marshlands got sick. Seeking to keep the peace, the General charged his engineers with finding a solution. After studying the problem for a year, his Legion engineers told him to cut a channel through the rock on high ground and divert the Velino River. With Dentatus' approval, they started by building dams on the river around a worksite. Then they chiseled away wagon loads of rock. Finally, they cut a notch along the clifftop and allowed the waters of the Nera and Velino rivers to joins. Together they fall five hundred and forty feet to the Nera River."

"And that dried up the swamp," Pollio guessed, "is now farmland."

"The channel on the high ground plus a trench down the middle of the valley did dry out the marshland and drain the lake," Grantian confirmed. "Your grandfather purchased our farm from the General when the land was still under a foot of water."

"How did he know it wouldn't make us sick?" Pollio asked.

"Stagnant water was the culprit," his father told him. "Moist earth is productive. It's as simple as that."

Three miles outside of town, they left the Viale Emilio Maraini. Once off the main road, the wagon trail became rutted and pockmarked with washouts.

"I should assign a few fieldhands to level this road," Grantian remarked as they neared a tree line. "They have nothing to do until spring planting."

"But this isn't our land or road," Pollio commented. "Our property line is ahead."

"We use the road. Therefore, we should take some responsibility for…"

Grantian Suasus ceased talking and reined in his horse. The servant halted the mule team and wagon. Young Pollio rode a few more paces before easing his mount to a stop. Something in the woods caught their attention. Then a Greek Hoplite emerged from the trees.

His bronze helmet, and bronze breast plate flashed in the afternoon light. Glowing from the reflective surfaces, the man stepped onto the wagon trail as if a fearsome spirit.

"Latian. Hold your caravan and pass over your coins," the highwayman instructed.

Other men stepped from around tree trunks. Folds of material over their faces hid their identities, and each held a spear. Knowing he was outnumbered, Grantian Suasus had no intention of fighting. But his Latin pride required that the insult of being robbed could not go unchallenged.

"Bronze Man, someday I'll see you crucified," Grantian swore. "If I had my armor, I'd ride you down like a dog and whip you."

"Well, Latian, I'm right here," the bandit argued. "Come test me."

With his bluff called, Grantian deflated in the saddle.

"That's what I thought. All you Romans quake in fear of an Etruscan warrior," the Bronze Man stated. "You are all cowards."

At the insult, Pollio Suasus squared his small shoulders, kicked his mount into motion, and charged at the highwayman.

"My father is not a coward," the boy screamed.

Within three strides, a spear arched up from the trees then tipped downwards before sweeping the boy off his horse. Pollio's small body jerked once as if trying to fight off the shaft that passed through his body. Then he relaxed, pinned to the ground like a bird brought down by a giant arrow.

"Pollio, Pollio," Grantian cried. He dismounted and ran to his son. With the little body in his arms, he asked. "Why? Why?"

The Bronze Man walked to the grieving father, reached down, and placed a quarter of a bronze coin on the boy's forehead.

"Because you are here," he whispered, "and your kind shouldn't be."

9

Grantian Suasus remained on the ground with his son in his arms. The highwayman and his gang took the horses and the wagon. When they had gone, Grantian scooped up Pollio in his arms. Rather than heading to his Villa, the father turned back towards Rieti.

"Proconsul Crassus, I am bringing you the latest victim of the Bronze Man," he bellowed into the darkening sky. "Do something, anything, to stop the murderer. But know this, nothing you do will bring back my son."

***

The servant followed Grantian through town and into the compound of the Governor's Villa. The farmer's arrival caused a flurry of activity. Before dawn, a messenger raced away with a letter to Praetor Blasio on the coast at Pescara.

In short, the letter begged for secrecy and help. While Proconsul Crassus could mobilize a Legion, he had no force to engage. And with the unrest in the Sabine Territory, all his staff members and Lictors were occupied with pacifying the locals and calming the citizens. If word got back to the Senate that one bandit had pushed a Proconsul to the breaking point, Otacilius Crassus' career would be over. He begged Praetor Blasio for the favor of silence and the blessing of a solution.

Three days later, the messenger returned with a letter. Written on the back of the parchment were five words.

'The scarred Lictor is in route'

Crassus bundled up the letter and threw it across the room.

"I have eleven Lictors at my disposal and a Legion," he roared. "What good will another bodyguard do?"

His chief of staff walked to the discarded letter and read the words. Then he pondered, "What does Praetor Blasio have in mind?"

Chapter 2 - Via Salaria

The gate sentry glanced at the sun and judged his shift to be half over. It meant another long, chilly afternoon of pacing from gate post to gate post. Then his eyes caught movement down the trail.

"What have we here?" he asked.

The stockade sat a mile from a crossroads. Most merchants and travelers used the throughfare of the Via Salaria to head south to Rome. Or they journeyed west to reach Umbria or the Sabine regions and beyond those the coast of the Adriatic sea. Few travelers journeyed north along the Tiber River to the city of Orvieto and deeper into Etruscan territory.

Civilian visitors, unless part of a supply convoy, were rare on the wagon trail leading to the Legion fort. One man on a horse cart offered a novelty for the bored sentry.

"Stop right there," the Legionary ordered as the wagon approached. "What's your business?"

"Dried and salt packed tuna and swordfish from the Adriatic Sea," the driver replied. When the Legionary shuffled his feet and frowned, the peddler advised. "Now if your Centuries don't want the opportunity, I can push onto Orvieto. I'm sure there are some rich men there who would enjoy dining on fish steaks."

"Orvieto is fifty miles up the Tiber," the sentry countered.

"That it is. But the fish are dried, packed in salt, and will keep," the seller remarked. Then he creased his eyebrows and inquired. "Or are you reminding me of the distance as a bargaining point? Possibly, to lower my prices. Very shrewd of you."

The gate sentry had no intention of bargaining. He mentioned the distance to the city on the plateau as a commonsense response. However, being identified as a man who could barter felt good.

"What's it worth to you if I allow you in?" the sentry inquired.

Before the vendor replied, the Sergeant of the Guard marched to the gate.

"Allow who in?" he asked.

"Optio, I was bargaining with the fish seller for a couple of tuna steaks," the sentry reported. "One for you and one for me."

"You forgot the Centurion," the NCO said. Then to the vendor. "It'll cost you three fish steaks to sell in my stockade."

The peddler touched the brim of his felt petasos in salute and snapped the reins.

"Sounds reasonable," he allowed as the horse and cart rolled through the gate.

Neither the sentry nor his NCO questioned why a fish seller from the Adriatic coast would bypass other forts and towns to reach their stockade. And they failed to note the horse wasn't a draft animal, but a stallion barely held in check by a tight hold on the reins.

"Good call," the NCO complimented the sentry. "Most guards would have let him in without extracting a toll."

"Gee, Optio, I might have a future in business," the Legionary suggested.

"Don't get a big head," the Sergeant of the Guard warned. "I'll keep your fish in the salt until you get off duty."

***

Alerio Sisera guided Phobos across the drill field towards a spot where his cart was visible to anyone leaving the barracks.

"A few years ago, you would have bitten the Optio," Alerio said to the horse. "I guess we've both matured and settled…"

The stallion reared up as they passed the animal pens. Inside the fence, cavalry mounts either shied away or issued a challenge to the stallion.

"He's fatigued and irritable from the trail," Alerio told a few passing Legionaries. "I guess the mounts frightened him."

"You should brush him to calm his nerves," a cavalryman recommended, "or he'll be on edge all evening."

"An excellent idea," Alerio responded while guiding the wagon around. "Can you send a stableman over with a bucket of water and some straw?"

"What do I look like," the man shot back, "your servant?"

Alerio had forgotten he was undercover and not traveling as a Colonel of the Legion. After positioning the cart, he climbed down and limped around to unharnessed Phobos.

"That's not a wagon horse," a youth observed.

He was dirty in the way an animal handler got soiled. Mud and other substances clung to his feet and lower legs while saliva and straw dust coated his upper body.

"Like me, he was once a war horse," Alerio told him. "I'll trade you a fish steak for some water and straw."

"What's a fish steak?"

"You've had mountain bass," Alerio offered. The youth shook his head in the affirmative. "It's like a section of the bass only as big as your face."

"For that, I'll bring him a bag of grain to go with the straw and water," the young stableman promised.

Alerio pulled a wineskin from under the cart's bench, strolled to the back of the wagon, and untied a tarp. He tossed back the cover exposing layers of salt and fish.

Lifting his arms, he announced, "Fish, fresh from the sea. And sea salt as sweet as honey. Fish steaks, fresh from the sea. Come, and get them."

***

During the afternoon, off duty Legionaries stopped by, bought steaks, and left. And while the load of fish and salt vanished, several Legionaries hung around the cart.

"It seems very peaceful here," Alerio mentioned while passing around a wineskin. "Not that I'm complaining. Years ago in this district, our Legion got stomped by the Etruscans."

"You were at Orvieto?" one asked.

"Back then we called it Volsinii, and yes I was with Gurges Legion when we were broken," Alerio replied. "But now, it's a wonder you don't die of boredom."

"Oh, we have some action," one informed Alerio. "Just two weeks ago, one of our auxiliary patrols had a tussle with some of the Bronze Man's gang."

Another grasped the wineskin and shook it as if strangling someone.

"At least we assumed they were in his crew," he whined. "Turned out, they were three Etruscan brothers returning from a hunt."

"Their father and the tribe's headman are coming to speak with the Tribune in the morning," the first Legionary stated. "That's going to be a messy meeting."

"Who is this Bronze Man and how did the brother's get mistaken for members of his gang?" Alerio questioned.

A veteran Optio pushed to the front and took the wineskin.

"The Bronze Man wears a Greek helmet and a chest piece both made from bronze," he explained. "But that's not where he gets the name. Every time he robs a Roman citizen, he leaves a quarter of a piece of a bronze coin."

"They say, the Bronze Man is never really seen when seen, never found when found, and never caught when caught," an infantryman volunteered. "It's why the brothers were executed. The Optio thought they were sneaking back across the border."

"Why would the patrol expect the gang to cross the border?" Alerio asked.

"Because, the Bronze Man boasts that Roman citizens fear Etruscan warriors," the NCO replied. "It's only logical that he and his brigands would flee home after the murdering and pillaging."

"Have you encountered gang members in the area before?" Alerio asked. "Or found their trails?"

"No. But the mountains are big and it's easy to lose them in the valleys up there," the Optio pointed to the peaks rising to the northeast of the fort.

"Never really seen when seen, never found when found, and never caught when caught," the infantryman repeated.

"Keep the wineskin," Alerio told the group. "I've got to go and have a talk with your Tribune."

"Are you sure a staff officer will want to talk with a fish seller?"

"He will," Alerio said as he went to the cart's bench, reached under it, and pulled out a wrapped object. "What's his name?"

"His name is Miratoris. For all the good it'll do you," the Sergeant commented.

Alerio smiled at the NCO, rested the wrapped object on his shoulder, and limped to the headquarters building.

***

Inside the administration office, Alerio looked over the staff until he located a Senior Centurion.

"I'll speak with Tribune Miratoris," he announced.

"Tell me fish seller," the senior combat officer inquired, "why would my staff officer want to speak with you?"

"Tell him, Praetor Blasio sends his regards."

The fish seller was Latin, and most likely a citizen. He had those going for him. But the real reason the Senior Centurion carried the message back to the Tribune's office was the mention of a Praetor of Rome. Few men would chance the punishment that came with casually throwing around the name of a chief magistrate.

"Wait right there," the combat officer ordered.

"Yes, sir," Alerio confirmed.

After years of trudging over rough ground, the Senior Centurion didn't so much march as he swayed. The same stiff kneed gait that took him down the hallway, brought him back moments later.

"Tribune Miratoris will see you," he declared. "Do you need me to hold that until you're done?"

The Centurion pointed to the wrapped object resting on Alerio's shoulder.

"No, thank you, Centurion," Alerio replied.

He limped across the office floor and the combat officer noticed.

"Legion injury?" he asked.

Alerio stopped, glanced down at the knee brace, and nodded.

"An Iberian spear in Sicilia," Alerio lied.

"That'll do it," the Senior Centurion acknowledged. "I caught an arrow in my hip a few years back. Still hurts in wet weather."

"That'll do it," Alerio observed before continuing down the hallway.

***

"You better have a good reason for mentioning Praetor Cornelius Blasio," a middle-aged staff officer threatened.

Based on the Tribune's age and location, he was either the youngest son of a wealthy family or a career military man. In one case, the patriarch parked him in a garrison command until the family required his presence at home. If career, he was waiting for an assignment to a Consul's Legion where he could earn glory and advancement. Neither scenario addressed the staff officer's competence.

"I need four things," Alerio instructed while he untied the bindings on the object he carried.

"You didn't answer my question," Miratoris countered.

"Tribune, you didn't ask a question," Alerio remarked. "Just as I didn't ask one."

In Alerio's experience, weak staff officers became unhinged when corrected. He didn't have to, but he couldn't resist poking at the Tribune to evaluate the man.

"You're right, I didn't ask a question," Miratoris confirmed. "And you aren't a fish peddler, are you?"

"No, sir," Alerio said as he stripped the fur wrap from a double-bladed ax. He placed the ax on the Tribune's desk.

Miratoris reached out and with reverence traced the gold and silver inlays on the ax heads.

"You're a Lictor from Rome," he guessed.

"All enforcers are from Rome," Alerio told him. "No matter the chief magistrate we're assigned to, our authority comes from the Senate."

"I've seen Consul processions. The head Lictor carried an ax bundled with a ring of birch rods. It was over five feet long and tied with strips of red leather. This is a little less imposing."

"Can you imagine a field investigator lugging around a ceremonial fasces?" Alerio asked. "This double blade is less intrusive. But it still symbolizes my Lictor's authority to enforce the law and punish the guilty."

"Why bring it to me?"

"As I stated, I require four things," Alerio responded. "I need information on the latest victims of the Bronze Man. A letter to Proconsul Crassus stating that I left the ax with you. And your assurance that the ax will be protected."

"You're here to stop the Bronze Man," Miratoris commented. "How can you do that when others have failed?"

"I'll start with the bronze coins he's leaving with the victims," Alerio answered. "And because I'm unknown to the citizens in this area and the Sabine tribesmen, I can move around without drawing attention to myself."

"What's the fourth thing you need?"

"A bed for the night," Alerio replied. "I've been on the road for five days sleeping on the ground. I'm sick of being cold and feeling rocks in my spine when I roll over."

"You'll of course join me for dinner?"

"I'm afraid Tribune that would ruin the surprise."

"What surprise?"

"The one for the Bronze Man when I run my blade through his heart," Alerio told the staff officer. "Until then, I'm just a Legion veteran with a bad knee looking for work."

"What else do you need?"

"Sir, I need you to loudly throw me out of your office," Alerio said. "Maybe with a mention that you don't care how many Naval Crown medals I have."

"Do you have a Naval Crown?"

"Two, actually," Alerio answered.

The staff officer wrote on a piece of parchment then waved it in the air to dry the ink. While Alerio reviewed the letter, Miratoris jotted down on another piece the names and villas of the latest victims. Alerio rolled both and put them under his shirt.

"Now, sir."

"Get out of my office," the Tribune shouted. "I don't care how many times you led attacks on enemy ships-of-war. I don't have anything for a cripple. Get out of my office. And I want you off my post first thing in the morning."

Alerio saluted and dropped his shoulders in resignation. He marched out of the Tribune's office and into the chest of the Senior Centurion.

"Don't you worry about him, sir," the combat officer assured his Tribune, "I know how to manage his kind."

With gentle pressure on the small of Alerio's back, he guided them out of the administration office. Outside the headquarters building, they turned in the direction of the Senior Centurion's quarters.

The peddler might have to leave in the morning. But the senior combat officer wasn't about to let a decorated veteran sleep outside in the dirt on a cold night.

Chapter 3 – Pieces of Coins

At mid-morning, Alerio nudged Phobos over the top of a long steep grade. Under the horse's hooves, the well-traveled dirt track of the Via Salaria transitioned to stone pavers. Along with the road improvements, a town appeared where the trail split.

Alerio reined in Phobos and scanned the ancient structures.

"What village is this?" he asked an old Sabine man sitting beside the road.

"It's Pallatium," the oldster replied. "Forty miles from the Latian Capital. And eight from Rieti."

"Seems like a nice place."

"It was," the old man griped.

"Was?" Alerio asked. "What happened?"

"Your General Dentatus happened," the man replied. "Twenty-two years ago, he marched his Legions through here, and the place hasn't been the same."

"I think that's called progress?" Alerio teased.

"Call it what you want," the Sabine scolded. "Everyone is rushing to Rome for who knows what. Or their dashing off to Rieti. In my day, we backpacked salt from the marshes at Ostia and sold it here in the market. These days, you Latians run salt carts right by here without stopping."

"You could always move," Alerio suggested.

"Pallatium has been here for hundreds of years and I for seventy of them," the man explained. "I only hope I die before the town does."

"I hope you get your wish," Alerio said as he urged the stallion forward.

Then he caught himself and wondered if wishing death on the old Sabine was a good thing or a bad thing. He'd have to trust the Goddess Nenia to make the judgement.

At a creek, he dismounted, brushed Phobos, and allowed the horse to graze. Looking around, Alerio could see old foundations and rotten boards on the outskirts of the village. From the placement of the ruins, he could tell this spot of civilization along the salt trail was vanishing little by little.

***

The hub of Rieti came into view shortly after midday. Behind the government and commercial buildings and the residential structures, cultivated fields spread to the north. The entire area reflected an abundance of timber and agricultural wealth. Some fields were brown after the harvest, while others displayed winter grain, greens, and root crops. The produce stretched from one side of the valley to the other. It was good land and Alerio grew a little jealous of the rich soil.

He located a café and dismounted.

"I'm looking for the Suasus farm," he mentioned to the waiter as he sat at a table.

"Oh, the Suasus estate, such a tragedy," the server told him. He dropped his head in reverence for a heartbeat but brightened quickly. "Take the center road for three miles and turn left. Three miles on, you'll find a road to the farm. Today, we have lamb and vegetable stew."

The jump from commiseration to business wasn't lost on the Lictor. Apparently, the Sabines weren't terribly enamored with their Roman neighbors.

***

After the meal, Alerio took the Viale Emilio Maraini out of Rieti. At the three-mile marker, he guided Phobos onto a wagon track. As he rode, he admired the farmland. Now he could see the richness of the soil that made the abundance in the valley possible. As the son of a farmer, he was envious. But the rough surface of the trail in the middle of such prosperity annoyed him. Then he recalled the murder of the Suasus child and replaced the criticism with analytical thinking.

By the time he neared a grove of trees, Alerio had reached the extent of his knowledge on the issue. His mind thirsted for new information. He pulled Phobos to a stop.

"This must be where it happened," he said while patting the stallion's shoulder.

A brick and board altar stood beside the dirt road. Flowers lay scattered over the surface around a clay idol of Orbona. Alerio wasn't sure if the Goddess of Children had done her job by allowing Pollio Suasus to die. Then again, she had given the boy seven years of life.

He dismounted and walked through the trees. At spots, he noted areas of crushed grass. He counted the places where the robbers had waited and found a larger space where they collected around a set of ruts from a cart. Based on the damage done to the grass, he figured the robbers had waited a long time for their prey. How would highwaymen know the road and the traffic patterns well enough to lounge around before an attack?

With only questions after the inspection, Alerio went to the altar. As a sacrifice, he sprinkled salt on the clay image of the Goddess Orbona.

But his pray went to a different deity, "Goddess Nenia, I hope you took the boy quickly."

After showing his respects, Alerio mounted Phobos and urged the horse back onto the wagon track. As the waiter described, he easily located the next turn off. Guiding Phobos onto the farm road, he headed for the Suasus estate.

***

At the front of the villa, a servant intercepted Alerio, "Can we help you, sir?"

He reached for the bridle, but Phobos nipped at him. Jerking back, the servant avoided the stallion's teeth.

"You're lucky. He usually kicks," Alerio told the man as he slipped from the saddle. "I'm here to see Master Suasus."

Alerio led Phobos to a grassy patch under a stand of trees.

"Sir, the Master isn't receiving visitors," the servant pleaded. "If you leave your name, I'll pass it to him."

"That doesn't fit my schedule," Alerio informed the man. He marched towards the front steps while advising. "You might want to get ahead of me and warn him."

On the way to the porch, the servant ran by Alerio, sprinted up the steps, and raced through the doorway.

"That helps," Alerio mumbled. "If he had closed the door and bolted it, I'd have to kick it down."

A middle-aged man in a stained tunic appeared in the doorframe. Besides the state of his garment, his eyes were red and swollen.

"Grantian Suasus?" Alerio questioned.

"Yes, that's me. Who are you?"

"In the Table of Laws, Table VII states under Land Rights and Crimes," Alerio recited, "people who live near the road are charged with maintaining it. If the road is not well maintained, then carts and animals can be ridden where the riders want to travel. Your road is a mess, Suasus. I'm surprised your neighbors aren't riding through your garden in protest."

"I know the law," Grantian growled. His eyes showed a little fire. "I asked who you are?"

"Lictor Alerio Sisera and we need to talk."

The farmer straightened his back and focused his eyes on the woolen travel clothing and the felt hat.

"How do I know you're a Lictor? Where's your fasces?"

"About the fasces, it's a long story," Alerio responded. "Don't make this difficult. I need to ask you about the Bronze Man."

At the mention of the murdering bandit, Grantian Suasus stepped aside and gestured for the Lictor to enter.

Alerio wanted to feel badly about quoting the law to a grieving father. But it helped snap Grantian Suasus out of his melancholy. Comforted by that thought, Lictor Sisera entered the villa.

***

Later in the estate's office over mugs of vino, Grantian Suasus told his heartbreaking story.

"I am sorry for your loss," Alerio said acknowledging the sad tale. "But I'm not a priest. My job is to find the Bronze Man and bring him to justice."

"The point of your blade is all the justice I want for him," Grantian responded.

"If it comes to that be assured, I won't hesitate," Alerio promised. "Right now, I want as much detail as you can remember."

Grantian reached to a side table and picked up a small porcelain bowl. He placed it on his desk in front of Alerio.

"Latians quake in fear of an Etruscan warrior and we are all cowards," Grantian recalled. "When I cried and asked why he murdered my son, he placed this quarter of a coin on my son's forehead. Because you are here, and your kind shouldn't be, were his words."

"What did he mean by that?" Alerio asked while fishing the small piece of bronze from the bowl.

On one side, the slice of coin had the imprint of a wheat shaft along the edge with what appeared to be clouds at the center of the coin. Turning the wedge shape over, Alerio noted a pair of legs stamped on the reverse side. A few letters rubbed smooth by use were illegible.

"I have to think he and his outlaws are Etruscans angry about the last war," Grantian replied. "They have no reluctance to injuring or killing during the robberies."

"Do you recognize this coin?"

"No. But truthfully, I've barely looked at it," the farmer admitted. "It reminds me too much of that day."

"Can I keep it?"

"Yes, of course. What else do you need, Lictor?"

"A note of introduction and directions to the villa of another victim."

"Do you really think you can catch him?" Grantian asked while scratching a note on a piece of parchment. "I'd like to be there if you do."

He handed the letter to Alerio.

"Fix your road Master Suasus and take care of yourself and your farm."

"Yes, Lictor Sisera," Grantian replied.

***

By the time he got back to the main road, a chill in the air warned of a cold night. Alerio pulled a fur jacket from a pouch and slipped it over his woolen shirt. He should be heading for Rieti to find a room for himself and a stable for Phobos. But the next villa lay due west and was only a mile farther down the road.

Pulling the reins, he turned the stallion north and pushed the animal to a trot.

"This'll warm us up," he said to Phobos.

The beast took the road in quick strides and the four-mile marker came into view moments later. Allowing the stallion to maintain the pace, he guided Phobos onto another farm road and they rapidly approached a large villa.

But there wasn't a single servant in the yard to greet him at this one.

"Turn around and leave," a man instructed, "or draw your blade and die."

He held a steel tipped spear in a proper guard position. On one side of him, an older man brandished a gladius, supported by a large servant, and on the other side two servants with harvesting implements completed a defensive line.

To spare the stallion an injury if he moved forward, Alerio tuned Phobos to the side and spoke directly to the man with the spear.

"Good posture and foot placement," he observed, "shaft held loose, and shoulders relaxed. You're Legion trained. And from the lowered head, I'd say a heavy infantryman."

"How does your head position tell him that?" the older man inquired.

"A Legionary can only see just above his shield and below his helmet, grandfather," the man replied. "After a while, you tilt your head down and look forward with your eyes before any fight."

"And how does he know that?"

"Well, sir," Alerio answered, "I'm a Legion weapons' instructor. Or rather I was before I got promoted."

"Promoted to what, Centurion?" the grandson inquired.

"Let me introduce myself," Alerio said holding out the note from Grantian Suasus. One of the servants took it and carried the letter to the old man. "I am Alerio Sisera, and I'm a Lictor from the Senate of the Republic."

"I know all of Crassus' enforcers," the elder challenged. "But I don't know you."

"You wouldn't," Alerio informed him. "They're too well known to catch the Bronze Man."

"And you being a stranger gives you freedom of movement?"

"That is the plan, sir."

"Siponar, Grantian's note vouches for him," the grandfather stated.

"I'm Siponar Della and this is my grandfather, Rovere Della," the grandson said. "Let's go inside, grandfather doesn't handle the night air as well as he once did."

"I'm as fit as any man," Rovere Della boasted.

"I'm sure you are, sir," Alerio offered. "But I've been on the road most of the day and the chill is effecting my knee."

"In that case, come inside and we'll talk by the fireplace," Rovere directed. "Siponar, have the stableman take care of his horse."

"He's a bit temperamental," Alerio warned while slipping from the saddle. "I better take him."

"I'll walk with you," Siponar volunteered. "We'll be along shortly, grandfather."

"Fine, fine but don't tell any Legion stories without me being there to hear," Rovere requested.

The old man shuffled slowly to the villa with the help of a servant. Siponar rested the spear on his shoulder while he and Alerio walked Phobos to the stable.

"I was with Proconsul Florus' Legion in Sicilia," Siponar Della explained. "Twenty-Second Century, Fourth Squad."

"So, I was right, you were a heavy infantryman," Alerio noted. "What happened between you and the Bronze Man?"

"It wasn't me," Siponar replied. "It was my grandfather and probably a good thing."

"Why is that?" Alerio asked while he guided Phobos into a stall.

"I would have fought and died," Siponar suggested. "Because everyone who has resisted the Bronze Man has been killed."

"No one wounded?" Alerio inquired.

He closed the stall door and leaned on it for a moment.

"Everyone who resists him is murdered," Siponar assured him.

Alerio pushed off the door and headed for the villa. His mind spun around the information. What bandit intentionally escalated the reason to be hunted? More questions, and still no answers.

***

After dining, the three relaxed with wine in front of a fireplace. And much to the delight of Rovere Della, Siponar and Alerio told stories from their days in the Legion. Eventually, Alerio turned serious and addressed the older man.

"Master Della, tell me about the Bronze Man," Alerio encouraged.

"Not much to tell," Rovere responded. "My manservant and I were in my coach heading back from a neighbor's villa. Suddenly, five men, one with a Greek helmet and a bronze chest piece stepped in front of the horse."

The old man shook his fist at the fire.

"They took the coach and horse and his coin purse," Siponar finished answering for his grandfather. "But they didn't harm anyone."

"Did they leave a piece of a coin?"

Rovere pushed out of the chair, then stopped. "They did. I can't remember where I put it. But, if that Etruscan crook was here, I'd show him we Romans aren't cowards."

"That tidies up my next question," Alerio stated.

"That's it," Rovere announced.

He left the room leaving Alerio and Siponar puzzled. They sipped from their mugs until the old man strutted back into the room.

"When Siponar returned from Sicilia, my wife put his medals in a box to tidy up his dresser," Rovere declared. "I dropped the bronze coin in the box when I got home."

Alerio took the quarter of a coin and examined it. Like the first one, the lettering was rubbed smooth. But he made out what appeared to be a bunch of grapes on a vine on one side, and another pair of legs on the reverse.

"Were you robbed just before Grantian Suasus?"

"No, Lictor," Siponar informed him, "there were two other holdups between them."

Alerio held the edges of the coins together. They were from the same coin or at least from the same minting. But all he had were a bunch of grapes on one side, and two pairs of legs on the other half of the coin.

"You'll stay the night, Lictor?" Rovere asked.

"It will be my pleasure, Master Della."

Act 2

Chapter 4 – Order of incidents

In the morning, Alerio guided Phobos to the Viale Emilio Maraini. After turning north, they followed the road as it curved to the east. The mountains drew closer and Alerio pondered the richness of the forest and the excellent soil in the Rieti Valley. But for all his early morning ponderings, he couldn't visualize a swamp covering the acreage. Or imagine how much water it would take to bury the farmland. At the seven-mile marker, he and the stallion took a farm road towards a villa built on a raised finger of land.

The elevation wasn't much more than a steep mound, but it allowed the residents a commanding view of the fields, the Viale Emilio Maraini, and the path to the house. When two men stepped into the roadway and blocked his path, there was no doubt of their military training.

"We don't get many strangers around here," one said over the top of a Legion shield. "State your business."

His spear rested on the rim as steady as if an Optio would be along shortly to review his shield and spear drill. A second man with the same war gear stood to the speaker's right. His shield tucked in close to protect his partner's flank.

"I wanted to ask about the Bronze Man," Alerio replied. "But seeing you two, I'll ask for an exercise session first."

"Legion?" the speaker asked.

"I was once a Colonel, and before that, a weapons' instructor," Alerio replied. He extended Grantian's note. "But I have a new job."

The right-side man stepped forward using the scutum as cover. He took the note and stepped back before reading it.

"He's a Lictor."

"I know Proconsul Crassus' Lictors, but I don't recognize this one," the other man replied.

"They brought me in from the Adriatic coast to hunt the Bronze Man and his gang," Alerio explained.

"One man to find the murderers?" the infantryman questioned. "How can you succeed when the entire Northern Legion can't?

"Because the Legion commanders are seeking an enemy to battle," Alerio clarified. "I'm looking for the tracks of a Lynx."

"The Lynx is a crafty animal," the flanker noted.

"I'm Smalt Semitalis and this is my brother Lentul," said the man with the centered spear. He lowered the weapon. "Come to the house and we can talk."

Alerio dismounted and walked with the brothers to a patio garden between two buildings. He tied Phobos to a post. While Lentul brought over a bucket of water for the stallion, Alerio joined Smalt at a table.

"Our father had relieved me on watch," the older brother described. "Ever since the robberies began, we've rotated one man to keep an eye on the fields and our flocks."

"I was up in the hills collecting a few stray goats," Lentul added. "We both saw riders come from the road. They dismounted and surrounded our father. Then one threw a spear."

"They were gone before I could get back," Smalt uttered. "Our father was dead when I arrived."

"What did they take?" Alerio asked.

"Nothing. Except our father's life," Lentul replied.

A servant brought a pitcher of watered wine. While he filled mugs, Alerio ran the details over in his mind.

The bandit didn't rob the senior Semitalis. Until now, he used resistance as a reason to attack. But the Bronze Man and his gang seemed to have stopped at the Semitalis' farm just to kill.

"Was your father also a Legionary?" Alerio inquired.

"Unlike Lentul and I, who served with heavy infantry Centuries," Smalt answered, "our father was a lamb. As he put it, he was a sheep who raised a pair of wolves."

Was it a stroke of luck that the bandits had arrived while the father was on guard duty? If they had attacked an experienced infantryman with a shield and spear, either Smalt or Lentul could have held them off until the other arrived.

"Because they didn't take anything," Alerio probed, "did the Bronze Man, by chance, leave a piece of coin?"

"Bronze Man my hairy cūlus," Lentul swore. "I fought Macedonian raiders at Crotone. He may have bronze sheeting on his helmet and breast plate for show. But no one wearing real bronze could move that easily or as fast as an unarmored man."

"He left a piece of a bronze coin on our father's forehead," Smalt answered.

But Alerio wasn't listening. The picture being painted by the victims of the Bronze Man didn't fit with a bandit out to get rich robbing Republic citizens.

"Would you like to see it?"

"See what?" Alerio asked.

"The piece of bronze coin?"

"Yes, please."

***

Curved lines as if cucumbers placed side by side on a display stand took up most of one side. Flipping the piece of bronze over gave Alerio a jolt. He pulled out Grantian Suasus' piece of coin and position the legs under the new image.

"It looks like a man carrying another person," Lentul observed. "But a cross body carry isn't practical so it can't represent combat."

Adding the third piece to the coin showed a second pair of legs.

"The legs are the same," Smalt commented. "Want to bet the missing piece will have another person carrying someone?"

"Do either of you recognize the coin?" Alerio asked. "Or the artwork?

"Nothing that I've seen," each brother replied.

The servant brought out a platter. On it were portions of thinly sliced ham and chunks of cheese along with a pile of olives.

"Try the cheese," Smalt suggested. "We make it with milk from our goats using an old Sabine technique. Isn't that right, Ulpia?"

The servant hesitated as if not aware of his surroundings. After pulling his eyes from the coin pieces, the Sabine replied, "The cheese is a tradition of the Rieti Valley,

Master. And I'm proud to say my family has been cheesemakers for generations."

Alerio selected a piece and bit into the aromatic cheese.

"Delicious," he exclaimed.

***

Alerio and the brothers ran gladius and shield drills. When their arms and legs stiffened, they went to the villa's baths and cleaned up.

"I haven't had a workout with a weapon's instructor for months," Smalt recalled while rotating his shoulder to work out a stitch.

"Father bought this land and the hills from a Sabine family who fell afoul of fate," Lentul described. "Once he realized it was too big a job for one man, he called us back from the Legion."

"You aren't third generation on this property?" Alerio inquired.

"No, Colonel," Smalt answered. "Unlike most farmers in the valley, we're newcomers."

The Sabine servant brought clean towels and the men dried off. While the brothers slipped on tunics, Alerio dressed in his woolens, and tied the knee brace on his leg.

"As much as I enjoyed the exercise, I apologize for the bad knee and not being a better opponent for you," Alerio remarked as he tied the last strap.

"Lictor, you inflicted enough pain," Lentul assured him. "I feel for the Centuries you trained before your injury."

"They did not have sweet things to say behind my back."

"Of that, I'm sure," Smalt offered. He took a mug of wine from the servant, took a sip, and saluted Alerio with the vessel. "Now Lictor, you wanted to speak with another victim."

"Yes. Is the villa close by?" Alerio inquired. He scanned the houses and fields in the valley. "I thought maybe a couple more today."

"That's going to be difficult," Lentul warned. "Their villas are out of the valley."

"West of here?" Alerio assumed. He turned and peered at the mountains west of the valley. "That's towards Etruscan territory, right?"

"No, Lictor," Smalt corrected. "The other victims are to the east along the Via Salaria."

Alerio took a moment to ponder the order of incidents and to compare them with the Bronze Man's comment, *"all you Romans quake in fear of an Etruscan warrior."* If the bandit was bragging about his heritage, why not attack easily reached citizens. Why circumvent the valley to reach victims far from your safe harbor?

"I better go," Alerio said as he strolled to Phobos.

"Last week, we sent a letter to the Proconsul demanding justice," Smalt told Alerio as he mounted. "His return letter said he was planning just that."

"Then you arrived, and we feel better," Lentul said. "He is doing something."

Alerio nudged the stallion into motion. His thoughts turned over what he knew. In the turmoil, he didn't remember the ride down the hill or reaching the main road.

"Let's head for Rieti," he told Phobos while guiding the beast to the south. "I believe it's time we got a second opinion."

***

The town had been calm and almost empty when he passed through the day before. It wasn't the case when Alerio rode in that afternoon.

"Use the side streets," an NCO instructed. "The main roads are for the movement of the Legion."

"What's going on, Optio?" Alerio asked.

"We're going to seal the Etruscan border," the NCO replied. "Let's see that murderer try to cross over with our blades blocking the way."

An image of an undefended valley and an unrestrained band of ruthless killers flashed through Alerio's mind.

"What's the best way to reach the government house?" he inquired.

"Go over five streets, enter the city, and hook a left before the main road," the Optio directed while indicating the way. "It'll keep you off the Legion's route and bring you in behind the offices of the Proconsul."

Alerio saluted the NCO, turned Phobos, and kneed him forward.

"It appears, we'll require more than a second opinion," Alerio said to the stallion. "We need the ear of someone in authority."

***

The compound reflected the importance of a chief magistrate. Rather than rough stone, the walls were coated in clay and painted. It might have been a waste of resources, but with a Proconsul in residence, no one would question the expense.

"I'm here to see the Chief Lictor," Alerio told the Legionary at the gate.

"Do you have an appointment?" the unarmed sentry asked.

Alerio didn't respond. He sat glaring down at the infantryman.

"Maybe you didn't understand me," the gate guard insisted, "is the Chief Lictor expecting you?"

Putting a hand over his forehead as if experiencing a shooting pain, Alerio pointed with the other hand.

"Get your spear and your shield out of the guardhouse," he ordered. "Stand properly to make your challenge. And it would be wise in the future, when someone comes to visit the head enforcer, that you be more respectful."

"More respectful of who?" the sentry demanded.

"Call your Centurion," Alerio told him. "Get him now before the medic arrives."

"What medic?"

"What's going on here," an NCO asked.

The Sergeant studied the man on the horse. The wide brimmed hat, the woolen shirt and pants, and the thick soled sandals told him nothing about the visitor.

"Optio, he was threatening me," the gate guard whined. "At least, I think he was."

"And who is he?" the Sergeant of the Guard inquired.

"I don't know?"

"Well then, what does he want?"

"The last thing was for me to get the Centurion."

"The last thing? What was the first?" the Sergeant inquired.

"The very first was to see the Chief Lictor, Optio."

"There were other requests?" the NCO questioned.

"Just one," the gate sentry reported. "He told me to get my spear and shield from the guardhouse. Oh, and to be respectful."

The last two comments sounded like those of a senior Legion officer. In response, the Optio saluted Alerio.

"Sir, how can I help you?"

"For reasons I can't go into, I will not give you my name or my rank," Alerio informed the NCO. "However, I do need to speak with the Chief Lictor in private."

"Sir, he's been known to sneak into the cookhouse for a snack on occasion."

"Can you pass the word that he needs to get a snack?"

"I can do that, sir," the Sergeant of the Guard assured Alerio.

Before he left, he had words with the sentry. As Alerio rode across the compound to the cookhouse, the Legionary retrieved his shield and spear from the gatehouse.

***

The man carried heavy muscles on his frame and a gladius on one hip and a long knife on the other. He came into the cook shed quickly. So smoothly and fast, no assassin could have been prepared for those moves from a big man. He spotted Alerio chewing the meat off a bone and the Sabine cook calmly stirring a pot.

"How's the pork?" he asked while gliding away from the doorframe.

"It's delicious, but could use some salt," Alerio stated. "Where's your fasces?

"It's a long story," the man responded. "Where's yours?"

"I'm Alerio Sisera and I don't rate a fasces. The Senate only authorizes me to carry a double-bladed ax."

"Cerialis, Chief Lictor for Proconsul Crassus," the big man reported. "You're the scarred Lictor from Pescara. Why the nickname?"

"Praetor Blasio walked into the baths one day as I was climbing out of a soak," Alerio told him. "He saw my war wounds and started calling me his scarred Lictor."

The head enforcer for the District went to the spit and yanked a meaty rib from the roasting boar.

"What can I do for you, Sisera?" he inquired. After gnawing off a mouthful of pork, he agreed. "It does need salt."

"You've mobilized the garrisons in the valley to block the border," Alerio said. "I believe that's exactly what the Bronze Man wants."

"To be trapped in his own district?"

"I don't think he's an Etruscan warrior, or even a bandit," Alerio summed up. "His victims are too far from the border to be optimum for an Etruscan outlaw. And he kills almost pointlessly. Almost as if he's looking to provoke a response."

"What kind of response?" Cerialis questioned.

"Maybe the removal of Legion Centuries from Rieti Valley," Alerio suggested. "Leaving the farmers unprotected."

"That would be a raid, an act of war," the District's Chief Lictor stated. "And who wants war with the Republic?"

"If I knew that, I'd have his motivation and from that I'd have a path to bringing the Bronze Man to justice."

"Look, I'm sure your logic is well considered," Cerialis complimented Alerio. "But the farmers have been hounding the Proconsul for action. I can't walk into his office and say the scarred Lictor said you mustn't mobilize the Legion. I need solid reasons to stop the repositioning of the Centuries."

Alerio set the bone on the edge of the butcher block table, pulled out a pouch, and dumped the pieces of coin on the surface.

"The only other thing I have are these," Alerio told the Chief Lictor while positioning the three wedges.

Cerialis rested his bone next to Alerio's. Then with his finger, he pushed each piece over.

"Those are familiar," he said.

The Chief Lictor extracted a pouch from inside his tunic, opened it, and pulled out two more tiny wedges. He added them to Alerio's three. One of the new pieces was the missing quarter to Alerio's puzzle.

Fitting them together produced two figures carrying objects. When Alerio flipped the four pieces over, they created a bust of a man. The curves of the cucumbers became his wavy locks, and the bunches of grapes the man's curly beard.

"Who is he?" Alerio questioned.

The Sabine cook swung the pot off the fire, strolled over, and peered down at the completed coin.

"Is that?" he asked before flipping the four pieces over. "Oh, dear me, just as I feared."

"What is it, chef?" Cerialis demanded.

"The man on the reverse side is Sabine King Titus Tatius," the cook explained.

"So, it's an historic coin memorializing a King," Alerio guessed.

"Stamped on the coin is the depiction of men toting off women," the chef explained. With the description as a guide, Alerio could make out the details. But he still couldn't grasp the significance of the coin. Then the cook helped. "It's more than a coin honoring a dead King."

"What does the coin mean?" Alerio asked.

"The coin recalls the Abduction of Sabine Women by you Latians. It's a symbol of Sabine resistance."

Chapter 5 – Acquisition by Force

"There was once a single Sabine nation," the cook described. "But a band of criminals, led by a Latian warlord, broke the bonds and divided my people."

"Stop right there, chef," Cerialis barked. "You will not slander King Romulus."

"Romulus? As in the first King of Rome?" Alerio questioned. Picking his bone off the butcher's table, he pointed it at the pieces of coin. "These go back to the founding of the Capital?"

"They symbolize actions from back then," the cook confirmed. "All the way to when your Rome was no more than seven hills, a swamp, and a flood plain. A brutal landscape conquered by a gang of merciless young thugs."

"Don't make me warn you again, chef. Those are my ancestors you're denigrating," Cerialis growled. He snatched up his pork rib and waved it in the air. "King Romulus took a group of downtrodden Latins, pulled them together, and founded a home for them. But you were correct about one thing. Most of them were young men."

"Then you tell the story, your way, Chief Lictor," the cook snapped. "I've got soup that needs tending."

The chef moved to the fireplace, swung the pot back over the flames, and returned to stirring the contents.

"Other disassociated men flocked to King Romulus and the Latin tribe swelled," Cerialis stated. "They cleared farmland, planted, and built homes and constructed businesses. But the King had a fear."

"What fear?" Alerio asked.

"While the city's strength protected it from attack, Romulus knew that in a single generation Rome would fall," Cerialis replied. "There weren't enough children to replace the men as they aged. To produce heirs, the Latin tribe needed women. The King sent out emissaries to neighboring tribes to barter for women of childbearing age."

"Barter? Is that would you call the abduction of the Sabine women?" the chef mumbled.

"If you weren't a superb cook, I would put you on the spit and roast you," the Chief Lictor threatened.

"Didn't mean anything, just commenting about the soup," the cook lied. "Don't mind me."

The District's head enforcer bit off, chewed, and swallowed a piece of pork before continuing.

"When all the trade delegations returned, they had the same story," Cerialis reported. "The neighboring tribes feared that adding to Rome's population would endanger their independence. Romulus was at his wits end with no idea how to solve his population problem. Deep in thought, he walked the fields brushing his hands against the green plants, oblivious to the storm clouds gathering overhead. When it started to rain, a servant ran to him with a cape. But King Romulus pushed the servant away and stood uncloaked watching the rain as it fell and nourished the soil. From that experience, a bold solution formed in his mind."

A loud clang came from a corner of the cookhouse. Both Alerio and Cerialis snapped their heads around to see what made the noise. An iron top for a pot rolled on the floor before spinning down to the floor.

"It slipped out of my hand," the cook said from the far side of the building.

In a huff, Cerialis started towards the doorway.

"What was the bold plan?" Alerio begged. "Please Chief Lictor, finish the story."

Cerialis spun around and glared at the chef. He stood with his fingers balled into fists for several moments. Then, he relaxed his hands and smiled.

"You're right, Sisera. It's a tale you need to know," he stated while staring at the chef. "To honor Neptune for delivering the idea with the water falling from the sky, Romulus declared an extravagant festival. He sent the emissaries back to the neighboring towns and invited prominent men from the tribes and their wives and daughters to come and enjoy feasting and drinking."

"I take it one of the tribes was the Sabine," Alerio ventured.

"Our ancestors in the lowlands," the cook confirmed. "Ill-fated, they took their families to Neptune's Festival."

"Sabines, Caeninenses, Crustumini, and Antemnates arrived to see the new city and to partake of its bounty and King Romulus' generosity," Cerialis told them. "Without a cloak, Romulus sacrificed to the God Neptune then encouraged his guests to eat their fill and to drink to their hearts' content while betting on the chariot races. All day the guests did just that. Deep into the night, Romulus stood sipping his vino and shivering in the evening air. Finally, when half filled mugs listed in limp hands and heads lulled to the side in drunken stupors, the King called for his cloak. He folded the material, then snapped it open, throwing it around his back, before making a grand gesture of settling it on his shoulders. At the signal, the Latin men moved through the Sabine encampment taking the daughters before fleeing with them into the dark."

Cerialis indicated the coin and the images of men carrying the women.

"Only the Sabine women?" Alerio questioned. "What of the other tribes?"

"Our women have wide hips for birthing children and pretty faces to lure men home from the fields at night," the chef bragged. "If nothing else, you Latians have good taste in females."

"I imagine they didn't abduct from tribes adjacent to Rome," Cerialis offered while ignoring the cook's observation. "The Caeninenses and Crustumini were close neighbors while the Sabines and Antemnates were farther away. In fact, Romulus took Hersilia, a woman abducted from the Antemnates, as his wife."

"Chief Lictor, how is it that you know so much about the history?" Alerio inquired.

"After the women were taken, the tribes attacked Rome," Cerialis went on as if disregarding Alerio's question. "Romulus and his Latin warriors were victorious after each battle. The first tribe to test the Romans was the Caeninenses. Their King fell in the fight and Romulus took their major city. Upon returning to Rome, he used the spoils to build a temple to Jupiter on Capitoline Hill. It was the first temple built in the new city. My family has been honored to supply priests to Jupiter for hundreds of years. I was raised on the story of King Romulus and the temple."

Alerio flinched at the mention of Jupiter's temple. Although he had issues with the priests of the Sky Father, he remained mute on the subject.

***

"I'm surprised, Lictor Sisera, that you aren't curious about the Sabine's response," Cerialis remarked after noticing Alerio's silence.

"Sorry Chief Lictor," Alerio apologized, "I was recalling my last visit to the Temple of Jupiter. Please tell me about their response."

"It is a breath-taking temple," Cerialis confirmed. Then with a pained frown, he continued. "The Sabines were the last to go against the Latin Tribe. Their King Tatius marched a huge army into the city, and they fought all the way to the citadel on Capitoline Hill. Stopped before the walls, his advance seemed stalled. The goal of taking back their daughters and punishing the Latins a lost cause."

"I didn't know that we captured Rome," the cook exclaimed.

"Your tribe almost did because the daughter of the Roman Governor made a deal with the Sabines," Cerialis described. "Tarpeia asked for all the things on the left arms of the Sabine warriors. They agreed. Believing she would receive the gold armbands from the army, she opened the gates of the citadel."

"Traitor," Alerio bellowed. "To turn against your city for gold is unforgivable."

"Interestingly enough the Sabines felt the same way," Cerialis agreed. "As they attacked through the portal, Tarpeia was bashed to death by the shields of the warriors. In truth, she did receive everything on their left arm. The breach caused the Latin defenders to flee. Now the tables were turned. The Sabines controlled the citadel and the Latins attacked from outside. But when the Roman General fell, the Latin fighters retreated across the city. Only King Romulus' appearance stopped their flight."

"The issue of panic in the ranks isn't new," Alerio noted. "Even back then it appears, the terror of one Century can infect and break an entire Legion."

"That was long before the Legions," Cerialis clarified. "Under command of their King, the Latins marched back and engaged with the Sabines. During the fighting, the Sabine General fell, and the Latin fighters began to dominate the battlefield. Romulus gathered his war band leaders and set the final battle plan. They positioned their men, but just as they clashed with the Sabine line, the fighting stopped."

"Hesitation kills momentum," Alerio observed. "I've seen Tribunes hold off too long and lose their advantage against an enemy. But stopping once you're locked in combat is difficult. Why did King Romulus do it?"

"Let me set the scene," Cerialis proposed. "The bloody, sweat soaked warriors stood facing each other. The only thing separating the Latins and the Sabines was a field littered with spear shafts. Cries of challenge rang out and war screams designed to boil the blood rose from both sides. Young men waved their weapons and prepared to butcher each other at the whim of their commanders. When the order was given, they ran at each other and began hacking and slashing. Then a vision walked into the nightmare. Romulus' wife Hersilia and the captured Sabine women marched into the slaughter and began pushing apart the combatants."

"Ah, the reason for the hostilities came to the battlefield," Alerio gasped. "What were the women thinking? That's madness."

"Madness indeed?" Cerialis pondered. "But consider Hersilia's speech. Once the women had inserted themselves between the sharp blades, her voice rose above the cries of the wounded and the threats flying back and forth over the lines. Hersilia is reported to have shouted, *fathers-in-law and sons-in-law should not contaminate each other with immoral bloodshed. Nor should a grandchild on one hand, and the child on the other stain their descendants with the sin of patricide. If you are dissatisfied with the connection between you, and if our marriages offend you, resent us, but not each other. We are the cause of this war. And understand, we suffer with each wound and every drop of blood shed by our husbands and our fathers. For in the end, isn't it better for us to perish than to live widowed or fatherless."*

"After that, our lowland brothers turned to Rome and abandoned the Sabine people in the mountains," the Chef complained. "All over women. Although, Sabine women are beautiful."

Alerio couldn't help but laugh at the cook's remark. After a glare from Cerialis, he collected himself and asked.

"If the coin is a symbol of Sabine resistance, what symbol represents Rome in the valley?"

"That's easy," the Chief Lictor ventured, "the roads, farms, and villas. Definitely, those are the improvements that demonstrate the superiority of Roman civilization."

From the fireplace, the cook cleared his throat.

Alerio raised an eyebrow and inquired, "Well chef, is it the roads, farms, and villas?"

The cook lifted the dipper from the soup and allowed it to hover over the pot.

"We have roads, farms, and houses," he answered. Then while slowly pouring soup from the ladle back into the pot, he explained. "The true symbol of Rome's interference in Sabine lives are the waterfalls at Marmore."

Cerialis stared at the ceiling lost in thought at the remark. Alerio called him back to the present.

"I have a motivation and a direction for the Bronze Man," Alerio announced. "What you need to do, Chief Lictor, is convince the Proconsul to stop the mobilization. Or do I need to present the case myself."

"No scarred Lictor, I can handle the issue," Cerialis assured him. "What will you do?"

"I have one stop to make," Alerio replied as he walked to the doorway, "before I chase down the rebel and his confederates."

Once Alerio had gone, Cerialis flipped the rib bone, still half covered in meat, into the fireplace.

"It needs salt," he grumbled.

"There's a bag on the shelf," the chef said while pointing to the salt. "All you had to do was ask."

The District's head enforcer scooped the pieces of the coins off the butcher block table, dropped them into a pouch, and stomped out of the cookhouse.

It wasn't that he didn't have good reasons to call off the Legion maneuver. His problem was organizing the information to make him look good in the eyes of the Proconsul. He did appreciate Lictor Sisera, but this was politics. And no one, especially a Chief Lictor, gave away credit when they could claim it for their own benefit.

***

Alerio put his knees to the stallion's ribs, sending Phobos out of Rieti and up the Viale Emilio Maraini. Seven miles later, he reined in the beast at the farm road. Moments afterward, they climbed the hill and were met outside the villa by the Semitalis' brothers.

"Come back for more cheese?" Smalt inquired.

"In a way," Alerio acknowledged. He slipped from the saddle, draped his arm around Lentul's shoulder, and bent his head to the younger brother's ear. "Don't point. Tell me where Ulpia, your Sabine cheesemaker, is?"

"He's in the house cleaning up before the evening meal," Lentul answered. "What's going on?"

"I'm not absolutely sure," Alerio admitted, "but I suspect he's part of a rebellion."

"How can you say that?" Lentul questioned. "He's been with my father since he bought the farm."

"And how long has that been?" Alerio asked.

The brothers had grown comfortable with the staff. To them, they were as much a part of the farm as their father had been.

"Not that long," Smalt admitted. "Even so, I'm not comfortable with accusing a man of wrongdoing unless you can prove it."

"Ulpia is a valuable member of our estate," Lentul told Alerio. "We will not allow torture for a confession, Lictor."

"I have no plans of cutting off his fingers or ears," Alerio advised. "But I need to search his quarters, and for you to be sure he doesn't escape."

"We can do that," Smalt pledged. "His rooms are through the second door in back of the Villa."

***

Alerio eased open the door and peered into a three-room suite. They were nice quarters for a servant. Yet, considering his skills as a craftsman of cheese, the room wasn't out of line with Ulpia's specialty. Good cheese brought a premium price at the market.

Unlike apartments Alerio had searched before, he wasn't looking for a hidden compartment containing contraband or stolen jewelry. Going straight to the bedroom, he dumped a dish of coins. After stirring them and not finding what he wanted, Alerio turned over a second bowl.

Mixed in with a few pretty stones were six quarter pieces of the bronze coins used by the rebels. Why would a cheesemaker have extra symbols of resistance? With his expectations exceeded, Lictor Sisera revised his search strategy.

Overturning the bed allowed him to test the floor tiles. Finding no hidden compartment in Ulpia's bedroom, he shifted to the study. The corners were solid, as were the tiles under a sofa. But after shoving aside a desk, he located loose flooring blocks.

Alerio placed the bronze pieces to the side, pulled his knife, reached down, and pried up the first loose tile.

Kneeling, he peered under the tile and noted the compartment under the floor wasn't empty.

Chapter 6 – Never Really Seen When Seen

"I have no idea why your friend would accuse me of being a rebel," Ulpia protested. "I'm just a household servant and a cheesemaker."

"He is a Lictor," Lentul stressed. "We're obliged to follow his instructions. I hope you don't hold a grudge against us."

"Plus, he hasn't accused you of anything, yet," Smalt offered. "If he did, it would be painfully clear. I'm sure it's a misunderstanding."

"I served your father faithfully," Ulpia boasted. "Surely that stands for something."

"Of course, your loyalty counts," Lentul comforted him.

A sound uniquely heard in armories drifted in through a back room. Usually, the noise came from an armload of wooden shields, iron and steel blades, and helmets, all banging together.

Alerio carried the contraband war gear through the doorway and across the room to the Sabine servant. After dumping the load at Ulpia's feet, he held out a fist and opened his fingers to reveal six bronze wedges.

"The punishment for being an accomplice to murder is death by drowning," Alerio advised. "It's a fast way to die and just slightly worse than strangulation."

Ulpia sat up straighter and stared at the pieces of coins. The Sabine's hands trembled but he didn't say anything. Neither did the brothers.

"The punishment for rebellion against the Republic is crucifixion," Lictor Sisera informed the servant. "It's an agonizing way to die, and the Goddess Nenia comes for you in her own sweet time. People have been known to hang on the wood for days trying to catch their breath while balancing on a heel sized piece of slick wood."

Smalt Semitalis made a sound as if to speak but was silenced by a slash of Alerio's open hand. As if they were blown back by the force of the hand, the brothers stepped away.

"Or I can begin cutting off your fingers, one at a time," Alerio threatened.

"Why would you do that?" Ulpia whined. "You haven't asked me any questions."

"Questions leave open the possibility for lies," Alerio informed the Sabine. "I'd rather you confess without prompting."

To emphasize the statement, Alerio kicked a helmet. It flew across the room and crashed to the tiles before sliding to a stop against a wall. In the silence following the violence, cheesemaker Ulpia howled.

"Go ahead, take my fingers, take my toes," the Sabine swore. "You Latians have already taken my heart and stolen my family's farm."

The Semitalis brothers exchanged glances. Drawing the conclusion that Ulpia had something to do with his father's death, Smalt reached for his dagger.

"Still your hand, Legionary," Alerio cautioned. "It's not your place to seek vengeance for your father."

"If not me?" the older brother demanded. "Then who?"

"The law gives that right to a Lictor," Alerio replied. He drew his knife and the afternoon sunlight reflected off the wide, steel blade. "It also grants me immunity for my methods in bringing the lawless to justice."

As quick as a serpent, Alerio caught the back of Ulpia's head with his knife hand and shoved the bronze pieces into the servant's mouth with the other. Then he hammered the man's knowledge knot with the pummel of the hilt. A strike to the boney ridge on the back of the head did two things. It momentarily scrambled Ulpia's brain and the impact caused him to swallow.

Cheesemaker Ulpia started to scream but blood from the cuts down his esophagus flowed upward. Coughing, he spit blood leaving a trickle on his chin.

"Water?" the Sabine begged.

"You ask for water," Lentul bellowed. "Was my father granted a last request?"

In a hoarse voice, Ulpia replied, "He wanted to kiss and nuzzle his favorite sheep one last time."

The younger brother yanked his dagger from the sheath and leaped at the servant. Hooking Lentul around the waist, Alerio flipped him over his hip, and threw him to the floor.

"That's what he wants," Alerio scolded. "Calm down and let me work or leave the villa."

Tears flooded Lentul Semitalis' eyes, and his lips trembled.

"I understand, Lictor," he acknowledged. "I'll leave this to you."

Alerio nodded, turned to Ulpia, and slapped the servant's forehead.

"So far, I haven't injured you, but…," Alerio said.

"But what? I can't talk, I need a drink."

"That's a lot of words from a man who can't talk," Alerio told him. "And the but? It means I can change from hurting you to injuring you at any moment. Tell me about the Bronze Man."

"He's never really seen when seen, never found when found, and never caught when caught," Ulpia responded.

"I've heard that secondhand from a number of people," Alerio stated. "I'd like to test the theory myself. Where can I find him?"

"Never found when found," the Sabine repeated.

"Have it your way," Alerio said. Then to Smalt, he instructed. "Ulpia is thirsty. Bring me a jar of vinegar."

"You are inhuman," the Sabine screamed.

The expulsion of air from his lungs and the stress of his rage forced more blood into his mouth. What started as a cry of defiance ended in a dirty coughing spell.

"Smalt, hurry with the beverage," Alerio encouraged. Moments later while reaching for the jug, he teased. "What kind of host are you to keep our guest waiting?"

"Nothing you do to me will change anything," Ulpia murmured. "The Bronze Man is everywhere. And he will bring down vengeance on you Latians and return my farm."

"He's everywhere you say. I haven't seen him around here," Alerio noted. He pushed back Ulpia's head and dribbled vinegar into the Sabine's mouth. "Where was he again?"

The pain of the vinegar on wounds to the delicate flesh of the Sabine's throat caused Ulpia to fold his body in two.

"He is never really seen when seen," Ulpia moaned, "never found when found."

"No, No. You said he's everywhere. Not, never found," Alerio corrected while pouring vinegar over the back of Ulpia's head. "Make up your mind. Is he everywhere or is he never anywhere?"

"Never found when found," Ulpia repeated while shaking his head to throw off the liquid.

"So, he's a no body," Alerio summed up by pouring more vinegar over the Sabine's head. "A joke, just a jester to amuse you weak Sabines on cold winter nights."

Alerio poured more vinegar over the back of his head. Ulpia violently shook in frustration before exploding out of the chair.

"He is not a joke," the Sabine screamed into Alerio's face. "When he blocks the channel and floods the valley, all you dead Latians will be swept away."

Alerio put two fingers into Ulpia's chest and pushed him back into the chair.

"I need one of you to take Ulpia to Rieti," Alerio instructed the brothers. "When you get there, have Chief Lictor Cerialis send a cavalry troop to your villa and Centuries of infantry to farms outside the valley."

"Could the Bronze Man be hiding at the falls?" Smalt ventured.

"No. He and his conspirators will be close by your farm," Alerio replied. He pointed to the blades and armors piled on the floor. "The dream of every rebellion is for the people to rise up and join them. These weapons will arm the population. However, before that, the Bronze Man needs to make a strong showing. Once he kills you two, he's hoping for the rest of the Sabine's in the valley will flock to him and join the revolt."

"You got all that from Ulpia's answers?" Lentul questioned.

"Once I realized the Bronze Man was a Sabine Rebel and not an Etruscan bandit, your father's death, although tragic, made sense," Alerio explained. "He was the first actual victim of the rebellion. Those murdered in the misleading thefts were to raise support among the Sabines. The Bronze Man used robbery and brutality to demonstrate that the uprising was a serious cause."

"Let them come," Smalt said, "we'll kill them all. But first let me stab this savage in the heart."

"We need Ulpia alive," Alerio advised. "The only reason to stash an arsenal in your villa is to arm the masses. And since Ulpia had the extra coin pieces and the weapons, he must have knowledge about the organization. If we're going to end this rebellion, we need Ulpia in Rieti, alive."

Lentul stared hard at the Sabine cheesemaker.

"Accept that your father's death was probably a favor for Ulpia," Alerio told the brothers the harsh truth. "But understand, the Proconsul needs the information Ulpia has in his head to stomp out the entire rebellion."

"I'll take him," Smalt volunteered.

Lentul spun and faced the side of the house. Lifting his head, he seemed to be gazing off into the distance.

"You said the Bronze Man will be nearby," the youngest of the brothers offered. "Our father had a cabin built for the herders in the mountain. It's only used in summer when they take the animals up for grazing."

"He called it Morning Shelter," Smalt added. "It's on the east side of the ridge and catches the light of the rising sun."

"How far away is it?" Alerio inquired.

"By road, the cabin is only six miles from here," Lentul answered. He used an arm to point. "But that's around the mountain. Morning Shelter itself sits directly west of our villa, over the summit."

"Take care of my horse," Alerio requested.

"Where are you going?" Lentul inquired.

"To see if it's true."

"What's true?" Smalt asked.

"If the Bronze Man is never dead when dead."

"It's never caught when caught," Ulpia corrected.

"Maybe in your world," Alerio growled as he walked to the exit. "In my world, when you murder a child to make a political point, you are definitely dead, not maybe caught."

***

Alerio removed the saddle and fought with the disgruntled horse. Phobos sensed he was being left behind and let Alerio know he was displeased. After putting the stallion in a stall, he pulled his dual sword rig out of a pack, strapped it to his back, and covered the weapons with a fur jacket. Late afternoon in the valley was chilly. He knew a night on the mountain would be colder. Once dressed, Alerio unstrapped the knee brace.

"If you're going to climb, you'll need support for that leg," Lentul offered.

"The time always comes when a disguise has served it's purpose," Alerio remarked. "Hold the cavalry at the villa. If I miss the rebels, I want them here to stop the rebellion before it gathers momentum."

"I understand," the youngest Semitalis brother acknowledged.

Alerio jogged away from the barn, moved off the mound, and once on flatland, paced at a Legion shuffle. A mile from the villa, the ground rosed sharply. From a steady pounding of his feet, Alerio was forced to scramble using his hands and feet. The higher he climbed, the colder the air got, and the steeper the face of the mountain. He didn't mind the physical exertion, it kept him warm. But he knew once the sun went down, the night would be uncomfortable.

***

Nineteen hundred feet higher, Alerio rolled over on the first piece of almost level ground he encountered. It wasn't his first break in the climb, but it was the first opportunity to lay on his back and look at the cool, crisp sky and the twinkling of the stars.

"I will try to get home by Saturnalia," he promised the night sky and by extension his wife, Gabriella.

He wondered what the twins were doing. Then, realizing the lateness of the evening, he knew his children were tucked in their beds, warm and cozy. Pushing to his knees, Alerio judged whether to stand or go forward on his hands and knees. To his delight, he managed to stand and walk up a gentle slope.

In the weak rays of a rising moon, Alerio noted the bright snow on the mountains adjacent to the lower range. Any higher and he would be hiking through it. But the grade ended, as did the need to climb, at a ridgeline. Below the crest, he spotted a dark cabin in a clearing.

Typical of most Legion maneuvers, the hard part had been getting to the site where the actual work would take place.

***

More temporary refuge than a lodging, Morning Shelter was a large box constructed of roughhewn boards with a slanted roof. Alerio circled the structure searching for signs of occupancy. After two circuits, he eased up next to the cabin and listened at a window opening.

"Either no one is home, or they are the quietest sleepers I've ever encountered," he whispered.

Then slowly, Alerio rose and peered inside. Seeing no shadows of sleeping bodies, he entered to get out of the night air.

***

A farm boy's days were full of chores. Livestock tending, uprooting weeds and stones, somedays in equal measure, plus working the fields and mending storage buildings were just a few of his responsibilities. To complete the tasks, the son of a farmer had to get up before the sun.

Alerio's habit of early starts on his father's farm gave him an edge. Already awake when he heard the rattle of wheels on a rocky stretch of wagon track, he slipped from the shelter unobserved. Having only Lentul's description that the road ran below the shelter, Alerio low crawled from the building to a thicket with a view of the entrance. He still couldn't see the road, but he heard the cart stop below his hiding place. Rushing from the cabin and scrambling to the bushes provided one benefit, he wasn't quite as cold.

For a long spell, the wagon sat unmoving. Then following a grunt from the driver, Alerio heard sandals on the wagon bed. The sounds of boards being moved drifted up from the road, then nothing.

Could it be a fieldhand sent to collect firewood? Or a hunter looking for small game? There were any number of reasons for a cart to be in the mountains at dawn.

Horse hooves clopping on the trail from a distance reached Alerio. Soon snorting announced the arrival of several more horses on the road below.

"We have a problem," a voice, faint but distinct, carried up the slope.

"Let's go to the cabin and talk about it," another man suggested. "And grab the Bronze Man's armor."

Alerio felt a smile pull at the sides of his mouth. There was nothing pleasant in his situation or humorous about a rebellion. But now he had the collaborators of the uprising, if not the leader. To identify the men, Alerio crawled deeper under the cluster of bushes. Once positioned so he could see the front of the cabin and the faces of the men as they arrived, he relaxed and waited.

The first to reach the cabin had the face of a statue carved by a Greek artist. Following the Hellenic god, a heavy-set man hauling a bronze helmet and breast piece struggled up the slope. A harness knife on his belt, light sandals, and the shiny material at his butt identified him as a wagon driver. The handsome man took the bronze armor and hung the pieces from hooks beside the door to the cabin.

"Do we need those anymore?" a third man questioned.

Rangy in form, the rebel moved in a fluid fashion. Alerio identified him as a fighter by his stride up the slope. To confirm the suspicion, a knife scar across one ear and on the back of his left hand confirmed it.

The last Sabine up didn't fit anyone's idea of a rebel. Slight in build, he wore a scholar's robe, soft sandals, and had no visible weapons. But on his head, he sported a nice felt petasos. Alerio appreciated the man's choice in headwear.

"That depends on the news from our teamster," the handsome one said as he traced a finger down the bronze chest piece.

"The garrison didn't march out last night," the driver explained. "If they were heading for the border this morning, there would have been movement. But the night at their bivouac passed quietly."

Alerio was pleased at having convinced Chief Lictor Cerialis to stop the Legion operation. Also, knowing the faces of the gang members would allow him to hunt them down. His solo part of the investigation required only one other item - the identity of the Bronze Man.

"That forces us to delay activating our cells," the fighter declared.

"Then we'll need the Bronze Man to maintain the expectations of our followers. Without our activity, they won't hold onto their passion for long," the scholar ventured. "So, who wants to be the Bronze Man for today's robbery?"

Lictor Alerio Sisera mouthed five words, "Never really seen when seen."

And for good reason, the Bronze Man wasn't an individual. He was a character played by these three men. A made-up hero of the Sabine revolution to rally the populace.

"I wore it at the Semitalis farm," the fighter stated. "Let someone else."

Act 3

Chapter 7 – Never Caught When Caught

The downhill segments of a journey usually went faster and easier than the trip up. But the western slope angled steeply, and the descent proved difficult. To keep from launching himself off the face of the mountain, Alerio used vegetation to break his fall. Trunks of small trees, low hanging branches, and wide bushes broke his momentum as he grabbed while hopping, tumbling, and sliding down the incline.

Near the base, Alerio allowed his body to sprint headlong onto the flatland. He managed to move faster than his legs could sprint for several steps before sprawling face first into the dirt.

There were no congratulations to himself on surviving the controlled fall. Somewhere in the valley, a wagon hauling a bronze helmet and a breast piece trolled for a victim. Pushing off the soil, Alerio jogged for the Semitalis' villa.

***

"Identify yourself," a dismounted cavalryman challenged.

"Lictor Alerio Sisera," Alerio replied as he struggled to the crest of the mound.

"A Lictor?" the Legion horsemen asked. "Where's your fasces?"

"It's a long story," Alerio responded. "Where's your officer?"

"Centurion Salubris is in the house. Wait, you can't…"

But Alerio used the last of his energy to run to the villa. He dodged through the doorway before the horseman could tie up or mount his horse and catch him. Inside, he reached the first empty sofa and collapsed on it.

"Centurion Salubris," Alerio snapped, "we need to get moving."

The officer almost spilled the content from his mug at the sudden intrusion.

"Who are you to barge in here and begin issuing orders?"

"He's Alerio Sisera. And might I say, Lictor Sisera, you look exhausted," Lentul offered. "Can I interest you in a beverage?"

"That would be most welcomed," Alerio replied. "Centurion, you need to scour the roads for a heavy-set wagon driver."

"And why would I do that?"

"To prevent another murder of a Republic citizen," Alerio shot back while taking a mug from Lentul. After several gulps, he added. "And even if he fights, you must take the teamster alive. He knows the identities of the Bronze Man."

The mention of the notorious bandit brought the officer to his feet.

"You mean the identity," he corrected.

"Round up the wagons on every road and take them to the turn off for the Suasus farm," Alerio instructed. "I'll be there to look over the drivers after I've cleaned up."

The Legion officer ran from the room and Alerio shifted his attention to Lentul and asked. "Where's Smalt?"

"He got back early this morning," the brother reported. "They questioned him for most of the night before he was allowed to leave. Should I wake him?"

"Only as a precaution. I think the revolt has been put on hold," Alerio responded while pushing off the sofa. "I'm going to clean up and ride to the crossroads. Hopefully, the cavalry will have the driver in custody by then."

"I want to know when you arrest the Bronze Man," Lentul insisted. "I need to be there when he's crucified."

Alerio knew men, especially warriors. Of the three playing the Bronze Man, the one Lentul wanted for killing his father was the least likely of the trio to be taken alive.

With that in mind, Alerio risked, "If I can make it happen, you'll be there."

On stiff legs, Alerio hobbled outside to wash up.

***

Five wagons rested beside the Viale Emilio Maraini, facing south. Six more sat across the road facing north. While the draft horses and mules stood calmly, the drivers and a handful of citizens who were escorting their drivers howled and threatened the cavalrymen.

Alerio trotted to the crossroads and into a storm of angry civilians.

'We've rounded up everything moving this early," Salubris reported. "I hope you know what you're doing, enforcer."

"Let me get a look at them, Centurion," Alerio responded. "Then I'll give you my opinion on if I know what I'm doing."

Guiding Phobos, Alerio rode south examining the drivers and the riders just to be sure he didn't miss the man hauling the Bronze Man's gear.

"Now see here, I need to get to the market," a farmer scolded. "Who are you to arrest my driver and hold up my load of squash."

Alerio saluted to show he heard the complaint. But he didn't stop to engage the man in conversation. To halt would slow the progress of capturing the rebels. And to stop and explain the reason for the detention, would be the same waste of the morning.

He urged the stallion along the line of carts and the collection of disgruntled drivers and their employers. The rebel driver was not among those heading south.

At the end of the wagons, he nodded to a mounted Legionary, turned, and signaled the officer.

"Centurion, you can release the southbound ones," he shouted.

While that caravan began pulling onto the road, he swung Phobos around and caught a glimpse of a body jumping into the back of a moving cart.

"Stop the wagons," he bellowed. Kneeing the horse forward, Alerio quickly reached the transport where he peered down at the chunky teamster. "You might want to climb down and get back to your wagon."

"I was just," the driver stammered. He paused and his lips quivered. "I just quit my employer and was getting a ride to Rieti."

"No sense riding in that uncomfortable cart bed, Sabine," Alerio offered the rebel wagon driver. "I'm sure we can get you a horse to ride. After you answer a few questions."

***

Alerio and the Centurion stood on either side of the driver. Behind him, three floorboards had been removed from the wagon bed, revealing a hidden compartment. Displayed next to the misplaced boards were a chest piece covered in a thin sheet of bronze and a helmet with the same outer layer.

"I'm sure there's a good reason you have those in your wagon," Alerio suggested. Then he inquired. "Why use sheet metal?"

The easy question was to get the teamster talking and loosen the man's tongue. While Alerio knew the tactic, the cavalry officer didn't understand it.

"It's lighter," the driver replied. "Have you any idea how heavy real bronze armor is? And let me explain…"

"We don't care about weight," Salubris growled while poking the teamster in the chest with his finger. "Who is the Bronze Man?"

A change came over the teamster. From a talkative driver, his spine stiffened, and he lifted his chin and stared into the Centurion's eyes.

"Poke me again and I'll break your face," he promised.

With the driver's hands lashed behind his back, and mounted Legionaries around the wagon, the cavalry officer couldn't imagine the prisoner fulfilling the threat. Alerio stepped back to allow the drama to play out. He would take over as a friendly alternative after a few moments.

"I asked you…," Salubris questioned while poking the man's chest with his fingers.

The driver bent his head down and to the right. Capturing the offending fingers under his chin, he dipped at the knees, yanking the officer's fingers out of joint. Then in a smooth transition, the teamster snapped his head up, jumped into the air, and pounded his forehead down onto Salubris' face. Crushed by the blow, the Centurion's nose flowed red.

Alerio's admiration for the overweight Sabine's skills caused him to miss the Legion dagger. Not until the blade was buried in the teamster's gut, and given a killing twist, did he realize the loss.

"Goddess Nenia, no," Alerio swore to his personal deity. Using his shoulder, he shoved the Centurion away, dropped to his knees, and cradled the teamster. "Stay with me, Sabine. Come on, it's just a scratch. Who is the handsome man?"

But the Goddess of Death had already taken the man's soul, leaving just a dead body in Alerio's embrace.

"He broke my nose," the Centurion moaned.

"And you killed our only link to the Bronze Man," Alerio replied while standing.

"And you are the only witness to it," the cavalry officer noted.

Although pointed downward, the dagger remained in the Centurion's hand.

"I'm not a Sabine wagon driver with his hands tied. I am an infantry officer, a weapon's instructor, and a Lictor of the Republic," Alerio warned. "Try and stab me, and I'll ram that dagger up your cūlus and break the blade off at the hilt. Then make you ride back to Rieti to report to the Proconsul on your reverence for Coalemus."

"I don't worship the God of Stupid," Salubris protested.

Alerio glanced down at the dead Sabine, at the naked blade, and up to the officer's dripping nose.

"You could have fooled me," Alerio remarked.

"What are you going to do?" Salubris inquired as he cleaned and put away the dagger.

"Not me, but you and your cavalrymen," Alerio instructed. "You're going to every farm and community in the valley where you will arrest the teachers and tutors."

"There are dozens of educators and philosophers in the district," Salubris complained. "How do we know which...?"

"It wasn't me who killed the rebel transporting the Bronze Man's armor," Alerio reminded the officer. "Bring the educators here to the crossroads. I'll eliminate them until we find the next link to the bandit."

***

At midday, Grantian Suasus rode to the Viale Emilio Maraini. Curious as to why cavalrymen were coming and going to a place near his farm, he rode to Alerio.

"Come look for yourself," Alerio offered when asked about the activity.

He removed a blanket to display the helmet and breast piece. After spitting on the Bronze Man's armor, Grantian galloped back to his farm without saying anything.

"Obviously overcome with emotion," a cavalryman suggested while he hung the blanket back over the armor.

Centurion Salubris had remained with Alerio at first. But the disruption of citizens' lives when Legionaries raced up to villas, and arrested the tutors in front of the children, required the presence of an officer.

"Who can blame the farmer?" Alerio commented to the pair of cavalrymen left at the crossroads. "He did lose a son to the Bronze Man."

A short while later, a cart came from the turn off to the farms with refreshments of wine, an assortment of food, and a note.

Lictor Sisera,

My constitution will not allow me to be in the presence of that evil armor. But know this, my heart is begging for your success.

Grantian Suasus, farmer, citizen of the Republic, and grieving father.

"You were right," Alerio told the cavalryman, "the farmer was overcome with grief."

***

The afternoon came and a weak sun hovered in the sky just beyond noon. The mounted Legionaries and Alerio pulled capes over their shoulders against the chill. Periodically, trios of Legion horsemen arrived with scholars who were brought before Alerio. After questioning them, the Lictor released the teachers and sent the cavalrymen on to the next villa.

Between sessions, Alerio and two men waited for the next search team to arrive. They had a fire to warm their hands and clay mugs of Suasus' vino to warm their bellies.

"Another three weeks until Saturnalia," one cavalryman mentioned. "When this is over, I'm going home to my family in Tivoli. What about you, Lictor Sisera?"

Alerio owned half a travertine quarry in Tivoli. But he didn't tell the Legionary because it would sound like bragging.

"By mid-December and the holiday," he answered, "I hope to be home with my family in the Capital."

"You'll have captured the Bronze Man and be home long before Saturnalia," the mounted Legionary remarked.

The idea rocked Alerio. For all the manpower expended by the Proconsul trying to locate the murderer, this cavalryman assumed Lictor Sisera could accomplish the task in under three weeks.

"I'll do what?" Alerio commented. "You seem to have a lot of confidence in me. Why?"

"The servant Ulpia was spouting death threats and swearing curses on Lictor Sisera when the farmer brought him in," the Legionary replied. "No one else has gotten this close to the Bronze Man. We figured if you got this far, you'll finish the bandit."

"We have confidence in you, Lictor," the other cavalryman added.

In politics, as Alerio had learned, allowing your superiors to take credit was beneficial for a career. The only thing better than a sponsor above, was having the adoration and support of the masses from below.

One of his cavalryman tossed a branch in the firepit. For a moment, the flames climbed higher than the men. Then, the limb popped, sending embers and sparks out in a radius. Alerio and the cavalrymen hopped back and away while beating on their capes.

"That was…"

A loud, angry voice carried from the south. Eight men and a young boy rode along the main road. Centurion Salubris rode at the front and beside him, based on the man's rich tunic, rode a nobleman. The Legion officer did not appear happy.

"Lictor Sisera. I will have words with you," the Patrician sneered.

He slipped off his horse and marched to Alerio.

"This cavalry officer insisted that my son's teacher, tutor Fuficia, accompany him," the nobleman complained. "When I protested, he said I would have to take it up with a Lictor. Since when does a man of my position have to answer to an enforcer."

"Your name?" Alerio demanded.

"Titus Menenius Lanatus. My family goes back to the founding of the Republic," Lanatus informed Alerio. "And I don't appreciate this intrusion into my son's studies."

"I'm sure we can get this resolved quickly and get you back to your villa," Alerio assured him.

"This may be the edge of the northern frontier, but even out here on the fringe of the Republic, my name requires respect," Titus Lanatus stated. "I will not stand for your insolence. Your name?"

Alerio was attempting to see around the boy and a pair of cavalrymen. But they had the tutor boxed in and out of view.

"I will have your name so I can report your ill manners to Proconsul Crassus," Lanatus vowed. "He is a friend of mine."

Before Alerio could answer, Grantian Suasus galloped from the wagon trail, circled around the group, and reined in at the Sabine wagon.

"I didn't want to, but it's praying on my mind,"
Grantian cried. "Why Bronze Man. Why? I curse you and
your armor."

He reached over and yanked the blanket off the helmet
and breast piece. As soon as it was exposed, a yelp came from
the cluster of riders and a cavalryman fell from his horse. The
high-pitched scream of a lad yet to reach manhood drowned
out the groans of the fallen man.

"Back away," the scholar from the mountain ordered.
Dangling from his arm but pressed close to the rebel's chest,
hung the son of Titus Menenius Lanatus. "Back away or I'll
cut this Latian piglet's throat."

"Tutor Fuficia, release my son," Lanatus instructed. "I'm
sure we can straighten this out. It's just a misunderstanding."

"Shut up, you blowhard," Fuficia spit back. "If you want
your son to live, order these dogs of the Republic to get out of
my way."

Titus Lanatus' body vibrated with indecision. The blade
against the throat of his heir, and the betrayal of a trusted
servant had crushed him.

"Back away," Alerio announced. He moved beside a
cavalry mount, and patted the beast's neck, then restated.
"Everyone, back away from the teacher."

"But, my son. My boy must be released," Lanatus
pleaded.

"I don't know about allowing him to take the boy,"
Salubris commented.

"Are you going to draw your dagger and act the fatuus
this time, as well?" Alerio questioned the Centurion.

"When have I ever acted the fool?" Salubris demanded.
Alerio indicated the blanket covering the body of the Sabine

teamster. Realization occurred to the cavalry officer, and he emitted a weak. "Oh, I see."

"Everyone, stand down" Alerio called to the Legionaries still mounted. "Dismount and back off the road. Let Tutor Fuficia have the way."

With a smug look, Fuficia urged his horse forward. He moved by the cavalrymen, Salubris, then Titus Lanatus, who sobbed, and finally Alerio.

"No one is coming after you," Alerio offered up to the rebel. "Just treat the lad kindly."

"I should cut off his ear," Fuficia stated. "I think I will take the ear before releasing him."

The tutor and his hostage rode beyond the turnoff at the wagon track.

"Do something," Grantian Suasus begged. He gripped one of his saddle horns as if preparing to give chase. "Can't you see he'll kill the boy just as he murdered my Pollio."

Fuficia's evil laugh floated back as did his words, "Never really caught when caught."

"Master Suasus, stand your ground," Alerio commanded.

More of Fuficia's laughter reached the men. Mixed with the maniacal humorless noise was the weeping of Titus Lanatus' son. The rebel's horse walked four lengths then five farther north while the cavalrymen, their officer, and the two fathers watched helplessly. They all voiced displeasure at the escape.

"You called him Master Suasus," Lanatus complained. "Yet for me, a nobleman, you granted no respect. And now you stand there doing nothing."

"Titus, not now," Alerio told him.

"Wait till the Proconsul hears about this," Titus Lanatus threatened.

But Lictor Alerio Sisera wasn't listening. While watching the retreating horse, he judged the distance and reached for the cavalry lance hanging from the Legion mount. As his fingers closed on the shaft, the whining and grumbling voices of the men faded.

Chapter 8 – A Wet Tumble

Throwing a lance, a spear, or a javelin was a stretch reflex. Starting with the shaft almost level, Alerio drew the lance back until the steel tip rested against the side of his face. To an onlooker, he appeared to be sighting along the metal head, but he wasn't. Next, he ran in giant steps while keeping his forward arm bent and loose. The elevation of the lance came when Alerio tilted his torso back. After three quick hops to build momentum, Alerio Sisera landed and planted his left foot. At the same time, his left arm straightened and rotated downward. With a snapping motion, Alerio rotated his shoulders, whipping his right arm forward. The lance left his hand. As orchestrated by the angle of his stretched body and the reflex action of his shoulders, the weapon soared upward.

Fuficia walked his horse slowly. Maybe because of the awkward hold he had on his hostage or possibly to show his Sabine courage, the rebel didn't rush away. It was his undoing.

The lance was in the air for about the same length of time it took for a sharp, short intake of air. And, when the steel head and heavy shaft tore into the top of the rebel's shoulder blade, it was the sound Fuficia made. High-pitched and turbulent, the agony ripped from his throat as the lance pierced his flesh.

Driven forward by the lance, the knife hand flew away from the boy's neck while the other arm released him. Titus Lanatus' son dropped out of the rebel's grasp just before the weight of the lance pulled Fuficia out of the saddle.

Alerio ran, and because the throw took the others off guard, he ran alone.

"Goddess Orbona, I beg of you," he pleaded with each pump of his arms, "don't let the Lanatus boy be injured."

He did care about the youth. But for a different reason than to spare the boy pain. Alerio needed to treat the rebel fast before he bled out. If the boy required care, Lictor Sisera might lose another link to the Bronze Men from the delay.

"Are you bleeding? Is anything broken?" Alerio questioned as he approached.

"No, Lictor," the boy replied.

"Good. Stand up and stop everyone right here."

On wobbly legs, the boy stood and extended his arms as if trying to stop the wind. Unfortunately, he didn't stop the wind or the crowd of men pounding after Fuficia. Alerio continued to the fallen rebel.

Skewered raw meat best described the rebel's shoulder at his neckline. Adding to the butcher's mess, the steel head poked out the front while the long shaft extended from behind. To Alerio's amazement, the wooden length supported Fuficia in an upright position.

"Tutor, you look a mess," Alerio noted while squatting in front of the rebel.

"My arm won't move," Fuficia complained.

With the other hand, he picked at the point of the lance as if he didn't recognize the object.

In battle, Alerio had seen men with severe injuries have difficulty acknowledging the reasons for their wounds. It seemed their minds couldn't grasp the horror of what happened to their bodies.

"I'm going to remove the lance," Alerio explained. He rested both hands on the mutilated trapezius muscle. "Breathe in and hold it."

Dazed, Fuficia had no idea what Alerio meant. It showed in the blank expression in his eyes. As the Sabine rebel contemplated the words, Alerio braced the rear of the tutor's shoulder and pushed the steel head back through the wound.

Fuficia screamed in agony. Titus Lanatus screamed in outrage and Grantian Suasus screamed in misery. Alerio threw his body over the rebel to protect him from the angry fathers and bellowed.

"Centurion Salubris, this is the last link we have," he warned.

After shouting voices, sandals and hobnailed boots shuffled away, Alerio relaxed. The two fathers and two cavalrymen, bent on revenge, were pushed back.

"Is he dead?" Titus Lanatus snarled. "Because if he's not, I'll gladly use my dagger."

"Salubris, kindly disarm the nobleman," Alerio instructed while inspecting the ugly wound. He reached under his tunic and began uncoiling a length of black silk. "I don't have time to explain."

"You're treating the Bronze Man?" Grantian Suasus asked in disgust. "Let him bleed. Let him die."

"Salubris, also take the knife from farmer Suasus," Alerio ordered.

To stop the bleeding, Alerio circled the material several times under the rebel's arm and over the wound. Then he wrapped it around Fuficia's chest. With the last piece, he created a sling.

"There, does that feel better?" he inquired. "The bandage isn't too tight, is it?"

The fall from the horse and the pain of the injury left the tutor confused.

"It's hurts, but I can manage," Fuficia replied. "Where am I? Where are the others?"

"The handsome guy said to bring you along," Alerio lied. "But he didn't say where."

"Alunni never gives a direct answer," Fuficia mumbled. "But what do you expect from an Umbrian Prince?"

Alerio had another name for the Bronze Man and a problem. Dealing with Umbria royalty added a new level of difficulty to the investigation. At that level of politics, it would be Proconsul Crassus' decision on how to deal with the Prince.

What Alerio wanted now was the name of the Sabine fighter. Afraid Fuficia might die, or go unconscious and awaken alert, Alerio rocked him gently.

"If Alunni wouldn't help us," Alerio ventured, "maybe the Sabine warrior will."

Then he waited for the words to soak into the wounded man's mind. The moments stretched out and Alerio began to worry his gentle interrogation had failed.

"At the first sign of trouble, Belliena will run to his cabin at Marmore Falls," Fuficia slurred. "If we hurry, we can catch him, before he vanishes into the mountains."

Alerio lowered the tutor to his back and stood.

"There was a group of men who assumed the Bronze Man's identity to stir up unrest for a revolution," he announced. "Fuficia was one. Another is a Sabine named Belliena. Centurion Salubris, use the wagon to transport the driver's body and this piece of filth to the Proconsul."

He intentionally left the name of Prince Alunni out of the discussion. Here was an opportunity to whisper the accusation into the ear of Proconsul Crassus. By keeping the name intimate, Alerio hoped his discretion would gain a favor from the Proconsul.

"If we're going to Rieti," the cavalry officer inquired, "where will you be, Lictor Sisera?"

"I'm going after Belliena before he vanishes into the wilderness," Alerio replied.

Alerio was four paces from the crowd when Titus Lanatus hooked his arm.

"Lictor, you saved my son. I owe you," the nobleman professed. He extended three gold coins. "Here's a reward for your actions."

Alerio stopped and stared down at the valuable coins and smiled.

"My name is Alerio Carvilius Sisera and my father was Senator Spurius Carvilius Maximus," he stated. "And you are correct, you do owe me. But your son is worth a lot more than three coins."

"Name your price," Titus urged. "Anything."

With a smirk on his face, Alerio told him, "I'll let you know the price when I'm ready. And then Titus Lanatus, I expect your complete backing."

"You have my word," Lanatus vowed.

The fuel that flamed politics, just as logs fed firepits, were favors. And Alerio had just banked one with Titus Lanatus, the patriarch of a noble family with ties that ran back to the founding of the Republic.

After the delay to talk, Alerio sprinted to Phobos. The falls lay fourteen miles away at the northern end of the valley. He had one advantage. Even if Belliena noted the searches and rounding up of teachers, the Sabine probably didn't realize a Lictor of the Republic was chasing him.

***

Six miles into the ride, Alerio pulled the stallion up on top of a riverbank. He studied the rushing river and imagined the frigid current of the Nera.

"Phobos, I don't want to do this," Alerio admitted.

He shivered at the thought of splashing through the cold water. Phobos picked up on the quiver, decided it was a command, and plunged down the embankment. Alerio howled when the icy water washed over the saddle, his legs, and his hips. Seventy feet of misery later, the stallion's front hoofs touched the far riverbed. With powerful strides, the beast climbed out of the current and charged up the embankment.

"That was fun," Alerio grumbled.

They traveled two more miles before the landscape changed and Phobos stopped. The horse quivered and refused to move. After several moments, as if nothing had happened, the stallion walked towards the steep grade.

From flatland, the grade became rolling hills that rose higher at each summit. As they climbed, the roar of a river falling hundreds of feet made Phobos skittish. And the mist that shrouded the trail, caused Alerio to huddle under his wet cape.

Five miles later, they reached the last dip and rise. The pathway came level with the top of the falls and Alerio reined in.

Between an opening in the trees, Alerio saw a slice of the fertile valley stretching to the south. After seeing the landscape with the farms and straight roads, he understood the resentment of the Sabine rebels. It didn't mean he sympathized with them. Twenty-two years before, the Sabines lost the war to the Republic and the right to rule themselves.

The trail ran beside a reservoir that fed the falls. On one end, a ribbon of water flowed into the lake. But there was no stream for an outflow. That job was handled by a torrent of water pouring over the top of the cliff, creating Marmore Falls.

Alerio reined in at a shack across from the lake.

"I'm looking for a friend who has a cabin around here," he mentioned to a fisherman at a firepit.

The man turned over a fish on a stick and poked the fire before looking up at the rider.

"If he's from here, I'll know him," the old fisherman assured Alerio. "Care to buy some smoked fish?"

"His name is Belliena and no thank you, I don't need any smoked fish."

"Young Quirinus," the fisherman replied.

"No, sir, his name is Belliena," Alerio corrected.

"Quirinus is the Sabine God of War," the man chuckled. "Belliena is always strutting around talking about the glories of battle and how he was born too late. I told him to join the Republic Legion, but he scoffed at the idea."

"And you don't feel that way?" Alerio asked.

"Only a few of us Umbrians want trouble with the Republic," the fisherman answered. "Mostly we want to be left alone to farm, hunt, and fish. But there are always young rebel rousers and Legion officers who want to come around and disturb our peace."

"Where can I find Belliena, the God of War?" Alerio asked.

"Him, the God of War? That's a good one," the fisherman acknowledged. "His cabin is around the lake. It's easy enough to spot. Look for the scarlet banner hanging over the doorway."

"A scarlet standard?" Alerio inquired. "Does the color have significance for the Sabine people?"

"Only those who believe the Spartan legend," the fisherman said. He lifted the charred fish out of the fire and took a bite. As he chewed, he clarified. "The story goes that a bunch of Spartans disagreed with their King. They moved to these lands and a bunch moved in with the Sabines. For sure, the Sabine tribesmen are surely mean enough and cheap enough to be Spartans."

"I think the word is frugal," Alerio offered.

"Cheap, frugal, it means they are coin pinchers," the fisherman snarled. "Plus, they can be cruel about it."

Alerio started to turn Phobos then looked back at the shack and the man.

"You know, if you hold the fish higher above the fire, it won't get burned," he advised.

"If I hadn't been a teamster for Gurges Legion when the Etruscans beat them in the field, and surrounded the survivors in the stockade, I wouldn't have a bad stomach," the man retorted. "And if you hadn't ridden up here to challenge Belliena, I'd have had a quiet afternoon to enjoy my blackened fish."

The near destruction of a Legion at Volsinii affected a lot of people. Alerio among them. But, for all the horrors that came with the defeat of a Legion, Alerio had met his adopted father. That meeting had changed his life.

After saluting the fisherman, he kneed the stallion, and proceeded to circle the lake.

***

Five hundred feet from the old fisherman's shack, Alerio noted a cabin through the trees. He turned off the main road and more details became apparent. It rested on a bulge of land that pushed into the lake. Besides a scarlet cloth hanging over the doorway, a pack mule and a mountain pony stood at the side of the small house.

"Looks like someone is planning a trip," he mentioned to Phobos.

The stallion snorted. At the sound, the mountain pony neighed in response.

"What's the problem?" Belliena asked the pony as he came around the cabin.

He stopped and stared at the stallion and the Latian coming down the pathway. The bags in his hands hit the ground and Belliena reached for a kopis. But he changed his mind. Rather than pulling the Spartan sword, he drew a hunting knife and sprinted to the pony. After slicing the line, the rebel leaped onto the animal's back.

"Your pony may out climb Phobos, but it can't outrun him in this muck," Alerio shouted. "You'd do better on foot. Let's race Olympic style."

The suggestion was aimed at disrupting the Sabine's chain of thought. Flight being primary, the escape route secondary, and his immediate actions at the forefront, Alerio hoped to overload Belliena's mind by adding in a Greek athletic event.

Even kicking the mountain pony couldn't force the shorter legs to pull ahead of the stallion in the soft earth. Belliena glanced back, scanning the trees for other pursuers.

"If I get off to fight, your patrol will overwhelm me," the Sabine remarked. "I'm not stupid."

They trotted along the lakeside drawing closer to the top of the dam.

"No patrol, just me," Alerio assured him.

The knowledge that he only faced one man took a few moments to sink into his brain. However, once he realized the advantage, Belliena rode by a trail that would take him away from the lake, the soft ground, and the dam.

As Phobos trotted in the mud along the shoreline, Alerio noted branches in the lake. The pieces drifted as if on a meandering river for most of the length. But the closer the limbs got to the top of the cliff, the faster they traveled. Although the water vanished immediately below the horizon, a white mist floated out front of the drop-off. And when the debris reached the dam, the branches were moving at such a fast rate that they hurled into the mist. The limbs seemed to hang for a heartbeat before dropping out of sight.

The pony was three body lengths from the dam when Belliena hopped off and drew his short sword and a hunting knife.

"I don't feel like racing," he challenged.

Alerio reined in Phobos, slipped from the saddle, and pulled his gladius and the Legion dagger.

"Good," he replied while rotating his shoulders to loosen the muscles, "because I don't feel like chasing you."

Chapter 9 – Leverage

Belliena crouched, held out his weapons, and walked forward, angling inland. Force to the edge of the lake, Alerio splashed into ankle deep water. While the lake would hamper the Roman's footwork, the Sabine had the freedom to dash around during the fight.

"Did you really think you could start a revolution and not attract the attention of a Lictor from the Republic?" Alerio inquired.

"I didn't plan on a revolution at first. The insurgency was Fuficia's idea," Belliena stated. He swiped with the knife. The weapon passed far from Alerio and left an opening for a counterattack. But Alerio noted the Sabine's sword hovered just out of the attack lane waiting for a chance to wound a foolhardy attacker.

When his ploy failed to draw Alerio in, the Sabine added, "It was the tutor who brought in an Umbrian and recruited the servant Ulpia. With their contacts, we were able to operate in secret."

"So, it was Prince Alunni's plan to create the Bronze Man?"

Belliena stumbled. He didn't expect the Roman to know the name of the Umbria Prince.

"Using the armor was my idea," Belliena bragged once he shook off the surprise.

Alerio stomped his right foot, splashing water to Belliena's left. The Sabine leaped right, thinking it was a precursor to an attack.

"Is life under the Republic so bad?" Alerio questioned.

"Sabine coins have lost their value. Our leaders have taken to wearing togas and spouting Latin phrases," Belliena sneered. "And the Sabine God, Soranus, has been absorbed by the God Apollo. My God is now an underling for music and dance in Apollo's temple."

"The God Soranus is recognized throughout the Republic and its territories," Alerio countered.

"We were the Wolves of Soranus," Belliena stated. "Our devotees were firewalkers. We strolled over hot ash and coals while wearing the entrails of sacrifices. During the ceremonies, we honored the God Soranus, and he protected us. But now, we have to pay Latian priests to worship a Sabine God."

They paralleled each other while moving south towards the top of the falls.

"Well, I can't," Alerio said just before stomping his right foot. The splash caught Belliena's left arm and leg. The Sabine hadn't moved with as much apprehension. "I can't blame you for not wanting to pay the priests. I feel the same way."

Not far from the combatants, the falls roared as water poured over the cascade. The leaves and branches that drifted on the surface became frantic as they raced for the drop off. Alerio stomped a third time.

The Sabine barely flinched from the splash. His mistake. Alerio exploded through the water droplets. Steel carved a slice from Belliena's left arm and the warrior stumbled away from Alerio's blade. He dropped his knife.

"I can treat that," Alerio offered while circling out of the ankle-deep water. "Put down your sword."

Alerio's path forced Belliena around until the Sabine stood in the shallows.

"And then you'll nail me to a cross," Belliena growled. "I'll not become an example of Republic justice."

The Sabine swiped his blade in a diagonal cut while rushing Alerio. But the gladius easily deflected the sword. Dipping to his left, Alerio sliced with his knife.

Blood flowed along the cut in Belliena's shirt and soaked Alerio's left sleeve. The Sabine staggered back into the water.

"Let me sew you up," Alerio offered. "We'll have a drink, eat some smoked fish, and talk."

"And then you'll put me up on the wood," Belliena slurred.

Red pooled around his ankles for a moment before the current whisked it away. Between the arm and his stomach wounds, the Sabine dribbled more blood into the river.

"I will see you crucified," Alerio admitted.

Belliena threw the sword. As Alerio ducked the spinning blade, the Sabine rebel hobbled into deep water. In a heartbeat, the current swept him off his feet.

He might have intended suicide and changed his mind or realized he couldn't swim across the reservoir that close to the falls. Alerio would never know which. Instantly, Belliena began to scream and thrash about in the water. The power of the flow took the Sabine to the crest and flung him out into the air. Flailing with his arms and legs, Belliena rode the spillover for a heartbeat before he tumbled out of sight.

***

Alerio reined in Phobos at the fisherman's shack. A jerk of the lead lines settled Belliena's pony and the pack mule when they pulled away from the stallion.

"How far downstream from the falls will a body travel?" he asked the fisherman. "Or is it lost to the Nera River?"

"I saw him go over. Not very graceful, was he?"

"It wasn't a dignified way to go," Alerio acknowledged. "About the distance?"

"He's most likely hanging on a tree root at the third cataract. But you'll need to crawl out and check all the drops to be sure."

The sun hung low, casting long shadows over the top of the falls.

"Will he stay until dawn?" Alerio inquired.

"Probably not," the fisherman replied. "Eventually, the strong current flushes everything down river."

"About that smoked fish?"

"I've already wrapped several in leaves for you," the fisherman said while offering up a package.

***

Just before midday, the guard at the Proconsul's compound noted three mounts heading for the gate. A big stallion led the procession followed by a mountain pony. The third animal, and most troubling, was a mule with a body tied over its back.

"Officer of the Day," the Sentry called out.

He didn't want any responsibility for a body being delivered at his post. To his relief, the officer and the trio of mounts arrived at the same time.

"Can I help you?" the Centurion inquired. Then he noted the rider had grass stains and dried blood on his clothing. "This isn't a temple if you need prayers for your dead friend."

"I fished him out of the roots and rocks, spent the night with his body, and loaded him on the mule this morning," Alerio listed. "He is not a friend or a companion. He is the Bronze Man and I need to speak with Chief Lictor Cerialis."

"If he's the Bronze Man," the Centurion inquired, "who are you?"

"Lictor Sisera," Alerio responded. "And no, I don't have a fasces with me."

He nudged Phobos forward, forcing the officer to step out of the way. The Centurion started to protest then reconsidered. He knew all the Proconsul's enforcers and stayed out of their way. And while he didn't know this one, he decided not to issue a challenge. Lictors were selected for their skills with weapons and had the authority to use them on citizens.

"Well, are you sending men to unload the body?" Alerio inquired as he moved into the compound. "Or will I have to unload the Bronze Man myself."

"Optio, send Second Squad to the stables," the Centurion ordered. "Have them take custody of the corpse."

***

Shortly after the Legionaries took the body, Alerio and the Chief Lictor stood outside a doorway glaring at each other.

"This is how it works in Rieti," Cerialis scolded. "You tell me. And if I decide the news has value to the Proconsul, I deliver the facts to him."

"The body is the Bronze Man," Alerio stated, "as is the wounded tutor."

"So, what else is there to tell?"

"That, Chief Lictor, is between the Proconsul and me," Alerio insisted.

"You need to stop being stubborn and trust…"

"Cerialis, I hear you in the hall," the Proconsul called through the doorway. "Get in here and tell me where we stand with the Bronze Man investigation."

Alerio shrugged his shoulders and smiled. Then he turned and headed down the corridor.

"Lictor Sisera, where are you going?" Cerialis demanded.

"I'm being trusting," Alerio replied.

"How is you walking away, any form of trust?"

"You want to act as a filter for Proconsul Crassus. Or maybe take credit for the investigation," Alerio responded, "then you go right ahead."

"But there are things I don't understand," Cerialis pleaded while chasing after Alerio. "I don't know the connection between the Bronze Man, the body you brought in, Fuficia the tutor, and the servant Ulpia."

"Or the third rebel," Alerio stated as he reached the exit to the hallway. "I need a bath."

"Lictor Sisera, stop right there," Cerialis ordered, "or I'll have you detained."

"Do you see the blood on my clothing?" Alerio asked. He pointed to the left sleeve where the red had been washed out, leaving an unmistakable blood stain. "I don't take kindly to being threatened. If this is a challenge, here's a hint, it's a bad idea."

Lictors were chosen from Centurions who used their combat skills one final time before retiring. Or they were brought in from noble families. For them, being an enforcer substituted for military service as the first rung of a political career. One had combat experience while the other possessed education, connections, and a few years of weapons training. The scarred Alerio Sisera projected the confidence of both types of Lictor.

"That's not what I mean," Cerialis said, changing his tone. "I'd like a full report before you leave."

"You have the bodies and a witness. Figure it out for yourself," Alerio instructed as he stepped over the threshold. "After cleaning up, I'm heading to Rome, my villa, and my family."

"First, you need to speak with the Proconsul," Cerialis stated.

"That's all I asked for," Alerio said while stepping back into the hallway.

***

Otacilius Crassus had been a Consul of Rome twelve years prior, making him around fifty-four years old. Although not an old man, the Proconsul had the stooped shoulders of a much older person.

Alerio thought the posture was strange. A standard of the Republic deemed that men of authority kept an overview of the situation but did not deal with *minima*, little things. They delegated mundane tasks to keep their minds and schedules free for bigger issues. Just as the Law of Twelve

Tables gave only guidance while leaving details for the courts to judge, the Proconsuls and Praetors kept their distance from minutiae. Crassus' stoop was an oddity.

"Proconsul Crassus may I introduce Lictor Alerio Carvilius Sisera," Cerialis announced when they stopped in front of the governor's desk.

"You're the one my friend Cornelius Blasio called the scarred Lictor," Crassus exclaimed. "It's about time you got here. Although you could have cleaned up before requesting an audience."

Alerio shot a hard look at the Chief Lictor. The Proconsul hadn't been informed of Alerio's arrival or that he was already investigating the crimes.

"Sir, I decided to get to work before reporting in," Alerio informed him.

"I like a man of action," the Proconsul stated. "I suppose it's too early to expect results."

"Praetor Blasio sends his regards," Alerio said filling the air as he collected his wits. Accusing a Chief Lictor of withholding information was not a good idea. Although Alerio was tempted. After a heartbeat to settle on a strategy, he remarked. "I've reported all but one fact to Chief Lictor Cerialis. He'll undoubtedly give you a full report on the rebellion."

"Rebellion? It's worse than I thought," Crassus whined. "I've got unrest from the Sabine and the Umbria tribes. And complaints from citizens in the region. A bandit was bad enough. But now I have to deal with rebels."

"No, sir. Lictor Cerialis and I have apprehended the Bronze Men," Alerio told the Proconsul. "The rebellion, except for one detail, had been stopped."

"What detail?" Crassus inquired.

Alerio moved to the side of the desk and bent to the Proconsul's ear.

"The last rebel and the third Bronze Man is Prince Alunni from the Umbria tribe," Alerio whispered. "I believe you'll find him in Terni."

Accusing a Prince of rebellion could put the Proconsul in an awkward position. Because Alerio wasn't sure how the information would affect Otacilius Crassus, he wanted to keep Alunni's name a secret between them.

The Governor sat straighter, slammed a hand on his desktop, and laughed.

"Chief Lictor, have a scribe send letters to the Umbria Chiefs," the Proconsul commanded. "I want them here in three days. Any who refuse, will be arrested and crucified."

"Sir, those are harsh terms," Cerialis noted.

Proconsuls possessed the authority to draw the regional Legion from their garrisons and march them to battle. It wouldn't matter if the mobilization was in response to an invasion, or to pacify an area. Proconsuls wielded the power based on their judgement. And they would not be questioned by the Senate, unless they lost the battle, or their territory fell into chaos.

"Ever since the Bronze Man began his crime spree, I've received delegations from the Sabine and Umbria," Crassus explained. "They made demands, and I considered each in the name of peace. When the Chiefs arrive, I want them to see four crosses with rebels up on the wood."

"Sir, we only have three rebels, and one is already dead," Cerialis offered.

"Four crosses on the road," Crassus repeated. "I want the Chiefs to see the wood. And I want them to wonder who the fourth cross is for. Now go and tell the scribe."

When the Chief Lictor had gone, the Proconsul stood and gripped Alerio's wrist.

"I was a friend of your father," Crassus stated. "Some of his political smarts must have rubbed off on you."

"Senator Maximus was a good teacher," Alerio acknowledged.

"I'll use the rebellion of the Prince as leverage," Crassus explained. "But now I owe you. What do you want?"

"When the time comes…"

Proconsul Otacilius Crassus held up a hand to stop Alerio.

"You'll have my backing, when you need it," he assured Alerio. "Now that you're done in Rieti, will you return to Praetor Blasio's services?"

"No, sir, I'm returning to the Capital," Alerio responded. "I'd like to be home for Saturnalia."

"Give my best to Lady Aquila," the Proconsul instructed.

Then he sat, returning to the sheets on his desk. But the stooped shoulders were gone, and the man appeared vigorous and lively.

Alerio marched out of the room. In the hallway, he met the Chief Lictor coming back from his chore.

"I don't know what you said to the Proconsul," Cerialis questioned. "But it brought him to life. What did you tell him?"

"I simply gave him leverage," Alerio replied. "If you'll excuse me, I have a ceremonial ax to retrieve. And then a long journey home."

They exchanged salutes and Cerialis entered the governor's office while Alerio marched down the hallway. The Chief Lictor would continue his duties as the chief enforcer for an invigorated Proconsul and Alerio would return to the Senate for another assignment.

Safe from the Bronze Man, the citizens of the valley and their families could travel safely from their farms to the market. Three bodies up on the wood and a fourth cross attested to it. In a few days, Proconsul Crassus would use that fourth cross to bring the Umbria under control. Secretly threatening to crucify one of their Princes had that effect on a tribe. Lacking the support of the Umbrians, the Sabines also would settle down for the time being. With the mystery solved, and peace restored to the valley, Lictor Sisera chose a detour before turning the stallion towards Rome and home.

Act 4

Chapter 10 – Chariot Races

Eight days after leaving Rieti, Phobos, the mountain pony, and the mule clomped off the main road that ran alongside the frozen Arno river. They climbed a low hill towards a cluster of buildings. Smoke rising into the cold, crisp afternoon air from one hinted at a warm destination for Alerio.

Two men came from the entrance of the structure. One was a short squat Latin while the other appeared to be Etruscan. They seemed surprised to see the small caravan approaching.

"The animals need a stable," Alerio stammered through frozen lips. "And I need a warm fire."

Statue like, he sat stiffly on Phobos wrapped in a blanket pulled over his Legion cape. A wool cloth tucked under his felt hat protected his neck and cheeks from the cold. Even with the layers, the chill seeped through the material and Alerio shivered.

"This is Legion Way Station number one from Fiesole. Or as the locals call it, Burchio Station," the Latin remarked. His breath sent billows of white fog into the air. "After the snow last night and the freeze this morning, we didn't expect any couriers or travelers."

"Most people stayed where they were comfortable," the other guy added.

"Last night, I had a thin tent and hard ground," Alerio told him.

"Then welcome to mile marker one hundred and ninety," the first man offered. "We are the last station before Fiesole."

Despite the cold, Alerio smiled. When he had been 'volunteered' for the Legion, fifteen years ago, he'd slept through the courier's first stop. Now that he saw Burchio Station, he was unimpressed, except for the smoke from the fireplace inside.

"Venthi will show you where to pen your animals."

"Follow me," the stableman directed. "I'll show you the fine facilities of the station."

He strolled around the building and Alerio nudged Phobos into motion. The pony and mule followed.

***

Phobos stomped the ground in challenge as they walked by corrals with horses, another pen with ponies, and a final enclosure with mules. All the animals faced the light breeze and were huddled together, sharing warmth. A few shied away from the stallion.

"That's a fine horse," Venthi complemented. He ran a hand along the warhorse's flank. "A few years ago, he'd have been the lead on a team."

The stableman tossed straw into a small, isolated corral.

"He's never been a draft animal as far as I know," Alerio replied while pulling bundles off the mule. "I've had him eight years. Never during those years would I attempt to harness him to a wagon."

"Too feisty?" Venthi questioned.

"Wait, I lied," Alerio admitted. "A week ago, I used him to pull a wagon."

"You couldn't have done that a year ago," the stableman suggested. "He'd have kicked his way free."

"You seem to know a lot about my horse," Alerio noted.

"He's Etruscan and bred for chariot racing," Venthi informed Alerio. "Didn't you notice he doesn't like other horses ahead of him? Or that he'll race to the front of any group of riders, but not run off?"

"I didn't know," Alerio admitted. "I just thought he was crazy."

"Crazy is the reason team owners sell hard to manage horses," the stableman confirmed. "Getting four hot tempered horses to work together is difficult. A few will snap from the discipline. Your horse is probably one of them. But not so much now."

"Why not now?" Alerio inquired.

"Old age," Venthi stated as he ran his hands over the gray on the chestnut stallion's muzzle. "But he's in excellent shape. You took good care of him."

"He's taken good care of me," Alerio replied.

"You cavalry?"

"I'm a Legion infantry officer," Alerio said. He didn't want to get into a Lictor conversation with the stableman. "My father has a farm at Cintolese. I'm going to visit."

"It's always nice to be home for Saturnalia."

"Unfortunately, I can't stay for the celebration," Alerio described. "I've got to be back in Rome by the seventeenth."

"You better hurry. The holiday is in fifteen days."

After brushing down the animals, they carried the bundles and the saddle into a storage shed. Alerio selected his bedroll and a large satchel with a strap. As he settled the strap over his shoulder, Venthi told him, "Your things will be safe here."

"I'm sure they will be," Alerio responded, "but some things are too valuable to let out of your sight."

"Come on," the stableman encouraged while rubbing his hands together, "Urbicus will have stew in the pot and enough wood on the fire."

"Enough to cook?" Alerio inquired as they rounded the building.

"A small flame will cook the stew. The station manager is cheap and doesn't want to pay woodsmen. So, the station is always cold. Unless you're sitting in the fireplace," Venthi responded. "But with a guest, he'll need to put enough wood in to warm the room."

The stableman opened the door and stepped aside to let Alerio walk in first.

"Sounds delightful," Alerio remarked at the threshold.

"What's delightful?" Urbicus asked.

"The aroma of fresh stew," Alerio answered the manager.

He didn't say anything about the fresh pieces of wood in the fireplace.

***

The three sat in chairs around the hearth. They ate and relaxed in the warmth with bowls of stew in their hands and mugs of wine by their legs. Alerio reached over the satchel, picked up his mug, and took a sip.

"What did you mean about Phobos being the lead horse on a team?" Alerio asked Venthi.

"A chariot quad rig has a post horse, two in the center that follow, and the lead horse on the outside," the stableman explained. "When the chariot turns left in a tight radius, the post horse slows and almost pivots around the pole. While the center horses follow by leaning, the outside horse must be the fastest to circle the outside edge. Then once on the straightaway, the beast has to set the pace for the team."

"Like a maniple line wheeling around to face a flanking enemy," Alerio suggested.

"Exactly," Urbicus, the station manager, agreed. "Think of the Legionary on the end of the line, jogging to keep up. Now imagine doing the maneuver while in an all-out sprint."

The stableman slurped the last of his stew and placed the bowl beside his mug of wine. He stood, bent at the knees, and bounced up and down as if driving a cart over a bumpy road. Then he held out both hands with his fingers spread, mimicking the grip of holding four reins.

"When the chariot reaches the marker pole, the driver retracts the reins on the post horse, pulling it around," Venthi explained while yanking his left hand back. Then he brought his extended right arm to the midline of his chest. The motion of his hands resembled someone turning a crank. "At the same time, the driver pulls the lead horse to the side. When I patted down your stallion, I felt ridges under the skin from the harness on his right side."

"Why hasn't anyone noticed that before?" Alerio questioned.

"My family has been racing chariots and breeding teams for a hundred years," the stableman boasted. "Few people, Etruscan or Latian, would recognize the subtle indentions caused by the turning leather."

"The Etruscans are really proud of their chariot racing," Urbicus added. "Although, they won't admit they took the practice from the Greeks."

"Greeks my butt," Venthi exclaimed. "My people were riding chariots to war long before the easterners showed up. Do you know why the racers turn to the left?"

"I don't," Alerio admitted.

"To place their sword hand towards the enemy," Venthi answered while swinging his right arm as if chopping with a blade. "After killing him, we rotate back before making another pass at the enemy. Chariot racers show the glorious use of war chariots."

"Your people don't use chariots in war any longer," Urbicus noted. "Now it's a sport for the wealthy. When I was in the Capital, I witnessed it firsthand."

"Some of the Celtic tribes up north still use war chariots," the stableman protested.

"And one day, the Legion will march north and beat them as well," Urbicus shot back.

"I've never attended the races," Alerio tossed out quickly, trying to prevent an argument. "What were they like?"

The station manager and the stablemen glared at each other for a moment before the manager replied to Alerio.

"The track was a third of a mile long and a thousand feet wide," Urbicus reported. "They placed a divider down the center to keep the returning chariots from running into those yet to make the turn. Embankments on both sides elevated the spectators."

"It sounds like you had a good view," Alerio remarked.

"It would have been," the station manager scowled, "but no commoner can get near the finish line. Those areas had been sectioned off for groups of rich merchants, growers, and Senators. Us Plebeians had to stand away from the Patricians."

"How do you know they were noblemen?"

"The fencing around the Senators were adorned with colored flags. On the track, the teams displayed matching colors," Urbicus replied. "Blue for blues, Green for greens, White for whites, and Red for reds. Each group rooting for the teams of the same color."

"But how were the races?" Venthi inquired

"The day started with the newer drivers racing pairs of horses," Urbicus stated. "After several races, the quad rigs came out. Four horses across, each horse blowing hard even before the start. And then, the wrecks as they rounded the posts with men and horses sliding around. And if they didn't go down from bad handling, the unlucky chariots were knocked over by their competitors."

"It sounds rough," Alerio said.

"It was," Urbicus agreed. "Three or four of the ten starters in each race had to be carried off the track."

"See," the stableman offered, "it's like war."

Alerio had seen enough war that he started to protest the remark. But three or four injured or dead, out of ten Legionaries, would be a bad day on any assault line. He decided to let the comment go.

Instead of correcting Venthi, he asked, "Is there more stew?"

***

As the sun came up, the three chairs, mugs, and the satchel remained around the fireplace. On the floor of the still warm room, the station manager, stableman, and Alerio Sisera slept in their bedrolls. Usually, the farm boy in Alerio woke him early. But a belly of hot food, several mugs of wine, relaxed conversation, and the cold finally leaving his bones, allowed him to sleep late.

The same environment kept Urbicus and Venthi in their blankets longer then normal. It's why all three were surprised when four men came through the doorway.

"Just like a bunch of lazy Plebeians," one boomed. "Sleeping the day away while others prosper."

"Is there any doubt why noblemen run the Republic," another stated.

Urbicus pushed to his feet, his cheeks red with embarrassment.

"Senior Tribune Scutulati, Tribune Marianus," the station manager greeted two of them, "give me a moment and I'll lay out refreshments."

While Urbicus vanished behind the counter, Venthi leaped to his feet and ran out the door to tend their mounts.

Alerio rolled over and sat up, still partly covered in the warm blanket.

"Maybe you should get busy, tidy up the room, and stoke the fire," Marianus directed Alerio.

"Sisera is a Legion infantry officer," the station manager informed the group. He cut slices from a cured meat roll and carved chunks off a cheese wheel. After scooping olives from a mounted amphora and dumping them in a bowl, Urbicus shoved the food across the countertop. "He's a guest. Wine, gentlemen?"

"Get on your feet Centurion," Tribune Marianus instructed Alerio. "You are in the presence of a Senior Tribune of Legion North, Western Sector. Show your respect."

Alerio yawned and stretched. After sleeping in his shirt while camping, he'd taken it off to sleep more comfortably.

"With all due respect Senior Tribune Scutulati, I'm not in your command," Alerio told the senior officer. "But I would advise that you get control of your staff."

At Alerio's remark, the other members of the party looked at Marianus. The Tribune nodded his approval and the two younger men, most likely Junior Tribunes, moved towards Alerio.

"You aren't on patrol, or you'd have NCOs along to wipe your noses," Alerio growled as he came to his feet. "And it's too cold for a joy ride. Where are you heading?"

The question was to identify the leader of this pack. Just because they were noblemen and officers didn't stop the four from thuggish behavior. Alerio wanted to know who he should put down first if they pressed their advantage.

"Not that it's any of your business," Marianus replied, "but we're going to the Capital for Saturnalia."

"Then, Tribune, I suggest you have a snack while Venthi changes your mounts," Alerio stated. He adjusted the blanket to bring it a little higher on his neck. "And leave me alone."

"I have combat officers in my Centuries like him," one of the Junior Tribunes announced. "Let me, I know how to put him in his place."

"I pity the men under your command," Alerio told him. "But I'm not one of them. Do not test me."

"He is arrogant for a commoner. It might be our duty to remind him of his place. I'm sure his next commander will appreciate it," Marianus sneered. Then the Tribune noticed the satchel. "What's a combat officer doing with such a finely tooled leather bag?"

The satchel rested on the other side of the fireplace with his chair and the mug. Alerio swore under his breath for leaving it there.

"You don't want to touch that," he warned.

"I've had enough of your insolence," Senior Tribune Scutulati exclaimed. "Seize the satchel. Let's see what he's stolen."

When Alerio allowed the blanket to fall from his shoulders, the four staff officers and Urbicus gasped. Marianus froze in mid step.

**

The impudent Centurion, although not an old man, sported a collection of marks attesting to a lifetime of combat. A double track from a gladius stab sat ugly on his right shoulder. Both forearms were marred, two separate wounds on his right hand warned that he knew blade work, and a round wound on his right hip exhibited where an arrow had entered his flesh. A small scar over his right eye was overshadowed by the crescent shaped blemish on top of his head. They were impressed with the visible marks. Clearly, the combat officer had faced enemies many times in his career.

When Alerio turned to pick up his shirt, they stopped breathing. Beyond the scar on the back of Alerio's left arm and the dimple when the arrow passed through his skin, he displayed the memory of a horrible episode. Lines of puckered skin from a whip crisscrossed his back.

Alerio dropped his wool traveling shirt over his head, spun on the Legion officers, and braced.

"I am Colonel Alerio Carvilius Sisera, a Lictor of the Republic," he declared. "If you touch the symbol of my office, I can guarantee this. None of you will get home in time for Saturnalia."

The station manager and three of the staff officers stood with their mouths hanging open. But one Junior Tribune drew his gladius.

"Ridiculous," he screamed while stabbing out with the weapon.

Alerio slapped the blade to the side with the back of his left hand while spinning forward. Once inside the range of a thrust, he brought his elbow around and slammed it into the junior officer's jaw. When the young man stumbled back, he did it without his gladius.

In the brief interval between the Tribunes responding to the assault on one of their own and the confusion at the sudden brutality, Alerio leaped over two chairs and landed next to the satchel. The single tie came loose, and Alerio's hand vanished into the bag.

"Home for the holiday, or a blood bath and stitches," he inquired.

In one hand Alerio held the gladius and in the other a double-bladed ax with ceremonial inscriptions and decorative scrolls.

"What's that prove?" the unarmed junior officer asked. "A Lictor carries a fasces. Where's yours?"

"It's a long story," Alerio replied.

"Where did you learn that disarming move?" Senior Tribune Scutulati inquired.

His eyes had an odd sheen, as if he witnessed something astonishing, yet out of place.

"When I was a very young man, a Centurion named Efrem took me under his care and taught me tactics and the gladius," Alerio answered. "And an Optio named Egidius instructed me in weapons and formations. Why do you ask?"

"Lictor Sisera, please return the blade to my junior officer," Scutulati remarked. "Accept our apologies and give my regards to Senior Centurion Efrem when you get to Fiesole. With your permission, Colonel, we'll take our leave now."

The door opened and Venthi started to enter while saying, "Sirs, your saddles have been moved to fresh mounts and your luggage transferred to fresh mules."

The stableman stopped when he saw the Centurion holding a fancy double-bladed ax and a gladius. It struck him as odd. He remembered seeing Sisera's sword in among his bundles.

"Senior Centurion Efrem?" Alerio asked. "I knew he was smart and a fine instructor. I never figured him for a command position."

"Efrem keeps up his training by punishing Tribunes on the practice field," Marianus uttered. "You learned from him. If we had time, we could compare bruises."

"I really don't want to be reminded of his methods," Alerio admitted.

He handed the young officer the gladius blade first. No one would return a weapon to a hothead in a manner that allowed for an impulsive stab.

The four Tribunes grabbed pieces of meat and cheese and handfuls of olives as they shuffled out of the station.

"Did I miss something?" Venthi asked.

"It's a long story," the station manager told the stableman. Then to Alerio, he inquired. "Refreshments before you leave, sir?"

Chapter 11 – Homecoming

Wooden structures, topped with clay roof tiles, lined the main streets. Behind several residences and businesses, Alerio saw a large Etruscan Temple. But it wasn't until he turned onto a side street that the thick stone walls of a citadel came into view.

"What's your business?" a sentry challenged when Phobos approached the gate.

With his spear held diagonally across his body and gripped in two hands, the Legionary displayed good training.

"I'm Lictor Sisera and I've come to see Senior Centurion Efrem," Alerio replied. "And please don't ask about my fasces."

"I wouldn't think of it, sir," the young infantryman replied. "You'll find the Senior Centurion in the headquarters building."

"That's it?" Alerio inquired. "Aren't you going to call the Sergeant of the Guard and question me?"

"No sir. It you aren't who you say, our senior combat officer will cut you to pieces," the guard responded while stepping aside. "It's not my place to deny him the pleasure."

Alerio laughed as he kicked Phobos into motion. Efrem hadn't lost his edge or the willingness to pass along his skills and attitude to the next generation. He guided his small procession around the practice field until he reached a cluster of structures. In front of the headquarters building, he tied up Phobos, the mountain pony, and the pack mule. After slipping the satchel strap over his shoulder, Alerio marched to the front door and pushed it open.

***

"Can I help you?" a duty NCO inquired.

"I'm here to see Senior Centurion Efrem."

"May I ask the nature of your visit?" the Optio responded. "The Senior Centurion is very busy."

Alerio glanced around the office. Two other NCOs sat watching the exchange. Their idleness demonstrated the lack urgency for the garrison command.

"I said, I'm here to see Efrem," Alerio bellowed while pulling out his double-bladed ax. "A Lictor does not answer foolish questions."

The duty NCO sat frozen from his mistake. He'd failed to ask the visitor's name and position. In the back of the office, another Optio rolled out of his chair, slipped, then used his hands for purchase on the floor as he scrambled down a hallway. Moments later, the tall lean form of the senior combat officer came rushing from his office.

"Lictor, we didn't expect..." Efrem stopped, and a tight smile crossed his lips. "If I wanted to talk to a weak, little, farm boy, I'd have sent for one."

"If you see a weak, little farm boy around here," Alerio countered, "slap him and send him home."

"How about I buy him a mug of vino and he tells me why he's a Lictor of the Republic."

"That's better than fending off one of your slaps," Alerio told his former teacher. "Because they hurt."

Nods from the office NCOs affirmed the pain of training with the Senior Centurion.

"But you remembered the lesson," Efrem offered as he came around the desk and gripped hands with Alerio. Over his shoulder, he instructed. "Optio, if anyone needs me, I'll be off getting drunk and telling lies with Alerio Sisera."

"It's a pleasure to meet you, Colonel," one NCO stated.

Alerio noted the wide-eyed stares of the other two Optios.

"You said my name on purpose," Alerio mentioned while they walked to the exit.

"I did. It'll give the staff something to talk about while I'm gone."

"But how do they know I was a Battle Commander?"

"Alerio, your father is so proud of you," Efrem explained, "he tells everyone who'll listen about the news from your letters."

Outside, the Senior Centurion pointed at an idle Legionary.

"These animals need rubbing down and put up for the night," he instructed.

The infantryman eyed Alerio as if judging something. Finally, he asked, "Where should I put them, sir?"

"In the Tribune's stable," Efrem answered. Then to Alerio, he explained. "Most Patricians mix well with the Plebeian class. But a few are hostile to commoners, and that bleeds into the attitude of the Legionaries. It's one of the problems of garrison duty. People have too much time to contemplate their own importance."

The Senior Centurion steered them to a small building next to a barracks.

"I like the NCO's pub," he exclaimed while holding the door, "they have better stew."

"Garrison duty is different than a Consul's marching Legion," Alerio commented. "I'm not accustomed to officers dining with NCOs. How do the Optios feel about this?"

"We're not eating, Colonel Sisera," Efrem announced so everyone in the pub heard. "We're here to drink."

When the Legion's Senior Centurion and a visiting Colonel took a corner table, the NCOs near them moved away.

"Now I see," Alerio observed, "you want privacy."

"That's correct," Efrem acknowledged. "No one here will want to join us and try to suck up to me."

A scarred veteran came over with two mugs and a pitcher of wine.

"Stew, sirs," he asked.

Alerio noticed a scar on the side of the server's head. The slice wasn't from a thick bladed knife or a Legion dagger.

"Where did you pick up that?" Alerio asked while pointing to the side of his head.

"You wouldn't know it, sir," he stated. "I was stationed in Crotone, and we tangled with a gang of rebels. One got his knife under my helmet."

Alerio lifted his petasos and bent so the server could see the crescent shaped scar on top of his head.

"I understand completely," Alerio told him. "You're lucky you survived."

"They came at us out of the darkness," the veteran mumbled, "in the night."

"They always do," Alerio confirmed.

The server moved away and quickly disappeared into the back room.

"What was that about?" Efrem inquired.

"On the east coast of the Republic, there are two kinds of enemies. Thieves disguised as rebels who use knives," Alerio reported while touching the top of his head. "And there are assassins who use thin curved blades. The old veteran is lucky to be alive."

"And you aren't?" Efrem challenged.

"Memento mori," Alerio stated after filling two mugs. "Remember you too must die. But not that day, nor this day."

The Senior Centurion gazed at his former student before picking up his mug. Alerio had matured and, more importantly, he'd survived because of the gladius and tactics training. With enthusiasm, they clicked their containers and took long pulls of wine.

***

A long while later, after a third or fourth pitcher, and with four empty stew bowls on the tabletop, the two senior officers leaned towards each other.

"I'm telling you, Sisera, you've got to start attending the chariot races," Efrem coached. "There are more deals made between the races than there are bets placed."

"I haven't had a lot of opportunity," Alerio admitted. "Besides, the track is always built away from the defensive walls. It's one reason I never bothered attending."

"If you're going to succeed at politics, you'll need to go where the factions are gathered," Efrem told him. "I was raised in Rome. My older brother and I went to the races with our father. While we watched the chariots and cheered, he talked about everything except what was happening on the track."

"Can we talk about something other than politics?" Alerio asked. "I've a feeling when I get back to Rome, it'll taint everything I do."

"Sure, what's on your mind?"

"You, Senior Centurion," Alerio responded. "You'll be retiring soon, and I can't imagine you as a farmer."

"Why not? I've got a cute little Etruscan wife," Efrem stated. "She's from a royal family and her father will give me acreage. Between the separation coin and the land, I will be the best farmer Saturn ever blessed."

"Does she have wide inviting hips, and a pretty face that makes a man want to return home at night?"

"Have you met my wife?" Efrem inquired.

They toasted Efrem's spouse. After placing his mug on the table, Alerio got serious.

"I'm having two triremes being built to protect my merchant fleet," he explained. "I need forty well trained Marines on each warship to fend off Illyrian pirates. And I need someone to train the Marines and a steady hand to manage the ships."

"Are you offering me a job, farm boy?" Efrem asked.

"Plus, a villa and land in sunny Crotone."

"I'm very happy here in the mountains," Efrem reported. But a twitch at the corner of his eyes told the tale of a nervous man. "When will the ships be done?"

"Hopefully, by late summer," Alerio answered. "Are you interested?"

"It just so happens, I'm leaving the Legion in the spring," the Senior Centurion stated. "And I really hate the idea of being a farmer."

"Saturn's loss is my gain," Alerio declared.

"Your father will be happy to have you home for Saturnalia."

"I'm not staying for the celebration," Alerio informed him. "I need to get back to Rome and my family."

"I'm glad you stopped here first."

"I had to," Alerio suggested. Although running into the Senior Centurion had been an accident, it saved him from searching out Efrem. "To thank you and to hire you."

"Mission accomplished on both counts," Efrem exclaimed.

He raised his hand to order more wine. But the old veteran was already heading for the table with a full pitcher.

***

It might have been nostalgia brought on by the familiar country, or the anticipation of seeing his father and mother again. In any case, Alerio woke long before dawn.

By sunrise he was heading off a flat plain and leaving the Arno River. Phobos, the pony, and the mule climbed into the hills. The trails that twisted into gullies and over spines of mounds might have confused a stranger. But Alerio had grown up hunting in the area and traveling the routes on the way to the markets in Fiesole.

He stopped to rest the animals at midday. As it did in this section of the Etruscan region, the cold was driven away by a warming sun. While the beasts ate, Alerio sat in a clearing and pondered his future.

In his quest for a seat in the Senate, he could depend on the legacy backing from Spurius Maximus' faction. Additionally, he had the support of Senators Lucius Metellus and Mamilius Vitulus. Although they controlled only a portion of their factions. But he had earned support from Praetor Blasio, Proconsul Crassus, and Titus Lanatus, patriarch of a powerful family. With those votes in hand, Alerio would be ready, on the Ides of March, to bargain with the new Consul for a seat in the Senate.

Feeling good about the future, Alerio returned the caravan to the trail. By midafternoon, they dropped out of the hills and entered a land of farms, vineyards, and orchards.

Almost as if he'd never left, Alerio identified landmarks and geographical features. He knew every detail of the road leading to the Sisera farm. What he didn't recognize, when he arrived, were the two large villas in place of the house where he grew up.

***

The chaos of his arrival settled when his mother got out the big pot and organized a slicing and dicing session in the kitchen. While preparations for a homecoming feast filled one villa with excited talk, Alerio's father grabbed his arm and walked him out of the house.

"See that hill to the west?" the elder Sisera asked.

"I do."

"Thanks to the coins you sent, we've expanded the farm to the top," his father informed Alerio. "Your sister's husband wants to plant olive trees."

"You don't seem happy about the expansion," Alerio noted.

"Balbus Choragi is a good man, and he treats your sister well," former Optio Sisera answered. "But he has boundless energy. Enough that I'm feeling useless."

"He built the other villa?" Alerio guessed.

Sergeant Sisera seemed to deflate at the mention of another of his son-in-law's accomplishments.

"Come with me," Alerio offered.

He switched hand positions and guided his father to the corral.

"The big fellow is Phobos," Alerio said introducing the stallion. "He and you are going to help me with my political career."

The usually standoffish horse trotted to Alerio and his father. Phobos stood patiently while both men reached over the wooden rails and patted his neck.

"Not to question a Battle Commander, but how can an old man and a horse past his prime help your new career?"

"All Senators are busy. They have investments, merchant ships, timberland, mines, or farms," Alerio replied. "The one thing they don't have is a moment to waste. Meaning the only way for a junior Senator to get heard is to have them come to me."

"And a chariot team will do that?"

"A winning one will," Alerio confirmed as he rubbed the stallion's muzzle. "Use Phobos and breed me a team of champions."

"I know just the plot of land for the stables and corrals," the elder Sisera remarked. "It'll cost. But I imagine you've thought of that."

"Cost is not a problem," Alerio stated. "Results are all that matter."

"I want to hear what command is like from a Colonel's viewpoint…"

A field hand waved and distracted the elder Sisera. Without finishing the idea, he strutted away from the corral. He failed to notice his son lingering with the stallion.

***

Three days later, his father, mother, Balbus his brother-in-law, and his sister, their two small children, and Alerio's youngest sister, plus two of her suitors filled the table. Inside, Alerio chuckled. He remembered the table being much larger.

"So, Alerio, you'll be staying through Saturnalia?" Balbus inquired.

"No, I need to get back to Rome. There's business that needs my attention, as well as my family."

"What's war like, Colonel Sisera?" one of his sister's admirers asked.

Alerio glanced at his father to see if the elder Sisera wanted to answer. But the former Sergeant dropped his eyes.

"War is like," Alerio began but stopped. After a moment of thought, he told the young man. "Blindfold yourself and walk into a corral of ibexes. Then have a friend, or an enemy, toss in a wolf."

"But I wouldn't be able to see the wolf," the man complained, "or dodge the horns with a blindfold on."

"Exactly," Alerio said as he reached for the platter of cooked cabbage and carrots. "In war, you never know the location of the sharp teeth or the ram that'll put you down."

"Just think, you were once an undersized practice post for bigger boys," the elder Sisera proclaimed.

When he didn't continue, his wife asked, "What are you saying, husband?"

"Alerio is more than a Legionary like I was," the former Optio stated. "Only a tactician could explain the madness of combat like that. Salute to you, my son."

He tipped his wine glass towards Alerio.

***

The next morning, Alerio mounted the mountain pony.

"Where's dad?" he inquired when his mother handed him the lead line for the pack mule.

"He's with Phobos," she answered. "Your father was afraid the stallion would miss you and act up."

"Have I asked too much of him?"

"That horse and your father are good for each other," she said. "You better hurry Alerio. It's only thirteen days until Saturnalia."

He bent over and hugged his mother. Then stiff backed with misty eyes, Alerio trotted away from the Sisera-Choragi farm, heading westward.

Chapter 12 – Saturn's Celebration

Thirty-four miles from the farm, Alerio rode into Viareggio. Located on the Tyrrhenian Sea, the town boasted a broad beach, shops, and warehouses for grain and grapes going out and hardgoods coming in. Unfortunately for Lictor Sisera, no vessels were beached or anchored along the shoreline.

"What'll you give me for the mule and the pony?" he inquired at a stable.

"A fair price," the stableman answered. "But what will you ride?"

"The next merchant or Republic warship to beach here," Alerio answered.

"Most merchants have headed for their home ports for Saturnalia," the stableman explained. "Warships, I don't know about. But they probably have too."

With no other place to go and not enough days remaining to ride to Rome for Saturnalia, Alerio sold the pony and the mule. Shouldering his bundles, he marched into town and found a pub. On a deck facing the sea, he located a table and dropped the load.

"I need two things," Alerio told the proprietor when the man came over.

"We aim to please. What do you require?"

"Food first. And then I need a place to sleep while I wait for a ship."

"Are you a ship's officer?" the owner inquired.

"No, just a merchant with business in the Capital," Alerio lied. It was easier and cheaper when dealing with tradesman to hide higher positions or lofty titles such as Lictor of the Republic. "I've been visiting my father's farm and overstayed my days."

"I own the small building next door," the proprietor offered. "The only other occupant is a priest. He's only taking up one wall. The other is yours if you want it."

"Renting rooms by the wall," Alerio tested. "What if two more people arrive? Will we end up with four tenants?"

"Like I said, it's a small building. Do you want it or not?"

"I'll let you know after I taste your cooking."

The owner walked away shaking his head.

As far as Alerio could tell, there weren't many options for dining in Viareggio. If he took the room, he'd be obligated to eat at the pub. And there was nothing worse than being forced to eat mediocre food. When he separated from the Legion, he'd left the requirement for limited culinary choices behind.

***

"Yo Saturnalia," the middle-aged man said in greeting.

Alerio carried the Lictor ax in a satchel, his bedroll, a small sack with clothing, and a weapons bag. A single piece of luggage rested on the floor beside the priest's leg.

"It's a little early for the salutation," Alerio remarked.

He dropped his load against the opposite wall and peered around the tiny room. A table with three chairs was shoved to the back wall. The fourth chair held the priest.

"The harvest is over, the days grow shorter," the priest responded, "and soon the winter solstice will be upon us. So, with good cheer and fellowship, I say Saturn is the reason for the celebration. And thus, I offer you, Yo Saturnalia."

After the speech, Alerio expected the priest to ask for a donation. Involuntarily, he touched his coin purse.

"Yo Saturnalia," Alerio replied.

"Our host said you're a sea Captain," the priest ventured. "But your face lacks lines from squinting into the sun. And although a young man, your eyes are harder than a man who passes over Neptune's realm. I can see scars from sharp blades on your arms. Seeing as we're sharing a room, care to tell me the truth?"

"I was a Legion combat officer," Alerio submitted. "Now, I'm just a man trying to get home to his family for the holiday."

"As am I, Centurion."

"But you're a priest," Alerio inquired. "Do you have a family?"

"Of course, I have a family. I have a father, siblings, and a mother," the priest countered. "But they're not why I want to be in Rome for Saturnalia. The Temple of Jupiter holds a gala festival for the clerics and the novices. And with great joy and humor, we'll honor the old ways of Saturn's day."

Alerio started to tell the priest his feelings concerning the clerics at the Temple of Jupiter. About the coin sucking rat who prayed on Lady Aquila on the day of her husband's funeral and the ploy of claiming they didn't have the coins to cash in his temple chits. But just before he lit into the priest, the festive words 'Yo Saturnalia' raced across his mind.

"Alerio Sisera," he said while delivering a Legion salute.

"Callum Farnese, Priest of Jupiter," the man responded. He lifted his hand and motioned as if reaching across the room and placing his palm over Alerio's forehead. "May the blessings of the Sky Father keep you safe in your journey."

Alerio laughed.

"Is it not a worthy benediction?" Callum questioned.

"It might be," Alerio told him. "But the last time I was in the Capital, several priests of Jupiter swore at me. I'm curious. Can a single blessing counter multiple curses?"

"Did you assault or rob them?" Callum Farnese asked. He shifted as if the chair was suddenly uncomfortable. "Those would be difficult to overcome without sacrifices."

"I didn't attack them, Priest Farnese. I withdrew my coins. And that seemed to upset several of them."

"Coins are necessary to maintain the temple," Callum explained, "and to feed and dress the novices and priests. We are not allowed to join the Legion or to go into politics. It would be bad form to call down the wrath of the King of Gods to fend off competition or to ravish a political opponent. So, we depend on donations and the profits we make from deposits to live. I can't imagine that withdrawing a few coins would elicit such a harsh response."

"I moved my coins to the Temple of Vesta," Alerio reported. "They have Lictors protecting the Priestesses and, by extension, my coins. Plus, as long as the holy fire burns in the temple, Rome will survive."

Alerio neglected to reveal that it took a cart to haul the weight of the coins away from the Temple of Jupiter.

"Then it surely was a couple of desperate clerics," Callum declared. "I'm sure my blessing will overturn their rash actions."

Alerio hooked a chair with his foot and pulled it away from the table.

"What did you mean by honoring the old ways of Saturn's day?" Alerio inquired while settling into the seat. "My father simply gave out gifts to the servants for harvesting the crops. And he sacrificed to thank Saturn for the bounty. Is there more to the celebration?"

"Saturnalia harkens back to an earlier age," Callum Farnese explained. "A place where King Saturn ruled over an open land, and no one slaved or worked for another."

"Who carried the hoe and beat the grain shafts?" Alerio questioned. "Who directed the planting, weeding, and the harvest?"

"It was an age of extraordinary bounty from the earth," Callum replied. "Without the need for labor, food grew, and people lived in a state of innocence. King Saturn ruled over this idyllic world."

"It must have been years and years ago," Alerio offered. "Because nothing grows in abundance without coaxing from farmworkers and an overseer."

"It was a Golden age and as you point out, no longer even a memory," Callum stated. "However, we honor Saturn by recreating the age at Saturnalia. Servants sit at the head of the tables and are served by the heads of the household. Everyone exchanges gifts, as you noted. And to push back the long night of the winter solstice, we light a multitude of candles. Each flame represents knowledge and truth. Therefore, I want to return to the Temple of Jupiter for Saturnalia. To share the once-a-year experience with my brothers."

"And I, to share the day and night with my wife and children," Alerio remarked.

"Perhaps you could share the blessing of your personal deity," the priest suggested. "Adding another voice to support our endeavor can't hurt."

"Priest of Jupiter," Alerio offered, "my personal goddess is Nenia, the Goddess of Death."

Alerio expected at least a disagreeable face or maybe a shudder from the priest. Callum Farnese did neither.

"I traveled to Etruscan land at the request of a family," he commented. "The head of the household was a big supporter of the temple and he had fallen deathly ill. They requested an experienced cleric to comfort him in his final days."

"Did your services cost the family much?" Alerio inquired.

Revealing the Goddess of Death as Alerio's personal Goddess, had no effect on Callum Farnese. The question about cost, however, caused the priest's jaw to set in a hard line while his hand rubbed his forehead.

"You aren't a religious man, are you, Alerio Sisera?" Callum questioned.

"I sacrifice and pray," Alerio replied. "I honor the Gods in my own way. And while most are decent, I have a problem with greedy and manipulative priests."

"The family paid nothing for my presence or my administrations," Callum assured Alerio. "But for three days, I remained by his bedside, beseeching Nenia Dea to come and relieve a good man of his pain."

"I've done that too many times," Alerio confessed.

"And what did you charge the dying?"

Anger stiffened Alerio's spine at the accusation. Then he noted the quizzical expression on Callum's face.

"I charged the wounded nothing for my prayers," Alerio answered.

"Just as I charged nothing for my prayers," Callum revealed. "Now, will you pray for our journey?"

***

The next day, they moved their chairs onto the beach and gazed out to sea, watching for approaching ships.

"You're thinking about going into politics," Callum remarked. "One part of me envies your freedom to choose."

"I wouldn't have choices if I hadn't been adopted by Spurius Maximus," Alerio told him. "Without the Senator, I'd still be an infantryman or working on my father's farm. There's not much a Plebeian can do except join the Legion or work in the family business."

"Things have changed," Callum suggested. "The Pontifex Maximus of Rome is a Plebeian."

"He's from a rich trading family," Alerio mentioned. "And he was a Senator and a Consul before moving to the exalted position as the head of the College of Pontiffs."

"Yet, he's not a nobleman," Callum Farnese insisted. "And among his many accomplishments, Tiberius Coruncanius is a scholar of the twelve tablets."

"Businessman, politician, scholar, and the manager of Rome's temples," Alerio listed. "Are you saying I should follow his path?"

"Not at all. I was merely talking about the unique journey of one man."

"When you examine his accomplishments, he sounds more Patrician than Plebeian," Alerio observed.

"In addition, Pontifex Maximus Coruncanius regularly holds lectures on the law in the forum," the priest informed Alerio. "And commoners are invited and encouraged to participate. Single handedly, Tiberius Coruncanius is making a difference in the class structure."

"As a Plebeian, he couldn't do that without his other achievements," Alerio commented.

"Imagine what a man could do if he started as a nobleman," Callum Farnese supposed.

Alerio didn't say anything. His mind was churning about his future. Until this moment, his plan to be a Senator was him following in the footsteps of his adopted father. In a sense, he was staying in the family business. But now, he wondered at the possibilities as the priest's words kept repeating in his mind, *Imagine what a man could do if he started as a nobleman.*

***

The third day in Viareggio brought a warship from the north and another from the south. Almost as if the sea lanes opened like mountain passes cleared of snow in the spring, merchant ships arrived along with the five-bankers.

"I believe we'll get to the Capital before the festival," Alerio said.

"Maybe you," Callum Farnese sighed. "As a Legion officer, you can claim a place on a quinquereme. I'm afraid spending Saturnalia on a slow merchant ship will be my fate."

"We'll see," Alerio remarked.

They walked to the pub, took seats, and waited. Once the warships were back to the shoreline, then were hauled onto the beach, the ship's officers and their Centurions marched to the pub.

"Terrible storms up north had us trapped on shore for three days," a ship's officer described to the other group.

"You think your storms were bad," a Principale countered. "Down south, the Sky Father dumped a lake on us for three days."

At the reference to the God Jupiter, Alerio glanced at Callum Farnese. The priest hovered at the edge of his seat. No doubt deciding if he should offer a prayer to the sky Father for delivering the ships.

"Centurion, a word?" Alerio called to the senior officer of the southbound warship.

"Do I know you?" the Centurion inquired.

"Lictor Sisera," Alerio told him. "Have you committed any transgressions against the Republic, lately?"

To settle any question, Alerio lifted the double-bladed ax from the satchel. The other ships' officers noted the symbol of an enforcer. They looked away as if afraid of eye contact. Only the selected Centurion and Priest Farnese remained fixed on the ceremonial weapon.

"You're a Lictor?" Callum asked.

Alerio acknowledged the priest's statement before waving the ship's officer to a corner of the pub.

"What can I do for you, Lictor?"

"I am Lictor Sisera," Alerio confirmed. "But I'm also a Legion Colonel. And I need two favors."

"What can I do for you, sir?"

"I want to get to the Capital before Saturnalia," Alerio answered. "And the priest of Jupiter needs a ride as well."

"Sir, we all want to get to Rome for the festivities," the ship's Centurion informed Alerio. "You're not a problem. But the priest is a civilian."

Alerio glanced at the warship and the sea. After several seconds, he asked, "Suppose he was my prisoner?"

"In that case, transporting a Lictor and a detainee would certainly be within regulations."

***

Callum rocked back in his seat when Alerio dropped a hemp cord over the shoulders of the priest.

"For the crime of speaking against the Senate of the Republic," Alerio exclaimed. "Callum Farnese of the Temple of Jupiter, you are under arrest pending further investigation."

"But. Wait. I don't understand."

Callum's pleas went unnoticed by the two ship's officers who yanked him from the chair. They marched him down the beach and handed him up to a couple of sailors. Deposited on the deck of *Veritas' Candor*, the priest spent the night in the open. As he slept, someone dropped his blanket over him and placed his travel bag beside his slumbering body.

In the morning, the five-banker launched and rowed away from Viareggio. Alerio Sisera and Callum Farnese were passengers on the warship as it headed south for Rome. They were nine days and seven stops away from celebrating Saturnalia in the Capital.

Act 5

Chapter 13 – Fundamental Political Problem

One hundred and twenty miles south and five days out from Viareggio, the warship *Veritas' Candor* rolled in the swells.

Her port side rowers saw nothing but sea water through the oar openings as the vessel dipped. On the opposite side, a vista of grey clouds and a stormed filled sky greeted the starboard rowers. On the lowest tier, the oars on the right became fully submerged and locked up. For two heartbeats, the rowers attempted to limit the water pouring through the oar holes by holding coats, capes, or rags against the hull.

"Second officer, steady your rowers," the First Principale shouted down to the rowers' walk. "We need forward progress to fight the waves."

"Stroke, stroke, call the count," the rowing officer boomed. He strutted down the narrow boards. "Stroke, stroke."

"Stroke," a voice from the stern bellowed. "Together, stroke."

Alerio Sisera's commanding voice reached the experienced rowers of the Stroke section. They added their voices and muscles to the chore.

"Stroke, stroke, stroke."

Soon, Alerio and the best oarsmen were churning their oars. Some uselessly in the air, others in deep water, but they had passed the phase of shock at the roll and were rowing together. With the stern rowers setting the pace, the Engine roared to life.

The center section picked up the count. And the most powerful oarsmen on the warship pulled hard, powering the five-banker forward through the waves.

"Stroke, stroke, stroke."

Finally, the lightest and inexperienced forward section dug their oars in, and the quinquereme went from a rolling log to a warship splitting the waves.

"Maintain that rate," Centurion Velius instructed. "Navigation let's see where we are. Take us closer to shore."

Veritas' Candor cut a path towards the socked in coastline.

"Sharp eyes, Third Principale," the ships First Officer warned. "We're angling landward."

On the bow, the ship's third officer peered into the driving rain. While he couldn't see a beach or trees, neither could he see rocks. What did catch his attention were brown streaks in the sea water.

"River signs," he bellowed to the stern.

One hundred and forty feet to the aft, the First Principale repeated the news to the Centurion.

"Take us closer in," Velius told the navigators.

The ram of the warship nosed towards the hidden coast. A few tense moments later, a beach became visible through the rain.

"First Principale, get us dry," the ship's Centurion instructed.

"Second Principale, starboard side hold water," the first officer commanded.

Below deck, the order was repeated, and the warship curved to its right. When she faced seaward, the rowing officer instructed, "Back her down."

Almost as if riding a bucking horse, the long ship rocked up and down on the swells. But nine feet below the surface, the keel touched the seabed, and slid up the beach to stabilize the warship.

"Shore party to disembark," the Second Principale exclaimed.

Alerio, staying with his rowing section, leaped from the rowing bench and followed the oarsmen up to the deck and over the side.

"Sir, you didn't need to get wet," the Third Principale remarked as he dropped into the waist deep water.

"I volunteered to row," Alerio replied as he placed his hands and chest on the hull, "and this is the section I joined. Besides, it's raining as much on the main deck as it is on the beach."

One hundred and fifty rowers leaned against the ship, waiting for the command.

"Call it," the first officer shouted down from the steering deck.

"On three, get our ship dry," the third officer cried out from the surf. "One, two, three."

And the combined might of half the oarsmen with assistance from the forward section of oars, lifted *Veritas' Candor* from the sea. Once moving, they ran her to higher ground until the bronze blades of the ram appeared.

"Rest," the Third Principale stated. "Good job."

Most of the shore party dropped to the sand. Between the rowing, and pushing, they were exhausted. But one man climbed back to the steering deck.

"Lictor Sisera, that wasn't necessary," Velius offered.

"I needed the exercise," Alerio replied while dropping his shirt over his head. He glanced around the deck and asked. "How's my prisoner?"

"Ever since the storm began, the priest has stood with his back against the mast, praying for guidance from Jupiter," the ship's senior officer replied. "I can't imagine why you detained him."

"That's between him and the Senate," Alerio stated. He dropped his shirt over his head and lied. "I'm just the enforcer."

For three days, they waited for the storm to blow itself out. When they finally launched from the beach at Albinia, the crew, Alerio, and Callum Farnese were growing impatient to be gone.

***

One hundred miles south, and two and a half days later, they beached at Ostia.

"Priest Farnese, step lively," Alerio urged.

The two men climbed off the warship and shuffled through the sand.

"Why rush? Saturnalia is the day after tomorrow," Callum complained. "There's no way a carriage can get us there before it starts."

Alerio didn't say anything. He marched ahead, leading them in the direction of the Legion headquarters building.

"Are you going to stash me in a supply room overnight while you arrange transportation?"

"No," Alerio responded.

They angled away from the administration building and walked around the corner to the stables.

"I need two horses and a mule," Alerio told the stableman while dumping his baggage on the floor.

"This is a Legion facility," an animal handler advised. "Civilians can get mounts in town."

"I'm a Lictor of the Republic and a Legion Colonel," Alerio shot back. "And I have a prisoner. Two horses and a mule, now."

Not long after they arrived, Alerio and Callum rode out of Ostia, heading for the Capital. The sun rested low in the sky and the holiday loomed just a day away.

***

Legionaries learned to ride horses. Priests were more comfortable in a carriage or on foot. Ten miles on horseback left Alerio's back stiff and Callum Farnese bent forward in the saddle with his eyes squeezed shut against the aches in his body.

By the time they reached the base of Capitoline Hill, the priest had no idea where they were and didn't care.

"All I want is off this horse," he whined.

"You had breaks when we changed mounts," Alerio reminded him.

At both way stations, Alerio had shouted for a stablemen. Then Callum remembered a flurry of activity before he was shoved back onto a fresh horse for more painful miles.

"Will this never end?" Callum begged.

"Hold on a little longer," Alerio coached.

"Then what? A cell for me?"

The horse clomped uphill for what felt like half the night. Then the ground leveled, and the horse's gait evened out.

"Priest Farnese, remember me in your prayers," Alerio said while reaching over and gripping Callum's shoulder.

He pulled the priest upright, steadied him, until the man realized where they had stopped. On the far side of a guard gate, the Temple of Jupiter towered over the landscape.

"Yo Saturnalia, priest," Alerio exclaimed. "Now get off the Legion horse so I can go about my day."

Pink streaks painted the sky as a new day dawned. Callum slipped off the saddle but had to cling to a strap for stability.

"All the abuse of your authority was to get me transportation?" Callum inquired. Then he smiled. "And to return me to the temple before Saturnalia."

"That does lend itself to a fundamental political problem," Alerio suggested. "Did my means justify the results?"

Callum Farnese hobbled to the pack mule to free his bag. Once he held it, he looked up at Alerio.

"I will pray to Jupiter to forgive you your transgressions," Callum assured Alerio. As Alerio turned the horses, Priest Farnese exclaimed. "Lictor Sisera. Yo Saturnalia."

***

The sun peaked over the hills as Alerio walked the horses off the boulevard and onto the driveway.

"Forgive me Bia," he acknowledged the statue in front of the villa, "but I've come a long way and still have much to do."

On most visits, he would stop and pray at the statue. That day, he walked the horses by the Goddess. When he came abreast of the front door, Alerio slipped from the saddle and walked stiff legged to the door. He knocked and waited.

"Who is it?" Civi Affatus inquired from behind the door.

"Optio Affatus, if you keep me waiting on these steps, I'm going to ship you off to Sicilia for the spring offensive."

"Thank you for the offer, but the Legion doesn't take over-the-hill Sergeants," Civi replied while opening the door. "Welcome home, Colonel Sisera."

Belen appeared out of the darkened interior.

"Will you be staying with us, sir?" the secretary inquired.

"Don't you ever sleep?" Alerio asked. Before Belen could answer, Alerio issued orders. "I need someone to return the mule and mounts to the Legion. Be sure they get a receipt. Then I need a driver and a wagon."

"Are you hauling bodies?" Civi asked. Seeing the look of confusion on Alerio's face, he added. "What I mean, sir, is how big a carriage, do you require?"

"A small one will do," Alerio replied. "As you can guess, I've just returned to the Capital."

"And you need a ride home, Master Sisera?" the Greek secretary inquired.

"No. I need a driver and a carriage," Alerio explained, "so I can go shopping for Saturnalia gifts."

***

The wagon had a fixed box on the rear of the bed and six feet of load space before a board separated the cargo from a team of horses. Alerio sat in a double basket seat mounted on the box. Civi Affatus stepped up and sat beside him.

"What manor of wagon is this?" Alerio inquired. "This box takes up the entire rear. There's no way to load from the back."

"Colonel, this is an antitheft wagon," Civi replied. He snapped the whip and the team walked down the driveway. "From here I can watch our load, stop anyone approaching, and prevent them from stealing our goods."

He reinforced the remark with a crack of the whip.

"Has the city always been this unruly?" Alerio questioned.

"There's always been bad sections," Civi responded. "But with the number of men our Legions are training then discharging after the campaign season, we have a lot of sharp blades and no commanders to control them."

"Legionaries?"

"No sir, mostly auxiliary troops who come to see the Capital," the former Optio answered. "And rural men looking for the easy life."

"The easy life. Like robbing citizens?" Alerio asked.

"Yes, sir, it's why we're sitting up here with a view of our surroundings," Civi stated. "Where are we going first, Colonel?"

"The Temple of Vesta."

***

Civi hauled back on the lines and settled the team at the base of the staircase. Alerio hopped down from the wagon and took the steps two at a time. After the Colonel vanished into the structure, the retired NCO studied the wattle and daub exterior. Spots where the clay had been replaced, puzzled him. Why repair it? The centuries old temple should be replaced by a more fitting building for the eternal flame of Rome and the Priestesses of Vesta.

In a few moments, Alerio appeared cradling three heavy coin purses in his arms.

"That didn't take long, sir," Civi remarked while taking and stowing the bags of coins in the box under the seat.

"It cost me a healthy donation to the temple," Alerio replied as he jumped into the wagon. "Drive on Optio. Our next stop is the harness maker."

***

The wagon rolled through the early morning. Making quick work of the empty side streets, they turned north on the boulevard. Blocks from the Forum, Civi pulled the team up at the harness maker's shop. Alerio jumped down and pounded on the door until he was admitted.

Through the open doors, Civi noted long sections of leather hanging and waiting to be carved, sewed, and shaped into harnesses, bridles, whips, and other gear.

Colonel Sisera lingered longer in the shop than he did at the temple. Eventually, he came out followed by two apprentices with midsized bundles. While Alerio climbed into the wagon, the boys deposited the packages in the wagon.

"We're off to the Golden Valley Trading House," Alerio instructed Civi.

The apprentices watched as the wagon rolled south towards the harbor. Their master was delighted with the early morning business, and the boys were excited for the feast the next day. Together they called after the wagon, "Yo Saturnalia."

***

To Civi, the compound seemed foreboding. High walls surrounded a two-story building. On the roof, he recognized an observation platform. What merchant needed a view of this section of the city and the harbor?

Few ordinary citizens did business with the Golden Valley. Their expensive merchandise may be desirable, but it cost more, a lot more. And rumor had it that the trading house dealt in assassins. The dark rumor sent a shiver down the NCOs spine.

While Civi's nerves twitched from the thoughts, Alerio Sisera hopped down and strutted to a door in the wall. He knocked, reached under his woolen shirt, and appeared to scratch his lower back. The door opened and a middle-aged man held it so Colonel Sisera could pass through.

Not long after he entered, the man and Alerio reappeared. Each held a crate with a sealed pot balanced on top.

"Yo Saturnalia," the man stated after placing his load in the wagon.

"The same to you, Favus," Alerio replied. "And thank you for opening so early."

"All you need do is ask, Senator Sisera," the man remarked.

"Whoa there, let's not get ahead of ourselves."

"There are whispers," Favus commented before walking back to the doorway. At the opening, he turned and declared. "I may be a lowly trading manager. However, who am I to deny the inevitable?"

Alerio climbed into the wagon and Civi snapped the reins.

"Where to now, Senator?" he asked.

138

"The cloth seller's shop near the Chronicles Humanum Inn," Alerio told him. "And keep the Senator stuff to yourself. It's two months before my birthday, and another after that before the Consuls are elected."

"Still sir, it's a well-deserved honor."

***

A little beyond the shop, the street hooked to the left. On the right side of the intersection, sat a unique building.

Terraces formed by stepping back the ascending floors gave each level a large balcony. Yet, as extravagant as the building appeared, the inn catered to Legion young officers and senior NCOs when visiting the Capital.

Civi halted the wagon. Alerio hopped down then reached into the wagon bed and lifted out the bundles from the harness maker.

"Need help, sir?" the Optio inquired.

"You stay here and guard the wagon," Alerio responded.

With the bundles in hand, Alerio went to the shop and kicked at the door until an old man opened it. After a few words, the Colonel entered the shop, and the door closed.

"Civi. Civi," a voice called from the porch of the inn.

"Yo Saturnalia, Master Harricus," the retired NCO answered.

"If Senator Sisera has a moment for the little people," Thomasious Harricus teased, "have him see me before you leave."

"Yes, sir," Civi assured the innkeeper.

It felt as if Alerio had just gone in when he reappeared.

"We'll need to wait," he announced.

"Sir, Master Harricus asked that you stop by the inn," Civi informed him.

"Stay here. I'll send over some refreshments," Alerio promised.

***

"Clay Ear, what do you hear?" Alerio asked while mounting the steps.

"The city is buzzing with the news that one Lance Corporal Sisera will soon be a Senator of the Republic," Thomasious Harricus answered.

"I haven't been a Decanus in years. And I'm not a Senator now," Alerio commented. "But I am thirsty as is my driver."

"Come in, I'll pour us a mug. Erebus will take vino to Civi."

They went into the main room and took seats at a table where Alerio could watch the wagon.

"I'm amazed to see you in Rome," Harricus admitted while pouring from a pitcher, "but not surprised."

"Can you explain the dual nature of that comment?"

"Amazed, refers to you, making it home. The word from the villas' servants was you were far up north, solving murders," Harricus described. "And not surprised, by your appearance, is a nod to your tenacity."

"Any news about an Umbria Prince?" Alerio inquired.

"What Umbria Prince?" Harricus questioned. He leaned forward and cupped an ear. "Is there a Prince involved in whatever you were doing?"

"Forget I mention it. The Clay Ear can't use that, even as a rumor," Alerio cautioned. Across the street, Erebus greeted Civi with a tray of refreshments. When the retired Sergeant picked up a slice of cured meat, Alerio realized he was hungry. "Can we eat?"

"Absolutely," Harricus responded. He waved over a server. "Meat, olives, cheese, and bread for the Senator."

"Again, you mentioned the position," Alerio noted. "Confirmation is three months away. But tell me, is it that solid?"

"There are only a few dissenting voices," the innkeeper replied.

"But there are some who don't want me seated in the Senate?"

"There always are," Harricus stated.

They ate and talked until the old cloth seller and his helpers emerged from the shop. Each held a bundle that they dropped into the wagon.

"I have a few more stops to make," Alerio announced. He dropped several coins on the table. "Before you protest, Thomasious Harricus, I will come back and let you treat me when I am a Senator. For now, I'm paying for food and information."

"The food you've had," Harricus said. "What information do you need?"

"The name and location of a wood carver. And the name of a gold metalworker that you trust."

***

Armed with the locations, Civi snapped the reins and drove away from the cloth sellers' shop.

"You're very popular, sir," he mentioned to Alerio.

"Why do you say that?"

"The old merchant returned the fee," Civi advised while handing Alerio a small sack of coins. "He said not to tell you until we were away. Should I turn around?"

"No, I'll accept his Saturnalia gift," Alerio responded.

"We have two more stops to make. A metalworker's shop and a barrel maker's compound."

"And it's not midday," Civi stated. "You've made good time, sir."

"But I'm not home yet, Sergeant."

"You will be soon, Colonel. I guarantee it."

Alerio folded his arms and closed his eyes as the wagon turned north and crossed the city for a second time that morning.

Chapter 14 – The Festival of Lights

"Husband of mine," the soft voice called to Alerio in his dream. A finger caressed his ear and traced along his jaw line. He leaned into the touch and the finger evolved into a palm cupping his face. "You can sleep the day away tomorrow."

When the warm blanket was snatched away and the cold of early morning washed over his skin, Alerio jolted upright in bed.

"I'm home?" he mumbled while blinking his eyes.

"Ever since late yesterday when Civi delivered you and those packages," Gabriella replied. She pointed to a pile of containers stacked in a corner of the bedroom. "If it were up to me, I'd crawl in next to you, wrap you in my arms, and we'd sleep the day away."

"That, my wife, sounds like the best idea of the year," Alerio remarked.

"For any other day of the year," Gabriella corrected, "but not today. Lady Aquila and the staff from Villa Maximus will be here soon and they'll need beverages and refreshments."

"So, have somebody serve them," Alerio growled as he reached for Gabriella.

"On any other day of the year," she directed, "but not today. It's Saturnalia and you are tasked, Lictor Sisera, with serving the guests. Now husband of mine, get your body out of bed."

She winked, turned, and sashayed out of the room. Laying down, he rolled over and sniffed the sheets. Her scent lingered and he started to call her back. On any other day of the year, he was sure, she would respond. But not today.

***

"I look ridiculous," Alerio complained.

"It's festive," Gabriella told him.

The light blue and green tunic with tiny trees bleached into spots on the material fit both descriptions. Before it got heated, a disturbance at the front door cut short the discussion.

"Colonel, the Maximus household has arrived," Hektor announced.

Alerio used both hands to indicate the tunic, smirked at the inescapable assault on style, and marched to the main entrance.

"Lady Aquila and company," he greeted the crowd, "welcome to Villa Sisera."

His adopted mother stopped, ran her eyes over his tunic, and looked across the room at Gabriella.

143

"You picked a good one," Aquila Carvilius complimented.

"It looks ridiculous," Alerio remarked.

"Oh no dear," Aquila said while patting his chest as if soothing a favored horse, "it's festive."

"Beverages?" Alerio inquired.

For a while, he rushed around filling and handing out mugs of spiced wine to servants, household guards, and Ladies Aquila and Gabriella. As Priest Callum Farnese described, Saturnalia harkened back to a golden age when there was no class division between people. Getting into the spirit of the day, Alerio teased, complimented, and made everyone, no matter their status, feel important.

"We have snacks on the patio," he exclaimed when everyone had a beverage. "Please help yourself."

Green garland hung around the veranda and every candle holder held an unlit candle. Standing off to the side with their drinks, the Ladies observed the proceedings.

"He's doing a fair job," Aquila mentioned. "With a little guidance, he might make a good addition to your staff."

"I am trying mother, but you know how hard they are to train," Gabriella noted. She linked arms with Aquila and nodded towards the patio. "Almost as hard as finding candles this year."

"I heard the war in Sicilia has disrupted the honey and wax supply," Aquila said. "It's a wonder you could find any candles at all."

"Shall we?" Gabriella suggested.

The Ladies strolled from the room and across the noisy veranda.

"On one hand, I always enjoyed watching Maximus do the serving," Aquila reminisced. "But I've always felt it was twisted to subjugate the authority of men like Spurius and Alerio."

"It's only one day," Gabriella commented. "And I think secretly, they enjoy being among the people."

"It's a far cry from their command positions," Aquila added.

***

When everyone finally migrated to the patio, Alerio hurried to the bedroom. It took three trips to haul the crates and packages back to the hall. Once he had them together, he began separating items.

Despite his complaints about the gaudy tunic and servant duties, Alerio appreciated Saturnalia. His adopted father had relished the role over the years. For him and Alerio, it provided an opportunity to show their gratitude to the people who made their lifestyle possible.

The first thing he did was unwrap and set up the fifty wax candles he bought at the Golden Valley Trading House. Then he uncapped the two big jars of honey and placed them near stacks of dishes and baskets of bread. From observing over the years, he'd learned that feeding the staff snacks throughout the day kept them from getting too drunk. And helped in avoiding the awkward apologies, they would have to make in the morning.

As if in order of importance, he laid out the gifts. Aquila's and Gabriella's appeared to be first and second. And they would be, any other day of the year.

Once the gifts were ready for the ceremony, Alerio struck flint to steel sending hot sparks to a stack of kindling.

Then he carried the brazier to each set of candles, and from the burning sticks, he lit the wicks.

***

While the master of the house served the guests and the guests were servants of the household, he didn't do the cooking. Alerio left the great room, closed the doors behind him, and marched through the patio.

"Can I help, Colonel?" Hektor inquired as Alerio passed him.

"Do you require assistance, sir?" Belen asked.

Both assistants were ignored. They didn't take offense. The questions were formalities and neither man expected an answer, let alone acceptance of the offer.

Shortly after crossing through the crowd, Alerio came back with the two cooks and their four helpers in tow. He paused at the door and spun on the food staff.

"Yo Saturnalia," Alerio proclaimed. He tossed open the doors, bowed, and ushered the cooks and their helpers into the great room.

Oohs and ahs, and other exclamations of wonder came from the cooks before Alerio closed the doors. Those on the veranda would have to wait to see the display that drew such a grand response.

"You did a good job with him," Gabriella remarked.

"I think a lot of people had a hand in forming Alerio Carvilius Sisera into the man he is today," Aquila offered.

***

The cooks and helpers gazed around the feasting hall. Everywhere they looked candles glowed and flickered. Garland caught the candlelight and cast shadows on the walls and ceiling between the bright spots. Alerio marched to the center of the enchanting room and held out his arms.

"Candles represent truth and knowledge," he lectured. "Today, on Saturnalia, the truth is we are working. Therefore, I will present your gifts, so that you can prepare, and I'll have platters of food to serve at the feast."

Both cooks knew Alerio and laughed.

"When I was a young infantryman, Senator Maximus would send me to the cookhouse for a meal," Alerio said while pulling a length of leather cord from a crate. Suspended in the center of the leather was a stitched bag. "For all the company and hot food while I waited for the Senators, I present you a gift of bronze. May you always have a reserve to fall back on in an emergency. This is my gift to you."

He tied the leather around the chef's neck. Then he dropped five bronze coins into the pouch. After the presentation, he waved the Villa Sisera chef forward.

"For your patience during my frequent visits to your pantry and ovens when I'm home," Alerio said to his villa's chef. He pulled another leather cord with an attached pouch from the crate. "I present you a gift of bronze. May you always have a reserve to fall back on in an emergency. This is my gift to you."

Again, he deposited five bronze coins into the pouch. Once finished with the chefs, he gave leather strings to the helpers before placing two bronze in their pouches.

"I present you a gift of bronze. May you always have a reserve to fall back on in an emergency. This is my gift to you."

The cook staff clustered around a honey pot, dipped bread in the sweet goo, held the pieces up and shouted, "Yo Saturnalia."

"Your service and loyalty to the Maximus and Sisera households is acknowledged and appreciated," Alerio assured them. "Now, go cook up a worthy feast. For this is Saturnalia."

When the room cleared, Alerio looked around to be sure all the candles were burning brightly before walking to the doors.

"Yo Saturnalia," he greeted the crowd on the patio. "Please come in for the celebration."

He stepped aside as the household servants and guards shuffled through the doorway. In the rear of the crowd, Gabriella and Aquila stepped through the doorway, hooked his arms, and walked him into the shimmering hall.

***

The cloth seller's bags on the harness maker's leather cords proved a big hit. At least that's what people said. In reality, it was the generous gift of coins. Bronze for the servants and men-at-arms, silver for Civi Affatus and Merula Mancini, and gold for Belen and Hektor showed Alerio's appreciation of their service.

As he presented each gift, he announced, "I present you a gift of coins. May you always have a reserve to fall back on in an emergency. This is my gift to you."

A long while after starting, Alerio reached out and took Aquila's hand.

"Come mother, I have a gift for you."

"A pouch on a string with coins?" she inquired.

"Not exactly," he replied. Reaching into a separate crate, he lifted out a small wooden box. After handing it to his adopted mother, he explained. "Provided you limit your donations to a couple of coins for each visiting priest, I'll refill the box. May you never be denied the comfort of a temple for the rest of your days. This is my gift to you."

Aquila hugged Alerio for several heartbeats.

"I do enjoy talking to priests," she whispered.

"I know you do, mother."

"Husband of mine, did you remember the children?" Gabriella questioned.

"Do we have children?" Alerio asked. He glanced around the room before commenting. "Because if we do, I don't see them."

Gabriella waved at the hallway, and a short while later, two pair of slightly unbalanced feet ran from a side room.

"Tarquin. Olivia. Yo Saturnalia," Alerio called to the twins.

They squealed and headed for him. Olivia arrived first. From a crate, Alerio pulled a polished box.

"This is a puzzle," he explained to the blank stare on the little girl's face. "You'll figure out that if you pull the center post."

He pulled the small dowl and the box fell into ten pieces. Olivia took a piece and held it up to an eye as if examining it.

"You may not appreciate it now, but you are your mother's daughter," he stated. "May you be clever for all of your days. This is my gift to you."

Gabriella collected the puzzle pieces. After a moment of studying them, she reassembled the box, inserted the dowl, and handed it to Olivia. The little girl held the box in her arms as if it would fall apart if she let go.

From the same stash he bought at the barrel maker's compound, Alerio took a likeness of a chariot with a four-horse rig. Unlike the puzzle box, there was no guess work in identifying the item.

"Tarquin. This represents our future," Alerio proclaimed, "at least part of it. For you, I give an opportunity to live life as a productive citizen of the Republic. This is my gift to you."

After moments of people fussing over the twins, Gabriella signaled a pair of nurses. As they took the four-year-old boy and girl away, their mother focused on Alerio.

"That ends the gift giving," he announced. Then he noticed his wife. "Did I forget anything?"

"Your wife, Master Sisera," she said, "should not be overlooked on Saturnalia."

"Really, wife of mine?" he asked. Almost absent mindedly, he tapped a pouched tied around his waist. "What's this?"

From the pouch, he lifted an object made of gold.

"For the mother of my children, my comfort on sleepless nights of worry, and the woman who manages the villa while I'm away," Alerio touted, "I give you the sun in gold. May you never face a sunrise without my companionship be it near or far. This is my gift to you."

The broach had an image in gold of Helios the Sun God with silver making up the scene around him.

"It's beautiful," Gabriella whispered.

Alerio reached out to hug his wife but stopped when a cook's apprentice stepped between them. Alerio might have gotten angry, but the young helper had a hand on his pouch as if it was his heart and a smile on his face.

"Colonel Sisera," the youth informed him, "the food is ready."

***

Beyond gratitude, the other part of Saturnalia that Alerio found satisfying had to do with quality of service. The day provided an opportunity to set an example for the attitude and mannerisms he'd expect from the servants for the next year. If he was sloppy, or impatient, and scowled at having to bring another platter of food, how could he expect anything different from his or the Maximus household staff.

"More radishes, sir?" he inquired at one end of the table.

"Ah, no," Civi Affatus replied.

A lifetime as a Legion NCO didn't equip him to sit while a Battle Commander dished out ladles of vegetables. But the example stuck. Civi would treat the house guards with respect and demand the same in return.

Alerio dashed around the table, filling mugs with spiced wine, plates with meats and vegetables, and moving stacks of flat bread to within reach of each diner.

***

At the end of the feast, Alerio led a procession to the garden.

"Saturn, God of Sowing, Sprouts, and Abundance, we pray that today has honored you," Alerio intoned while shoving wood onto glowing embers. Once the split logs caught fire, he pulled a sack of grain up next to the bonfire. With his hands, he lifted out kernels of grain and allowed them to flow between his fingers and fall back into the sack. Then, using the sack to hide his hands, he scooped a handful of grain dust from another sack. "To end our Saturnalia, please accept this offering of grain."

Rather than whole grains, Alerio threw the handful of grain dust. In a spectacular flash, the air above the wood burned like the sun. As rapidly as the grain dust caught fire, the flash faded.

In awe of the God's response to the sacrifice of grain, the household servants and guards gasped. Surely, the Maximus and Sisera households were blessed by the God Saturn.

"And that concludes the official celebration," Alerio told the assembled servants. "Please continue to drink and eat. But you'll serve yourself. I'm going to the cook shed and get a platter of food and eat my dinner."

Cheers followed Alerio as he marched to the edge of the garden.

"Husband of mine," Gabriella said intercepting him. "You've done our villas proud. But come with me I've something to show you."

"But I'm hungry," Alerio begged.

"Shortly," she promised.

With his hand in hers, she guided him into the great room, and down the hallway to his office.

Upon entering the room, Alerio immediately noticed the toga on his desk. Off white, the eighteen feet of fabric had a strip on one edge designating it as a Senator's toga.

"We aren't a Senator yet," Alerio protested.

"You have to be," Gabriella insisted. "The cloth seller charged a lot. We could have bought two draft oxen for the cost of that material."

"No wonder he gifted the pouches," Alerio sighed. Then with passion, he said. "I do appreciate the toga."

152

"And," she said in a drawn-out fashion. Accompanying the word, Gabriella lifted both hands to shoulder height and held them up facing a wall.

"And what?" Alerio asked.

He had a hand on the toga and his eyes on Gabriella.

"The wall, look at the wall," she insisted.

Shifting his focus, Alerio noted a new shelf with wooden stands. His double-bladed ax with the silver and gold scrolling rested on the stands.

"Between the Lictor's symbol and the Illyrian snakehead scroll," Alerio announced, "my walls are becoming crowded."

"You'll be home most nights and working on policy for the Republic and business deals," Gabriella predicted. "You need things in your office to impress visitors."

"I don't think that would be proper," Alerio informed her.

"What wouldn't be proper?"

"Having my wife standing around my office just to impress my visitors."

"I thought you were hungry."

"I am," Alerio confirmed.

"Then husband of mine, let's get you to the cook shed and fed," she directed. The candlelight reflected off the gold flecks in her brown eyes as she smiled and cocked her head to the side. "Afterward, Senator Sisera, I have something else to show you."

Chapter 15 – Political Clout

Alerio found it easier to keep the travertine operation and the farm's accounting with Belen. He relied on Hektor to keep the records for the merchant shipping and Noricum ore transportation. Although inconvenient, maintaining an office in each villa satisfied any complaint about him not being the male head of household for the Maximus and the Sisera villas. How could he not be? He was in both daily.

"Belen. Why haven't we filled these orders?" Alerio asked as he ran down a list of building sites requesting their stone.

"Sir, it was fall and now it's winter," the secretary explained. "In the spring, the snow will melt, the river will rise, and the flatboats will carry more travertine."

"You're right. I remember that river," Alerio acknowledged. He rubbed his eyes and stretched. "I think that's enough for today. Unless you have something else."

"No, Colonel Sisera, we have…"

Civi Affatus rapped on the doorframe.

"Noon approaches, Colonel," the former Optio advised. "I have horses saddled and waiting."

"If they aren't racing. Why am I going to the chariot track?" Alerio complained.

"It's a preview for next year's races," Belen told him. "It excites the bettors and gives them a look at individual stables."

"Why do I care to watch stablemates race?"

"Because the Senators will cluster under their favored banner," Belen replied. "And while politicians will say anything behind their hands, you need to know where they stand publicly."

Alerio walked from behind the desk and rested a hand on Belen's shoulder.

"Senator Maximus trusted you," Alerio complimented the secretary, "as do I. Thank you."

"I feel it's my duty to guide the next generation through the traps and pitfalls of politics," he said. "Both you and Hektor."

***

Alerio and Civi rode through the eastern gate. Once out of the congestion, they moved at a trot and were soon by the steel and brick making ovens. The Legion way station fell behind and they came upon a long mound of dirt facing a graded hillside.

"Where will you be, sir?" Civi inquired.

"Senator Metellus said he'd be under the red banner," Alerio answered as he slipped off the mount. "Although I may move to Quintus Vitulus' faction."

"What color is that, sir?"

"I can't remember," Alerio admitted while handing the reins to Civi.

"In that case Colonel, I'll meet you behind red when this is over."

Alerio marched to a guard standing at the rear of a roped off section.

"I'm a guest of Lucius Caecilius Metellus. The name is Alerio Sisera."

"Yes, Lictor Sisera," the guard acknowledged while waving a flag at a pair of guards stationed halfway down the red area. "The Senator is expecting you."

Unlike other red team supporters, Alerio was ushered through the second barrier. Metellus waited with other statesmen and successful businessmen closer to the track. He waved Alerio to him.

***

"Lictor Sisera, I'm so happy you could join us," Metellus exclaimed. "Today is important. We'll learn which of our stables have produced the best team for the red banner."

"Yes, sir," Alerio said. In the future, when he had a team, he might care about chariot teams. But not today. "Where is Senator Vitulus?"

Lucius Metellus jerked, looked around quickly, took Alerio's arm, and walked him away from the cluster of people.

"When you're in the red area, or under any banner, do not mention the enemy," Metellus scolded. "Here, among their faction, politicians are hyper partisans. Be careful what you say."

"I understand," Alerio whispered. "Where is Senator Vitulus?"

"He's in the white area," Metellus answered. "Quintus Vitulus is a gold grabber."

"A what?"

"Whites are for negotiating trade deals with enemies of the Republic," Metellus scoffed. "Going so far as to support treaties with the Qart Hadasht Empire. They don't believe in Rome's destiny to rule. Just in her as a commercial entity. Thus, he's a gold grabber."

"Yet, according to Senator Maximus, they support marching Legions," Alerio offered.

"I'll give the whites that," Metellus allowed. "Unlike the blues, which you'll have to cross through to reach the white banner."

"Is that going to be a problem?"

"Not for a Lictor of the Republic."

On the track, a dolphin symbol mounted on a pole dropped. In response, six drivers whipped their teams into motion. At first, because of the staggered start on the curve, it was difficult to tell which chariot was in the lead. Deciding which color took the track was much easier.

People in the green banner area screamed for their favorite stable. Even a few attendees in the blue and white areas cheered the green racers. In all the excitement, Alerio noted not one red gave any indication of support.

"The enemies," Alerio uttered.

Belen had been right. At the chariot races, Alerio could clearly see where the Senators stood publicly.

Seventeen laps later, a winner was crowned. At the spring chariot races, the driver and his four horses would be a favorite when he raced against the other colors. Alerio used the arrival of white teams on the track to slip out the side of the roped area.

"I'm a Lictor of the Republic," he informed the guard.

"Yes, sir, please crossover."

Alerio ducked under the rope and entered the blue banner area.

***

Most of the blue spectators were clustered in small groups. Only a few watched the activity on the track, the rest talked among themselves. Alerio had crossed to the other side when he noticed a large crowd. Backtracking, he angled to the rear of the mob.

"When I'm Consul, we'll see an immediate savings," a speaker exclaimed. "And not just in the Republic's gold that's pouring out of the Temple of Saturn. But also, in saving the blood of our citizens who spill their treasures on the soil of Sicilia. And for what…"

From the speech, Alerio understood the stance of the blue supporters. Anti-expansionist, they wanted to pull back from foreign engagement and create fortress Rome on the mainland. Out of curiosity, Alerio raised up and looked over the heads of the listeners.

It felt as if ice water trickled down his spine. Alerio ducked. But it was too late, the speaker stopped talking.

On the Punic coast, Consul Lucius Longus had attempted to burn Alerio to death in a supply tent. Crazed and believing people were out to get him, Longus had been shipped back to Rome. And now he wanted the power and the prestige of the position again.

"…And for what?" Longus stammered. "So, the reds can get rich on the corpses of our Legionaries. And get fat on conquered lands. And then invade more territory and start the cycle of waste again?"

Alerio fast walked to the rope, mumbled his status as a Lictor, entered the white area, and began searching for Quintus Vitulus.

***

The Senator stood with the other spectators watching the white teams shuffle into their spots. Trainers backed up teams or pulled horses forward to place the chariots on their marks. Once all six chariots were set, the dolphin dropped, and the drivers whipped their quads into motion.

Alerio waited for the teams to make it two laps around the poles.

"Senator, I hate to bother you during the race," Alerio apologized. "But this is important."

"Alerio, I didn't see you," Quintus Vitulus greeted him. He stepped back from the crowd of observers. "What's so important that you can't wait for... Melpomene, bless me."

At the mention of the Goddess of Tragedy, Alerio shifted his attention to the track. A team had rounded the end pole too sharply and overturned the chariot. The driver sprawled on the track where the chariot dumped him. Before he could move, a second chariot team ran over him. With an arm and leg twisted at bad angles he couldn't move. And a second chariot came around the pole.

Quintus and Alerio gasped. Surely the wheels on the second chariot would mean death. But the alert driver rocked his chariot onto one wheel while reining his thundering team wide. The raised wheel passed over the injured man.

Two assistants ran onto the track, grabbed the injured driver's arms and legs, and hauled him out of danger.

"That was miraculous," Alerio exclaimed.

"And bad for the white team this year," Quintus whined. "He was our best driver. Oh well, there's nothing to be done about it. What did you need, Lictor Sisera?"

"I passed through blue to get here and overheard Lucius Longus delivering a campaign speech," Alerio told him. "He wants to be a Consul this year."

"The co-consul with Pacilus? No, no that will never do."

"So, you can stop him?" Alerio questioned. Then quietly after checking that they were away from other whites, he added. "With Senator Metellus' help?"

"If Longus is publicly campaigning, he's already secured enough votes," Senator Vitulus informed Alerio. "A blue and a green in office in the same year will undermine our treaties. It'll take years to heal the damage and reclaim our place among other nations."

"I assumed that Metellus was popular," Alerio offered. "Can't he run against Longus?"

"Our friend Lucius Metellus has a weakness. He's seen as being inflexible by the old families," Quintus Vitulus remarked. "They would never take him over Longus. Besides, Metellus is slotted for next year. At least he was before this Longus thing developed."

The truth of it was if Longus became Consul, he would never allow Alerio to become a Senator. On the other hand, if Alerio waited a year, there was no guarantee that the next set of Consuls would grant him the appointment. In the meanwhile, pulling Legions back would throw the Republic into a near civil war. Alerio kicked the ground and groaned.

"I can deliver the patriarch of an old family," he explained, "plus, the votes of Proconsul Crassus and Praetor Blasio. And if need be, a portion of my adopted father's faction. Would that give Metellus the votes he needs?"

"Are you sure you want to get involved?"

"I don't have much choice," Alerio responded. "It's the Republic and represents the things I've fought for most of my life. Sitting back and praying for a good outcome, like a temple priest, isn't my style."

"Plan on writing the letters and calling in your markers," Quintus Vitulus coached. "I'll conference with Metellus about our strategy."

Not wanting to cross blue and having no interest in the chariot races, Alerio walked to the exit at the top of the mound and went to locate Civi and the horses.

***

The next day in Villa Sisera, Alerio sat at his desk. Next to the ink pot, three pieces of parchment waited for him to write the letters. A fourth scrap dangled between two of his fingers.

"You're working early," Gabriella noted.

"I'm afraid, I'm trading our future plans for the greater good," Alerio told her.

"You're selling the farm? Divesting of the travertine quarry? Or quitting the Noricum ore trade?" she asked in rapid succession.

"None of those. With these letters, I'm giving away my support and making an enemy."

"How bad could it be?"

"I really don't know," Alerio admitted. "But the letter to Praetor Blasio will free him of his debt to me. The one to Proconsul Crassus will absolve him of his commitment. And the missive to Titus Lanatus will burn a bridge to an old family. Leaving me with no more protection than any other citizen."

Alerio waved the fourth piece of parchment at his wife.

"More bad news?" she questioned.

"We have two months to dodge the wrath of Senator Longus once the support for Metellus comes in," Alerio remarked. "Senator Vitulus says he can protect my family, the villas, and our businesses. However, he can't stop Longus from abusing his authority as a Senator and bringing me up on charges."

"What will you do?" she asked.

"I could not write the letters and let the fates take control," Alerio replied. "Or I can go to Sicilia as a Lictor for Proconsul Florus until Spring."

Gabriella walked to the wall and plucked the double-bladed ax from the shelf. Then she pulled a chair around the desk and sat facing the door.

"What are you doing?" he inquired.

"I'm protecting my husband while he writes the letters," she replied. "And making his office look good."

"You certainly are," Alerio confirmed as he started to write the first letter.

***

Of everyone involved in the political gambit, the most vocal and critical was Belen. Every time Alerio visited Villa Maximus, the old secretary scolded him.

"Had you consulted me, I would have worked out the details with Senator Metellus' secretary," the Greek whined. "As it is, you are exposed."

"Lucius Metellus is a friend," Alerio said defending his decision. "We needed to stop Senator Longus and we have."

"Your results are hard to argue against," Belen admitted. "As long as the end result is what you expect."

As Alerio worked on business matters, he could feel Belen's eyes on him. The secretary might have agreed, but he wasn't pleased.

Letters take weeks to be delivered and answered. And seeing as the response wouldn't come to Alerio, he wouldn't know when the replies arrived. For him, it amounted to standing behind a combat line blindfolded. He knew spears would come. He just didn't know when, so he kept his bags packed and waiting in the stables.

***

On the morning Titus Lanatus' letter arrived confirming his family's support for Lucius Metellus as Consul, Alerio left the Capital. In a day, he would be in Ostia and by the next, on a warship heading south to Messina.

No matter the extent of the search by Lucius Longus' lieutenants, they couldn't locate Alerio Sisera. The Senator was aware that he couldn't get Sisera up on the wood. But he could get the troublesome Battle Commander exiled. Lucius even had the charges of treason already written up, all he required was Alerio to stand trial.

Having missed Colonel Sisera, Senator Longus dared to bring up the legitimacy of the Sisera/Maximus relationship in chambers. Senators of the Republic roundly criticized him for the attempt. Spurius Maximus might be dead, but his political clout extended beyond the grave to protect his family.

Act 6

Chapter 16 – New, Old Silver Chalice

Alerio took the wooden steps from the beach to the raised walkway. The stairs and boardwalk extensions were new improvements to the harbor. When he first arrived in Messina, the piers were wobbly, and the beaching areas separated from the cargo docks by footpaths. Fourteen years as the primary port for Legionaries arriving in Sicilia, the city of choice for commander meetings, and the main harbor for Legion fleet operations had forced changes on the city's infrastructure.

Two sailors with his luggage trudged behind him.

"You can leave the bundles here," Alerio instructed. "And thank you."

"No problem, Lictor Sisera," one acknowledged.

They set the bundles on the boards, jumped down to the sand, and hiked across the beach to their warship.

"Never had a Lictor take a shift on the oars during a voyage," one remarked.

"I've never seen one with that many battle scars," the other noted. "I wouldn't want him hunting me."

"Folks like us don't have to worry about the likes of him. Lictors enforce laws on the wealthy."

"I guess you're right," the other agreed. "If we mess up, our Centurion will handle it. Still, I wouldn't want Sisera coming after me."

They reached the quinquereme and climbed up to the steering deck. On the boardwalk, Alerio signaled for a porter with a cart to come and collect his luggage.

***

The compound of the Proconsul for Sicilia occupied a city block at the base of Citadel Hill. Like the harbor, the area around the government facility exhibited new construction.

"We captured Admiral Hanno where you're standing," Alerio ventured as he glanced around at the new privacy walls and paved streets.

"Captured who, sir?" the young Legionary inquired.

Alerio did the math. The year he and a handful of Legionaries seized the Empire commander on his way back from negotiating with Tribune Gaius Claudius, the sentry had been around six years old.

"Old news," Alerio said brushing off the remark. "I'm Lictor Sisera. And I need to report to Senior Lictor Ahala."

"Yes, sir. He maintains an office in the Legion headquarters building," the infantryman advised.

Alerio wore a fine tunic and quality sandals. Would the sentry have been as agreeable to a man dressed in a workman's shirt and trousers? People assumed many things about a person's status and situation based on their clothing.

Alerio strolled through the gate easily identifiable as a gentlemen with luggage. Not because he was, but because he dressed the part.

At the Legion headquarters building, Alerio told the porter to wait while he went inside.

***

"Can I help you, sir?" the duty NCO inquired.

"I need to speak with Chief Lictor Ahala," Alerio replied.

A tall, heavily muscular man with numerous combat scars separated from a group of men. Other than the difference in clothing, Ahala wore a fine tunic while the Legion officers had on matching tunics with red capes, the combat officers resembled each other.

Of the two types of Lictors, Ahala fit into the semi-retired Centurion category. And it explained why the Proconsul's chief enforcer had his office in the Legion HG. It was a familiar environment.

"I'm Ahala, what can I do for you?"

"Alerio Sisera, Chief Lictor," Alerio introduced himself.

Ahala examined Alerio, with an eye to the visible war wounds. "Centurion?"

"My last position in the Legion was Colonel," Alerio informed him.

"You took over Regulus Legion North during the operation on the Punic coast," Ahala stated. "What can I do for you, Battle Commander Sisera?"

"That was a few years ago," Alerio protested. "Now I'm a Lictor of the Republic."

The Centurions in the office heard the name and the Legion designation. They marched over to the Lictors.

"You commanded Regulus Legion North?" one questioned.

He was short and wore the insignia of a cavalry officer. Which wouldn't have been unusual except, the Centurion of Horse was very young.

"Yes, I did," Alerio asked. "Is that a problem?"

"No, Colonel," another combat officer assured Alerio. "We just wanted to say, if Legion North and you had been on the forward combat line, the invasion would have had a different outcome."

"I'm not sure about that," Alerio protested. "The Spartan General maneuvered his army with precision."

"We debate the operation often," a third combat officer told Alerio. "With Proconsul Regulus dead, there aren't many officers left from the Punic operation. Can we invite you to dinner for a discussion, sir?"

"That would be up to Chief Lictor Ahala."

"I approve of education for all Legion officers," Ahala stated. "But, can I ask Lictor Sisera, why are you in Sicilia?"

"I'm hiding from an angry Senator and looking for a job," Alerio reported. "Is that a problem?"

"We'll sort that out tomorrow," Ahala replied, ignoring the answer. "Tonight, you'll be a guest of honor at the officers' mess. So, let's find you a bed for the night."

"I've got room in the cavalry barracks," the Centurion of Horse volunteered.

"Lartha, I'll not have you pestering Colonel Sisera," Ahala warned.

"Would I do that, Chief Lictor?" Lartha countered. "Me? No sir, my people taught me manners."

"I've seen those manners during debates," Ahala said. Then to Alerio he warned. "Centurion Lartha Mystacis is relentless. It's how he earned a reputation of being a tenacious competitor. Unfortunately, his curiosity makes him a nuisance."

"It's served him well," Alerio conceded. "Being a Centurion of Horse at a young age is rare. I'd be honored to share quarters with such an officer."

"Come with me, sir," Lartha encouraged.

As they walked towards the exit, Alerio questioned, "Lartha is an Etruscan name. Do you know anything about chariot racing?"

"My Etruscan Grandfather married a Latian," Centurion Mystacis said. "He taught me about chariot teams and horsemanship. And my Grandmother instructed me in my rights as a citizen of the Republic."

"And your parents?"

"They died in a plague when I was a baby," Lartha answered.

Outside, Alerio waved the porter and his cart forward. They followed Centurion Mystacis to the cavalry barracks.

***

At dinner, Alerio learned that while Lartha Mystacis was brash and forward, he was untested. But the young cavalry officer wasn't alone. A good portion of the Centurions in the Proconsul's command had no combat experience.

"For all the skirmishes and light engagements on the other side of Sicilia by the marching Legions," Ahala explained, "Messina and the east coast have been calm. It's about as exciting as garrison duty with the Southern Legion, minus the adventure of rowing on the strait."

Alerio also discovered during the discussions, the young officers thirsted for an education. He wondered at the readiness of Centuries that guarded areas not far from the enemy but had to substitute lectures for war.

***

Chief Lictor Ahala wasn't the only one at home in a Legion environment. Although the talking and drinking went late into the night, long before sunrise, Alerio danced in front of a training post, exercising with two practice swords.

"Don't let the Legionaries see you wielding dual gladii," Ahala warned.

In his hand, he carried a single wooden gladius. At a second post, he began running sword drills.

"Early in my career, I was a weapon's instructor," Alerio told him. "The reason I have an extra, one is for my students."

"Good excuse," the Chief Lictor stated. "I always carried extra javelins to 'hand out' during an assault. The truth was, I'd rather throw and impale an enemy than waste strikes sword fighting. I had more important things to do."

Rules were made to keep uniformity in the Legion between fighting seasons. For most Legionaries, NCOs, and officers, the rules worked. For some experienced men, the guidelines were limiting.

When both Lictors were soaked in sweat and breathing heavy, Ahala stopped and pointed to the baths.

"Come and have a soak," he instructed. "Then you can tell me what I'm supposed to do with you."

Neither Alerio nor Ahala solved the riddle of what to do with Lictor Sisera. The solution came from Proconsul Aquillius Florus in the form of an invitation. It directed Alerio to attend the Proconsul's midday feast on the following day.

***

Alerio loitered by the sundial near the front entrance. With an eye to the etched numbers on the face, he watched the shadow from the sun creep by the fourth mark of the morning. And for the third time he read the motto chiseled into the base of the shadow clock.

If you dally at the sundial, you learn little while you idle, and you squander the day, leaving your mind dull, and your affairs in disarray.

Alerio couldn't argue with the logic as he stifled another yawn.

Just before the shadow on the device touched the midday mark, he marched to the entrance of the Proconsul's residence and knocked.

***

"Lictor Sisera, welcome to the home of Aquillius Florus," Grisha, the Proconsul's aid, greeted him before coaching. "Have a little to eat then rest your bowl. That will give the Proconsul an excuse to dismiss you."

Alerio stopped at the threshold, stared at the Greek secretary, and asked, "I presumed the invitation was for a noon feast. Yet, you're already trying to get rid of me."

"The Proconsul keeps a tight schedule and has important meetings all afternoon," Grisha responded. "You are a courtesy. Please don't abuse the privilege."

"Wouldn't think of it," Alerio responded.

He marched through the great room, and following the Secretary's directions, located the Proconsul in a garden.

"Alerio, please join me," Aquillius Florus invited. "I'm so sorry I missed your father's funeral games."

"It was a glorious affair and a proper send off for Senator Maximus," Alerio told him while stretching his legs out on a sofa. "You would have enjoyed the games."

"I'm sure I would have. But governing the populace of Sicilia and advising the Senate on the war with the Empire fills my days," Proconsul Florus stated. "How is Lady Aquila holding up?"

"She misses Maximus," Alerio told him. "I'll tell her you asked about her when I return to the Capital."

"Which brings me to why I wanted to speak with you," Aquillius revealed while waving to several servants. At the signal, they strolled into the garden with bowls of vegetable soup and stacks of flatbread. "I heard that you selected the Lictor path into politics. By now, I'd expect you to be in Rome negotiating for a seat in the Senate. Not here vacationing in Messina."

"I would be, or rather I was in the Capital, but Lucius Longus announced his candidacy for Consul," Alerio explained. "There was talk of preventing Consuls of blue and green ideologies from serving in the same year. But that's not the reason I blocked him."

"And how did you do that?"

"I pledged my supporters to Lucius Metellus," Alerio replied. "With my backing, he will become a Consul this year."

A shadow passed over Aquillius Florus' face and he inquired, "What written promise did you get in return for your votes?"

"Well, sir, not exactly a promise," Alerio confessed. "But it's verbally understood by Senator Metellus that I'll be elevated to a Senate seat once he's a Consul."

"If Senator Maximus were alive, he would advise you this. Verbal isn't worth the paper it's written on."

"Sir, both Lucius Metellus and Quintus Vitulus approached me about getting into politics," Alerio countered. "Why would Metellus go back on his word?"

"No matter your opinion of Lucius Longus, he controls a powerful faction in the Senate," Florus informed him. "Longus wouldn't go away without a fight, or written promises. I know your opinion of him. But, tell me, how does Lucius Longus feel about you."

"Longus would never grant me a seat in the Senate," Alerio responded. Then he stopped and paused for several heartbeats. "You don't think Metellus would agree to block me this year, do you?"

"I've seen politicians do worse to gain power," Florus remarked. "But now I know why you're hiding out in Messina. And seeing as you're here, I have a problem, you might help with."

"Can I get that in writing?" Alerio scoffed.

Instead of finding offense, Aquillius Florus beamed a smile at Alerio.

"Now you're learning," the Proconsul complimented him. He looked towards the corner of the garden. "Grisha, bring me that item."

Grisha bowed, turned, and walked away. Remembering the Secretary's advice, Alerio pushed his half-eaten bowl of soup away and waited to be dismissed.

"Finish your meal," Florus ordered. "I'm not done with you."

***

While Alerio soaked up the drippings of the soup with a piece of bread, Grisha returned and handed a cloth covered object to the Proconsul.

"If I decided to take up art collecting, I could pick a famous craftsman from a town with a reputation," Florus reflected. He grabbed the cloth and yanked it from a silver chalice. "Or I could invest in a few of these."

Alerio reached out and Florus passed it over.

"Beautiful workmanship," Alerio noted. He rotated the goblet and examined it from various angles. "This would be a good investment. Or, seeing that the cup is new, it would make an excellent addition to your festival dishes."

"Scholars tell me the chalice is three hundred and fifty years old," Florus advised.

"It appears new," Alerio reported. "It's been well stored."

"Well stored is the problem," Florus suggested. "Other than Punic craftsmanship, no one knows where the cup came from."

"Maybe from a lost temple?" Alerio offered.

"This new, old silver chalice is Punic, and it is ancient. It could be from a royal burial site or a temple," Florus answered. "Usually, unless the land was blessed by a Roman priest, I wouldn't care. But half the residents of Palermo have business associates or relatives in the Qart Hadasht Empire. The merchant who passed the chalice to me is upset. To keep the peace and prevent subversion around Palermo, I need the theft to stop. And someone has to be brought in to face charges."

"You need a Lictor who isn't attached to your staff to arrest the robber," Alerio ventured. "That way, no one can accuse you of drumming up a crime to remove a political opponent."

"An excellent observation," Florus allowed. "With that kind of forethought, I find it difficult to believe that you didn't get your agreement with Metellus in writing."

"I'll investigate the source of the chalice," Alerio assured the Proconsul while accepting the jab at his political prowess. "But I need several things before I go to Palermo."

Chapter 17 – A Rich Man's Pleasure

Master Philetus Smaltum,
Merchant and Citizen of the Republic,
I hope this letter finds you in good health and feeling spry.
The son of a deceased acquaintance is visiting Sicilia. Although he claims to be on vacation, I have a feeling Alerio Carvilius Sisera is avoiding troubles in Rome. However, the purpose of my communication has nothing to do with that speculation.
Sisera requires a villa while he is in Palermo. I would consider it a personal favor if you would secure housing for him and his staff. Also, since Spurius Carvilius Maximus' death, his son has access to large sums of coins. As any good heir, he seeks to expand the family's fortune. But he is inexperienced in commerce and requires guidance. He may look at farmland, mining opportunities, or merchant ships. If you would help Alerio and keep him away from bad investments, I will be in your debt.
May Sancus the God of trust, honesty, and oaths bless you and your household.
Aquillius Florus,

Proconsul of Sicilia, Senator of Rome, and Citizen of the Republic

Philetus Smaltum placed the letter on his desk, reached over the parchment, and caressed the figurine of the Goddess Kore.

"Decimia, come in here," he called to his assistant.

The Samnites walked in and spied the merchant's hand on the Punic Goddess of the Harvest and Fertility.

"Is Kore sending wealth our way?" the assistant inquired.

With a final pat of the tiny statue, Philetus drew his hand back.

"Indeed, she is," he replied. "See that the small villa off…No wait. Get the big villa on Via Roma cleaned and ready for a guest."

"Are you expecting an important politician?"

"Not a politician and I'm not sure how important," Philetus replied. "But he is rich."

"I'll include a cask of good wine in the setup," Decimia remarked.

"An excellent idea," the merchant agreed as he reread the letter.

***

The coastal trader nudged against the shoreline. Four crewmen and two others jumped into the surf.

"As close as you can get to the beach, please," Alerio requested.

The Skipper sneered behind his hand but didn't let his passenger see the expression.

"Palermo is a good harbor," he pointed out to Alerio. "The deep water runs close to the shore. But this isn't my stop, so we'll only get so far out of the water."

"You have to understand, my good fellow," Alerio whined, "trudging through sand is a bother and I hate getting my sandals wet. They are very expensive to replace."

The merchant Captain wanted to laugh. Most people just let their footwear dry. To replace a pair of sandals simply because they got wet was an extravagance beyond his understanding.

"Fidenas. Don't get too sandy," Alerio called down to the beach. "You'll get the luggage dirty."

"Yes, Master Sisera," the man servant replied. "I'll brush off before unloading."

A sailor next to the servant commented, "He sounds like a dainty gentlemen."

"Master Sisera is richer than most temples," Fidenas informed him.

Corporal Fidenas looked at the other undercover NCO. He received a smile and a nod from Optio Tatiana. They were both on loan to Lictor Sisera from the Sicilia Legion for the mission.

"Master Sisera is none of your business," Tatiana scolded the sailor.

After being reprimanded by the wealthy man's bodyguard, the seaman lowered his eyes and settled his shoulder against the hull.

"Get us dry," the Captain instructed.

Despite the original touch-and-go plan, the trading vessel slid out of the water and onto the beach. When it settled, the Skipper received a pair of silver coins from his passenger.

"Very nice, my good fellow," Alerio added after handing over the coins. "Now. If you'll have the crew climb up and lower the ramp."

***

Philetus Smaltum hustled around his office straightening objects and rearranging a pair of chairs. Once happy the space was ordered, he strolled behind his desk and called to Decimia.

"I'm finished with the correspondence, please escort Master Sisera in."

A man wearing a wide brimmed felt hat, a gray cloak, and a long tunic strolled through the doorway. He walked to the chairs Philetus had just repositioned and moved them to satisfy a different sense of style.

"Everyone wants guests to face forward," Alerio complained. "I prefer a more subtle placement. One not as garish as a direct confrontation over a desktop. Don't you?"

"Why yes, I do. I'll speak with the villa's staff and remind them," Philetus lied. "Welcome to Palermo, Master Sisera."

The merchant found it unnerving to speak to his visitor's profile. In an ungainly manner, he stood, rounded the desk, and took the chair opposite Alerio. Any feeling of superiority vanished with the move.

"I'm here to make purchases," Alerio explained.

"I've been alerted to the facts," Philetus assured him. "Farmland, mines, or merchant ships, if memory serves me."

"That is the story, isn't it," Alerio remarked. "But the truth is much different."

"How so, Master Sisera?"

"The truth, Philetus, is I am a bad businessman," Alerio confessed, "My mining operations are not producing. My farms are quickly turning to dust. And my merchant fleet is being hounded by Illyrian pirates."

"But you are the heir to a fortune," the merchant reminded Alerio. "You are expected to increase your family's holdings."

"I know that, and I have plans to. However, they don't include the mechanics of industry," Alerio stated. He leaned forward and locked eyes with Philetus. "Art increases in value. And does it without the sweat, the difficult personalities, and the travel. Therefore, I am in Sicilia seeking out unique pieces of artwork."

"There are many ancient temples on the island," Philetus assured him. "And, although I hate to brag, I have contacts in that class of merchants."

"I'm not looking to buy mundane statues or tiles," Alerio insisted. "I require rare art that qualifies as investments."

"I would expect nothing less from a nobleman like yourself," Philetus Smaltum offered. "Will you join me for dinner?"

"No. I am exhausted," Alerio begged off. "The travel from Messina was uncomfortable."

"I understand," Philetus commented. "Perhaps you'll be rested by noon tomorrow. I may have news about some art opportunities by then."

"Noon will be fine," Alerio said as he stood. "By the way, the villa at Via Roma is close to the defensive wall. I'm not going to have city guardsmen stomping through my garden all night long, am I?"

"You'll not have guardsmen in your courtyard unless the city is attacked," the merchant informed him. "And no one has invaded Palermo since the Sicilian Wars."

"That's good to know," Alerio acknowledged. He pointed towards the door. "Come Tatiana. I hope Fidenas has the villa clean and put in order by now."

"I'm sure he has," the bodyguard assured him.

"Do I need to remind you that he failed to prepare the villa in Messina," Alerio blustered.

He and the disguised NCO walked from the room, through a hall, and out of the house.

"The villa is clean and stocked and in order," Decimia told Philetus. "Imagine that delicate daisy flower worrying about my work."

Philetus didn't comment on his assistant's indignation. Rubbing the figurine of Kore, the merchant smiled and dreamed of the fat commissions he would receive from Alerio Carvilius Sisera.

***

A block away, Alerio glanced at his bodyguard.

"What do you think, Sergeant?"

"I've seen greedy merchants in my time, sir," Optio Tatiana replied. "In every city and town with a Legion garrison, they cluster like hungry birds around the Legionaries. This one has better surroundings, but he's just as vile."

"Do you suppose the Proconsul realized it, when he sent me to Philetus Smaltum?"

"That, sir, is between the Proconsul and you," the Optio said distancing himself from any splash of political mud that might erupt. Pushing the idea of a high-level confrontation further away, he stated. "I'm sure Fidenas has the villa in order."

"We can sleep on the floor for all I care," Alerio commented.

"I'd rather not, sir," Tatiana ventured. "Sleeping in a feather bed is a rare luxury."

***

As Philetus predicted, no city guards crossed the garden behind the villa. If they had, the patrol would have been drawn to the clash of steel blades and heavy breathing.

"Corporal Fidenas, if you drop your guard in combat," Alerio coached, "some barbarian will cut your head off."

"Yes, sir. I'll keep my blade up."

Soaked with sweat, Tatiana, Fidenas, and Alerio continued to duel until darkness ended the exercise.

"After we clean up, we'll walk the city's defenses," Alerio informed Tatiana. "When I visit, I like to know the layout of the defensive walls."

"It's only a mile and a half around the perimeter, Lictor," Tatiana stated. "Along the way, I'll show you the armory."

"Is the armory important?" Alerio inquired.

"The Legion stockpiles javelins, spears, bolts, and arrows in Palermo, sir," Fidenas explained. "With the wide harbor, the city is the best missile staging area for campaigns on Sicilia."

"Then we'll see the armory," Alerio agreed. "Corporal Fidenas, do we have a bath?"

"The villa comes with a wash, a rinse, a soaking pool, and a masseuse," he responded. "I had him set the fires before I ran the staff off."

"I apologize for that," Alerio stated, "but I don't want servants overhearing us."

"We'll wait until you finish, sir," Tatiana offered.

"When I served in the Legion I washed in mud puddles, rivers, lakes, and the sea," Alerio told them. "I never thought about washing separately in the field. Make no mistake, this is a mission. There are large sums of coins to be made balanced against an angry populace. We're inserting ourselves between the money and the mob. And both sides will defend their positions with blades."

"This way to the baths," Fidenas directed. He pointed to the side of the villa with his gladius. "After you, sir."

***

"The sauce is lumpy, and the fish is overcooked," Alerio complained while picking at the midday feast. Then he blinked as if realizing how rude he sounded. "Of course, I don't blame you, Master Smaltum. This far from Rome, it's hard to find a quality chef."

Philetus wanted to throw the platter of food at the arrogant nobleman. They were halfway through the meal and at every course, Sisera had found fault. Only visions of gold coins prevented the merchant from carrying out the action.

"I must apologize for my inadequate staff," Philetus responded. "Perhaps dessert will meet your approval."

"Sweets are not pleasing to my palette," Alerio announced. "Can we forget about this disaster of a feast and get down to business?"

In response to a wave, Decimia stepped to the side of the merchant's couch.

"We're retiring to my office," Philetus told his assistant. "Once we're settled, bring in the vendor."

"Yes, sir," the Samnites replied.

Philetus and Alerio strolled from the banquet hall and moved down a corridor to the merchant's office. Tatiana trailed behind a respectful distance. At the door, Philetus allowed Alerio to cross the threshold and enter the room first.

To Philetus' displeasure, Sisera crossed the room, circled the desk, and sat in the merchant's seat.

"You don't mind?" Alerio insisted. "I'm more open to negotiations from behind a desk."

Reluctantly, the merchant sat with his body sideways to Alerio. Only his head faced the desk.

"Now, what have you brought me?" Alerio inquired.

Decimia marched in followed by a middle-aged Greek. As Alerio had been insufferable during the noon feast, Tatiana braced and rested a hand on the hilt of his gladius. Alerio noted the aggressive movement and sliced the air with his hand to stop the Optio from drawing. Decimia and Philetus missed the hand motion. They were ogling a covered box cuddled in the Greek's arms. Their focus was so intent, Alerio was tempted to follow their gaze. If he had, Lictor Sisera would have missed Philetus' scowl of impatience.

"Pika runs a small trading shop here in Palermo," Philetus stated. "Pika, this is Master Sisera. What have you brought us?"

"Just what you…" the trader started to say.

Decimia cuffed his shoulder and instructed, "Stop wasting the day and show Master Smaltum what you brought."

"Yes, sir," the trader agreed.

He placed the box on the edge of the desk, removed the cover, and lifted out a silver chalice. Although different from the one the Proconsul possessed, the cup was beautiful. Alerio held out his hand for the chalice.

"It's cute," Alerio stated while thumping the rim of the vessel. A dull thud would have warned of lead filling. "The silver seems pure enough. And the gods and battle scenes are well crafted. But in Rome, I can buy these by the crate."

"Oh no, sir," Pika exclaimed. "See the markings on the bottom. Those are the symbols of King Mago the First of Qart Hadasht. Or at least one of the Kings silversmiths. That means the chalice is at least two hundred and eighty years old."

"That does change the prospective," Alerio noted. "But what am I to do with one? A set of four would have more value. Wouldn't it?"

"The likelihood of there being three more cups of that quality is immeasurable," Philetus proclaimed.

Alerio knew Aquillius Florus had an equally rare chalice. If there were two on the market, there had to be more someplace. Alerio needed to pressure Pika to go to the source to secure three more.

"If it's only a matter of coins," he boasted. "I have the funds."

A look of raw greed flashed between Pika and Philetus. At least Alerio assumed it was. But a second later, Pika slumped, turned to the merchant, and asked, "What should I do Master Smaltum?"

Philetus bristled at the familiarity of the question. But he played his part.

"I don't know," he deflected. "But my client is willing to pay handsomely for three more silver cups. I'd say give me a week and I'll try to complete a set."

Pika squared his shoulders and announced, "Give me a week, Master Sisera, and I'll try to complete a set for you."

The almost word for word response told Alerio that Proconsul Florus had not simply drawn Philetus Smaltum's name by chance. Florus had suspected the merchant and sent Alerio in to prove his hunch.

"Then gentleman, I'll see you in a week," Alerio stated. Heading for the door, he yawned and mumbled to his bodyguard. "Come Tatiana, we've wasted half a day. And I need a nap."

Rich, hapless nobleman Sisera and his bodyguard walked from the room. Once they were gone, Pika spun to Philetus.

"Master Smaltum, where can we get three more chalices?" he asked. "This was one of the only two we found."

"We found them. Open another and find three more," Philetus shot back. "I have a ready customer in Sisera. Plus, he's a Latin and won't go crying to a bunch of hysterical locals about insulting their ancestors."

Chapter 18 – Curses and Sources

At the villa on Via Roma, Alerio went to a table, glanced at the map he drew of the city, pushed the piece of parchment aside and, grabbed a pitcher of wine.

"What do you think, Optio?" he asked the bodyguard while filling two mugs.

"We'll know for sure when Fidenas reports in, sir," Tatiana replied while taking a mug. Before drinking, he added. "But I'd say Pika works for Philetus Smaltum."

"That's my thought," Alerio agreed as he began to pace. Stopping, he took a sip and inquired. "When is Centurion Mystacis due?"

"It's a four-day ride from Messina, Lictor. If all goes well and the weather holds, the cavalry troop should be here the day after tomorrow. But sir, not trusting the local Centuries is a nuisance. There are good men stationed here."

"Criminals spread coins around and it's tempting for Legionaries to collect a few by passing on information," Alerio countered. "I prefer to bring in men I can trust, rather than trust that I won't get a dagger in the back of my neck."

Tatiana jerked at the description, reached around, and rubbed at the base of his skull.

"Do you think it'll come to blades?" he questioned.

"When men walk the dark edge of civility for coins, they will kill to protect their reputation," Alerio offered. He picked up the roll of parchment. "Come on Optio, lets go find some food while we go over the map of the city. Being a smug urbanite and a food critic has left me hungry."

"Our pantry doesn't offer the same quality of food as you turned down at the feast," Tatiana warned.

"That's true. But here I can eat and not act like an insufferable dandy."

"Your performance was very convincing, sir. You could have a career in the theater."

"Thank you, I think," Alerio commented. He tucked the parchment under his arm and instructed. "Bring the wine, Sergeant."

They walked down the corridor to the pantry and selected items. While one began rinsing the crust off a salted pork loin, the other sliced vegetables.

Legionaries learned early to work together and to use everything they carried in their packs. Although they hadn't humped in the makings of the meal, the salt that preserved the meat would go into the pot to season the boiled vegetables.

"No grain, sir?" Tatiana inquired

"I'm hungry and spelt takes too long to soften," Alerio told him while banking the fire. Once the wood burned with enough intensity, he skewed pieces of pork and held them over the flames. In moments, the aroma of roasting meat filled the room. Alerio glanced at the Optio and smiled. "Remind me to save some for Tesserarius Fidenas."

"Yes, sir," Tatiana acknowledged. He inhaled, savoring the aroma. "I'll try."

***

Late in the afternoon, a hooded figure slipped over the garden wall. In three strides, he reached a pathway. After a quick march, Fidenas arrived at the rear patio.

"Did you do any good?" Tatiana questioned.

"After we talked, I identified Pika and followed him to his shop," the Corporal reported. He tossed the hood off and brushed his head as if some wool lint had stuck in his short hair. "It's full of ropes, hooks, and other nautical items.

There's nothing rare on display. Oh, and the shop is owned by Philetus Smaltum."

On the way from the Smaltum Villa, Fidenas had fallen in step with Tatiana for a city block. Once he had a description, the Corporal stepped off the street and waited to follow Pika.

"How did you learn that Philetus owns the shop?" Alerio asked from the doorway.

"Street vendor's love to gossip," Fidenas answered. "For the price of a bowl of wheat with honey, I learned about every shop on the block."

"We saved you some pork and vegetables," Tatiana informed him. "But if you're not hungry…"

"I can eat," the Corporal said quickly.

"What's Pika doing?" Alerio asked.

They were watching the trader looking for suspicious activity. If Pika moved to secure another chalice and no one was there to observe him, the entire exercises would be for nothing.

"The trader was preparing a meal when a pair of sailors showed up. Right now, Pika is busy haggling with them over the price of gear," Fidenas explained. "I figured it was a good opportunity to report in."

"Come into the villa. You can show us where the shop is located while you eat," Alerio directed. "I'll take the second watch on Pika."

"Sir, Optio Tatiana and I can split the duty," Fidenas suggested.

"You could," Alerio agreed. "Except, I'm not a follower of the Goddess Aergia."

The NCOs chuckled. They'd only known Lictor Sisera for a few day. In that time, they learned he was far from a follower of the Goddess of Idleness, Laziness, and Sloth.

Just before dusk, Alerio tossed a gray cloak over his shoulders and tugged the hood over his head.

"I'll see you at moonrise, sir," Tatiana assured Alerio.

Alerio walked the garden path to a section of wall between a pair of trees. He climbed to the top of the wall and paused in the overlapping branches. Seeing no one on the road, he dropped off the far side. Moments later, Alerio Sisera vanished into the streets of Palermo.

***

Five blocks along the Corso Calatafimi, Alerio turned off the main road. He strolled two blocks north before finding Pika's shop. As Corporal Fidenas described and pointed out on Alerio's map, the trader's shop sat on a corner in a commercial district.

Darkness had fallen, and the vendor used by the Corporal for information was nowhere to be seen. Alerio located a narrow alleyway with a view of the shop and snuggled against one brick wall. Conversations from second-floor residences fluttered down to street level. Arguments peaked and ebbed as tempers heated then cooled. Children babbled. Babies cried. And a feeling of homesickness swept over Alerio.

In hindsight, he should have consulted Belen, kept the political favors, and waited a year. Sure, his actions prevented Lucius Longus from becoming one of the Consuls. But they also renewed the animosity between Alerio and Longus. Exiled to Sicilia to avoid political backlash, he stood in a cluttered alley, on a deserted street, watching a closed shop. Despite the political threat Longus represented, it would have been more satisfying for Alerio to wait the year at home.

His remorse ended when a man strolled to the shop and pounded on the door. The shape seemed familiar, but Alerio couldn't place him. Then Pika with a candle in his hand opened the door. As the visitor turned sideways to enter, Alerio recognized Philetus Smaltum's assistant. Pika followed Decimia in and closed the door behind them.

An early evening visit from the merchant's assistant further tied Smaltum to the theft of the Punic holy items. This added to the anecdotal evidence against him but didn't give Alerio enough to present to Proconsul Florus. Alerio had to be sure of his stand before accusing a rich and powerful merchant of...

And there was the biggest issue. Taking religious items wasn't sacrilege, if the location hadn't been sanctified by a priest of a Republic temple. Technically, the chalice or anything else taken from a barbarian temple was simply an artifact. Unless, as Proconsul Florus pointed out, it disrupted the good order of a region. And having emotionally charged Punic items sold at market certainly qualified as disrupting.

During the mental exercise of what he needed to bring charges, Pika and Decimia left the shop. Alerio slipped from the alleyway and slinked after them.

***

A strong garrison in a secure location had one drawback, a lack of vigilance. Confident in their ability to respond quickly with force, only one sleeping sentry guarded the gate. The rest of the area's Century slept nearby. Alerio assumed it was the same at every gate leading into the city.

Or, he considered while following the assistant and trader through the gate, at every portal leading out of Palermo.

The road ran straight through a forest. Under cover of darkness, Alerio rushed forward closing the distance. Fortunately, his movement was covered by Pika's and Decimia's voices. And while he couldn't make out the topic of their conversation, the talking allowed Alerio to trail them when they left the main road.

***

The Legion had taught Alerio to measure distance by counting strides while on the march. As an estimate, he knew they had traveled twelve hundred and fifteen paces from the walls of the city, or three quarters of a mile.

Another quarter of a mile along the turnoff brought them to a cultivated area. Moonrise gave Alerio an impression of the size of the fields and forced him to hide in the shadows.

Before ducking down and stepping off the wagon track, he saw an outline of a farmhouse and work buildings. Based on the size of the house, Alerio figured the farm was the holding of a prosperous but absentee landowner. If a family owned the farm, they would have built a larger villa. He assumed Pika and Decimia would cross to the farmhouse. In preparation to follow them on a parallel track, he slipped through the rails of a new fence.

He could tell it was newly installed by the aroma of freshly cut wood which blended nicely with the green crops and turned soil. The smells reminded Alerio of his childhood and, by association, his own children. For a moment, Lictor Sisera almost returned to Palermo. He'd pack his bags, and sail for home at first light.

"Curse this," he growled, "let someone else find the source."

Then Pika and Decimia vanished.

***

The crops weren't high enough to block the men from his vision. Nor was the night black enough to shade them from view. Alerio scanned the field, before rotating until he faced the forest. Stooped low, he peered over the rail fence, and searched the shadows of the trees. One branch bobbed up and down, marking the passage of a body. Alerio hopped the fence and ran to the branch.

Lifting his feet to avoid entanglement, he tried to walk softly while easing limbs out of his way. Somewhere ahead, Pika and Decimia followed a hidden trail.

Alerio didn't have the luxury of knowing the destination. He did have the experience of serving in a Raider Century and the benefit of an association with a scout. Using his knowledge, Alerio walked several paces, stopped, and listened. Once he located the direction of snapping twigs and slapping branches, he moved towards the sounds before stopping and listening again.

Thanks to the method, Alerio didn't get lost when the rustling ahead stopped. He followed the last audio clue until two candle lanterns flared to life.

In the weak light, Pika with a long thin rod poked the forest floor. Behind the trader, Decimia pushed the blade of a shovel into the soil.

"This would be easier if we did it in the daylight," Pika complained.

"The fieldworkers would see us and come to investigate. Master Smaltum can't afford to lose any more of them,"

Decimia replied. He shoved the blade in another spot before continuing. "I had to dispose of the two who discovered it. They're buried and hidden a few trees over. If any more fieldhands disappear, the word will get out that the farm is cursed."

"Isn't it already?" Pika asked. He thrust the rod into the soil and pulled it out. A few feet away he stabbed again and observed. "Look at this rich topsoil. The land cries out for clearing and planting. Except it can't be used, can it?"

"Don't you start with the cursed talk," Decimia scolded. "We have a job to do. Stop talking and get on with the search."

Through the trees, Alerio watched the men dig and probe. They didn't seem likely to halt or to move to another location. Sinking to the forest floor, he listened and pondered what they expected to find in the forest in the middle of the night.

***

The grunts that accompanied each poke with the rod and the huff that came with each thrust of the shovel went on until deep into the night. Then the rod, the shovel, and the lanterns were covered by a piece of tent. Before the men hiked away, they sprinkled leaves over the tarp to camouflage the gear.

Alerio put his back to a tree trunk, crossed his arms, and closed his eyes.

***

The alignment of the forest provided two contradictory reactions to the sun. At dusk, darkness came on quickly, partially because of the hills to the west. Conversely, at the first light of dawn, the rays of the rising sun streamed through the trees, illuminating the ground. Alerio stood, brushed off dried leaves, and walked to the center of the previous night's labors.

Starting in the center of the poked ground, he began walking in ever widening circles. Soon he trekked through the trees with an eye to the center where Pika poked the earth and an eye to the ground searching for what got the farmworkers killed. It took several revolutions before he found a mound of fresh dirt under a scattering of leaves.

Thinking it was the murdered farmworkers, Alerio circled the pile. Then Decimia's words came to him, "Buried and hidden." A mound didn't fit the definition of hidden. Alerio bent and pressed fingers into the soil. Most of it was soft dirt. On the far side of the pile, his fingernails sank in as before, but on the second joint, his finger stopped. After removing a few handfuls of soil, he saw a board. Two yanks later, the board fell away to expose the opening of a tunnel.

Act 7

Chapter 19 – The Guilty

After retrieving a candle from under the tarp, Alerio returned to the opening. He struck steel to flint, sparked a piece of kindling, and lit the wick. Then, with a hand shielding the flame, he stepped into the tunnel.

Steps chiseled from the rock took him down to a flat area. There he faced a wall of rock on three sides. Turning around, he noted a narrow cut beside the steps. He squeezed into the gap, scraping his knees on the side of the stairs. Partway into the cavity, the rock against his knees vanished. Stooping, he saw another set of steps.

Ten tight steps down, the ceiling of the passageway ended, and the rock opened, allowing his candlelight to fill a burial chamber.

"Goddess Nenia, I can tell that long ago you came and took the souls of the departed," Alerio prayed while stooping to view the vault. "Please excuse my violation of their sarcophagus."

Two bodies wrapped in cloth lay on a ledge. Both had been disturbed as he could see from the odd angles of their dried bones and the rips in the internment fabric. He wondered what valuables had been stripped from the corpses. Further signs of invasion came from bare spots on a tabletop. The small, clean circles in a thick layer of dust matched the bases of the old Punic chalices.

"Only two in this one," he said while stepping onto the floor of the chamber. "It's no wonder Decimia and Pika were out searching…"

The candlelight illuminated the walls, and he stopped talking. A mural of finely cast clay tiles depicted a scene of a family and royalty by a fireplace. In the mural, Alerio recognized the tall headdresses of Qart Hadasht noblemen.

The artistry in the chamber identified it as the final resting place of an important man and his wife.

"Were you related to a Punic king?" Alerio inquired while looking at the shelf.

Based on the opulence of the vault, there was a good chance other Punic subjects were buried in the vicinity. After a final look around, Alerio climbed the steps. At the top, he reset the board and covered it with dirt and leaves.

Then, with everything left as he found it, Lictor Sisera dashed for the edge of the woods.

***

At the wagon trail, Alerio jogged quickly to the main road. But just as he turned towards Palermo, Legion skirmishers screening for an infantry Century warned him off the route. Before the Legionaries arrived, bowmen strutted by.

"Step to the side Latian, and make way for the Legionaries," an archer instructed.

There were twenty bowman, and each had two long leather carries over one shoulder and two hard sided leather arrow totes on the other. Beside the bows and arrows, some were armed with short swords while others had war hatchets on their hips.

"Where are you going?" Alerio inquired.

"There's a garrison in Poggio Ridente," the bowman responded. "We're moving there to make room."

"Make room for what?" Alerio asked.

He didn't receive an answer from the archer. The bowmen were far down the road by the time he finished the question. But marching far ahead of the unit, the Century's Optio heard and replied.

"Metellus Legions North and South landed and took all the available barracks," the Sergeant told Alerio. "Stay off the road..."

"And make way for the Legionaries," Alerio repeated. "I know."

The left stomp of an infantry Century shook the ground and in moments, the eighty Legionaries approached. As they neared, Alerio examined the unfamiliar armor and helmets. Although the shields and gladii were correct, the equipment was not Latin inspired.

In the Consuls' marching Legions, Legionaries were required to be citizens of the Republic with their own armor and shields. But due to the on-going conflict with Qart Hadasht, and the expansion of the Republic, more forces from Rome's client-states were drafted into garrison Legions. The Century marching on the road was an auxiliary unit of heavy infantry with a Latin Optio and Tesserarius.

Tomas Kellerian would not be pleased. In fact, the armorer to the Gods would be furious at witnessing foreign troops trained in Legion tactics. As Kellerian often warned, *"We don't teach potential enemies how to defeat our Legions."*

"Unfortunately, Master Kellerian," Alerio whispered to the ether, "the sons of Rome are too few to staff distant garrisons."

No matter the origin of the Legionaries, the one constant of a Legion Century on the march followed the infantrymen. In this case, it was fifteen goats loaded with tents and utensils. An equal number of servants led the pack animals. In his years, Alerio had seen mules, donkeys, and goats used for the same purpose. Men can only carry so much weight on the march and the pack animals and servants were essential for the comfort of the nightly bivouacs.

He stood peering down the straight road at the receding Legion Century and their caravan of animals. Then Alerio turned and looked at the tops of the defensive wall in the distance. Between him and Palermo, there was no sign of the Century's Centurion or other displaced officers. After several heartbeats, Alerio decided if he encountered riders, he'd have time to jump out of the way.

But the mounted officer never materialized. Alerio reached the city gate at mid-day. Oddly enough, he hadn't encountered anyone coming from the direction of Palermo.

***

Rather than one sleepy sentry at the gate, two armored Legionaries stood in the portal.

"What's the nature of your business?" one questioned.

"I've never seen the gates guarded this attentively," Alerio observed. "Has there been trouble?"

"Consul Metellus and Proconsul Florus are in residence," the other Legionary replied. "There's been no trouble and there won't be. Metellus Legions North and South are on the scene."

Delighted to have Lucius Metellus and Aquillius Florus in Palermo at the same time, Alerio took a step forward. The pair leveled their spears over the infantry shields. Alerio stopped.

"No one in or out of the city except for special cases," the other Legionary insisted. "What is the nature of your business?"

"Why is Palermo locked down?" Alerio asked.

"A Lictor went missing last night," the second sentry explained. "Proconsul Florus has ordered a house-to-house and building-to-building search."

Proconsuls had the authority to command a Legion if a Consul wasn't available. But Lucius Metellus' presence gave the Consul/General the overall authority. Why would the search command come from Aquillius Florus?

"You'll need to give a reason to enter the city, or you'll have to leave," one Legionary instructed. "Pick one, because you can't stay there blocking the gateway."

Alerio was thinking about the power shift between the Proconsul and Consul positions when the Legionary spoke. It didn't occur to Alerio that the infantrymen were out of patience.

"Leave it is," the second sentry announced.

The two stepped forward, forcing Alerio back to avoid the spears.

"Wait," he begged while holding up his arms. "I am Lictor Alerio Carvilius Sisera. I believe the search is for me."

The Legionaries didn't retreat or relax. One simply shouted over his shoulder, "Officer of the Day to the gate."

Then the three stood in the gateway gazing at each other over the shields. Obviously well trained, the Legionaries gave no sign that they would lower their guard until the situation was resolved. Alerio appreciated the professionalism of the men from Metellus Legion North.

***

Soon runners raced to alert NCOs in charge of the search that the Lictor had been located. As the hunt drew down, two horses galloped down Corso Calatafimi. A block from the north wall, they reined in at the villa on Via Roma.

"Thank you, Centurion," Alerio said to the officer escorting him.

"We're glad your safe, Lictor Sisera," the combat officer responded.

He took the reins of Alerio's horse and walked the mounts away. While the escort headed for Legion Headquarters, Alerio strolled to a sentry posted outside the compound.

"I'm Lictor Alerio Carvilius Sisera and I'm expected."

"Yes, sir, the Proconsul is on the patio," the Legionary responded. "It's near the garden. Do you need directions?"

"I know the way."

***

When only three men occupied the residence, the place seemed huge. Now, with Aquillius Florus' administrative staff, military attachés to the Proconsul of Sicilia, and household servants scurrying around, the hallway felt crowded.

"I can see why you chose to sit out here, sir," Alerio greeted Florus when he reached the patio.

Aquillius Florus put down a scroll, picked up a glass of wine, and tilted it towards Alerio.

"You're dirty but unlike other times I've seen you in disarray, you aren't bruised or bleeding," the Proconsul observed. "That speaks well for your night. Can I assume you weren't abducted?"

"I was not, sir," Alerio responded. "My night was spent uncovering the source of the Punic chalices."

"Chalices? There's more than one?"

"At least two, that they've found," Alerio told him.

"Ah, they've found. You've discovered the vendors of the artifacts?"

"I have, Proconsul," Alerio explained. "They raided an old, a very old Punic necropolis. It's in a wooded area a little more than a mile outside of Palermo. And I learned that Philetus Smaltum owns the land where the graves are located."

"Do you have enough to bring him to trial, Lictor Sisera?"

"Well sir, he wasn't at the sarcophagus, or in the woods probing for another tomb," Alerio admitted. "But he did make the introduction to a trader selling one of the chalices. And I overheard Master Smaltum's assistant admit to murdering two fieldhands to keep the secret of the Punic grave."

"So, you have a trader and an assistant," Florus pondered in a soft voice.

"Yes sir. But give me a few moments with Smaltum," Alerio promised, "and I'll get a confession out of him."

"Of that, Lictor Sisera, I have little doubt," Florus said. "But you have the guilty. Bring them to me and I'll pass judgement. Once they're crucified, the citizens will be pacified. And we'll have squashed any rumor of unpunished sacrilege."

"But, Proconsul, we can…"

Aquillius Florus held up his hand to stop Alerio.

"Philetus Smaltum is a wealthy and influential merchant with many friends," Florus told him. "And now, Master Smaltum owes me a favor. Just as I owe you one. Do you understand?"

"Completely, Proconsul," Alerio assured him. "I might suggest that you have the Legion clear the trees and have a Latin priest bless the graveyard. That will allow you to bring the full force of the law against any future offenders."

"A perfectly acceptable conclusion to the whole affair," Florus stated. "When will you apprehend the degenerate tomb robbers?"

"Not until this evening," Alerio replied. "If Smaltum's to be left out of this, I need to arrest his assistant when he's away from his master's villa."

"Take whatever force you need from the Sicilia garrison," the Proconsul offered.

"Sergeant Tatiana and Corporal Fidenas will be enough. Long before anyone knows they're missing, you'll have Decimia and Pika to judge," Alerio declared. "Now if you'll excuse me, sir, I want to go speak with Consul Metellus."

"Need I remind you that you're in the middle of an investigation for me," Florus remarked. "Please see this one to a conclusion before opening another inquiry."

"It's only a talk about my Senate seat," Alerio reminded Aquillius Florus.

"After your obligation to me is satisfied, if you please."

"Yes, Proconsul," Alerio agreed.

Disgruntled but committed to completing his commitment to Florus, Alerio walked from the patio. He had just secured a favor from a powerful politician, and he needed to protect that support. In the villa, he began searching rooms looking for Tatiana and Fidenas.

***

That evening, Decimia strolled through the dark streets of Palermo. He approached the shop on the corner, stepped to the door, raised his fist, and knocked. Holding a candle, Pika answered the knock. As soon as he opened the door, a shoulder pounded into Decimia's lower back. He and his assailant flew by Pika and vanished into the store.

Confused by the sudden violence, Pika held up his candle and peered into the shop. With his free hand, he reached for his knife. Before the blade cleared the sheath, Optio Tatiana hammered his forearm into the trader' neck. The light went out when the candle hit the floor.

Pika, off balance and stumbling, tripped and fell. In the dark, he tumbled into the fight between Alerio and Decimia.

"I'm a little busy, Optio," Alerio complained when the trader's body landed. While fending off a punch from Decimia, he added. "Handle him yourself."

"I'm on it, sir," Tatiana stated.

He kicked Pika then leaped on him. All four men rolled on the floorboards exchanging blows with fists and knees.

Infantrymen against merchants should not have been a contest. But in the darkness and confusion, getting control of the grave robbers was taking longer than expected.

Outside, Corporal Fidenas walked a mule cart to the entrance.

Unaware of the fighting, he called through the doorway, "Optio Tatiana, are we ready?"

"Thieves, thieves," Decimia shouted. "We're being robbed."

In response to the shouts, neighbors bellowed for the city guard. Pounding feet from around the corner announced the arrival of six Legionaries. One knocked Fidenas off his feet, flipped his spear over, and placed the tip on the Corporal's neck.

"Don't move. Don't speak," the infantryman warned. "Don't even breathe hard."

As if pinned to the ground, Fidenas lay in the street, unmoving and frightened.

The five remaining members of the patrol ran into the shop and began pulling the combatants apart.

"I am…" Alerio started to explain.

The butt end of a spear smashed into the side of Lictor Sisera's head. He dropped to the ground.

"We're with the Proconsul's Legion," Tatiana began when a steel spearhead snapped up and stared him in the face.

"Don't talk," the Optio of the patrol ordered. "I don't know how the Sicilia Legion handles thieves. But I know what Metellus North does and if you were one of mine, you would be dead before your body hit the street."

"You must release me," Decimia begged. "I am…"

"Conveniently, there's a mule cart here," the Legion NCO threatened. "Keep talking and you can ride along with the other sleeping guy."

In short order, Pika, Decimia, Tatiana, and Fidenas, along with the groggy Alerio in the mule cart, were marched to Legion headquarters.

***

Each horse stall was walled off, making them excellent holding cells.

"I need to see Chief Lictor Ahala," Alerio said while rubbing the side of his head.

"I don't know who that is," the officer in charge admitted.

"He's the chief enforcer for the Proconsul of Sicilia," Alerio told him.

"There's your problem," the Centurion snapped. "This is Legion North, not the Proconsul's horde. Sleep off the wine. We'll sort this out in the morning."

"I'm not drunk," Alerio protested.

"Then you've no excuse for getting into a street brawl," the officer scolded. "Optio, if that one continues to be a problem, have someone poke him in the head to shut him up."

Alerio realized nothing would get done until morning. After fluffing up the straw, he stretched out, and pondered the mess he made of the arrest. Ignoring the slight headache, he drifted off to sleep.

It felt as if he had just closed his eyes when yelling and running feet outside the stable woke him. Garbled shouting added to the confusion.

"All Centuries report to your assembly areas," one clear voice commanded. "Prepare to defend the walls."

Chapter 20 – A Hateful Deal

When the Legionaries left, Alerio realized the cells had transitioned to unguarded stalls in a stable. To test that theory, he reached over the half door and lifted the locking beam.

"Optio Tatiana, Tesserarius Fidenas, we're back on mission," Alerio informed his men. Once free of the cell, he walked to the other stalls and opened the gates.

"Pika, Decimia get out here. And know this, if you fight, I will hurt you."

"Master Sisera?" Decimia questioned. He walked from the stall rubbing sleep from his eyes. "What's going on?"

"You're being charged with sacrilege against a holy place," Alerio told him.

"First, the ground hasn't been sanctified by a Latin priest," the assistant listed. "Second, I work for Master Smaltum. Those are two reasons I'm walking out of here. Stand aside."

With more light than they had in the shop, it was easy for Alerio to catch the assistant's arm, twist it behind his back, and throw Decimia to the ground. Alerio kneeled on his back.

"I forgot to mention the murder of two farmworkers," he added.

Four Legionaries marched into the stable. They stopped and stared.

"I'm Colonel Sisera," Alerio told them. "Get me two lengths of rope so I can secure my prisoner. Optio Tatiana, do you have the other one."

"Yes, Colonel," the NCO replied.

The Sergeant appeared from a stall holding Pika by the neck. To demonstrate his control, Tatiana shook the trader.

"Sir, we were sent to guard the prisoners," one of the newly arrived Legionaries reported.

"And you will," Alerio assured him, "all the way to the Proconsul's residence."

With a pair of Legionaries in front and another pair behind, Alerio and his NCOs marched the grave robbers out of the sable. On the way to Via Roma and the villa, they saw teamsters moving wagons of javelins, arrows, and spears to distribution stations along the route.

"Shouldn't we ask what's going on, sir?" Fidenas inquired.

"No, Corporal," Alerio instructed. "Right now, we have command because the Legionaries think we know what we're doing. Let's not make them question the premise by asking about the obvious."

"The obvious, sir?"

"That the city is under siege," Alerio replied. He glanced at the dawn sky. "We may not understand the circumstances, but we know an enemy launched a pre-dawn attack."

Infantry runners raced from the walls. At the wagons, they collected arm loads of javelins and arrows, before sprinting back to their defensive positions.

"Based on the numbers of projectiles our defenders are using," Fidenas noted, "it's not a simple raid."

***

After weaving around reserve Centuries waiting to relieve those on the walls, they reached the Via Roma compound.

"Lictor Sisera to see Proconsul Florus," Alerio declared his purpose.

"The Proconsul is meeting with Consul Metellus about the defense of Palermo," the sentry at the gate advised. "Is there somebody else who can help you, sir?"

"Chief Lictor Ahala," Alerio replied.

An Optio ran to collect the enforcer. Moments later, Ahala and two junior Lictors arrived at the gate.

"The two prisoners are for Proconsul Florus," Alerio informed the Chief Lictor of Sicilia. "Unless you need them, you can dismiss the Legionaries, and Tatiana and Fidenas. Then tell me what's happening?"

"I don't need Legion North infantrymen. You four are dismissed. But you other two are Sicilia Legion. Collect your war gear and stand by to protect the Proconsul," Ahala directed. He indicated for Alerio to follow once everyone had dispersed. "Late yesterday, Centurion Mystacis and a detachment of thirty cavalrymen from Messina reached the far side of the Oreto River. That's about a mile east of the city. He planned to camp there overnight and ride into Palermo at first light."

Alerio looked at the sky and remarked, "This is first light."

"His troop ran into a Qart Hadasht army sneaking down the far side of the river," Ahala reported. "If not for Centurion Mystacis, we'd be fighting hand-to-hand and street-to-street by now. Instead, Legions North and South have pushed the mercenaries back from the walls."

"Where's the Proconsul?" Alerio asked.

"Proconsul Florus is meeting with Consul Lucius Metellus and has been since before sunrise," Ahala said. "Mystacis and twenty other lost and confused department heads are waiting for clarification from the commanders."

"What instruction is the cavalry officer waiting for?" Alerio questioned.

"What to do about the war elephants the Punic general brought with him."

***

Alerio located Lartha Mystacis pacing in a hallway off a crowded antechamber. The cavalry officer vibrated with pent up energy.

"They have elephants," Lartha gushed when he saw Alerio. "Colonel Sisera, they have elephants and I have cavalry. But I can't get orders to test my theory."

"What theory?" Alerio asked as he fell in beside the cavalryman.

They marched in step down the entire length of the hallway while Lartha collected his thoughts. On the way back to the room's entrance, he explained. "Elephants have four legs and a rider. My mounts have four legs and riders. It seems to me, elephants are nothing more than big, really big horses."

"With trunks that can throw you over the animal's back and armored tusks that can impale a horse," Alerio pointed out. "And they're not slow. During the Punic expedition, our Centuries encountered the brutes on many occasions. They can devastate an assault line if the Legionaries are forced to hold a position."

"That's the point, Colonel," Lartha declared while bouncing up and down on the balls of his feet. "My horsemen are not stationary. We are fast and mobile. And we have javelins."

"And the elephants are surrounded by their infantry," Alerio broke the news to him. "For the purposes of keeping cavalry, like yours, away from the elephants and their handlers."

"Oh, I hadn't considered that," Lartha admitted.

From inside the room, Proconsul Florus' voice cut through the clutter of those waiting. His first words sent Alerio rushing into the antechamber.

"Consul Metellus and I spent last evening and all this morning deciding on a course of action," Florus exclaimed. "The Sicilia Legion and our Centuries will stand back and leave the fighting to Metellus Legion North and South. We will of course be available to fill any breaches."

Alerio pushed into the room to find the Consul and Proconsul standing shoulder to shoulder. He edged his way closer until he made eye contact with Lucius Metellus. For a moment, their eyes met, and a flash of recognition passed between them. A brief instant later, the Consul dropped his eyes and turned away.

Taken aback by the brush off from a political ally, Alerio forced his way forward.

"Lucius, I'd like a word with you," Alerio shouted.

A pair of shields from Legion North's First Century slammed together blocking his path.

"Lucius, I'd like a word with you," Alerio repeated over the shields and armored shoulders of the Legionaries.

Almost as if a trapped rat who found an escape route, Consul Lucius Metellus scurried from the chamber, vanishing through a doorway. His First Century bodyguards scrambled to keep up with their General. And Alerio Sisera stood alone with his mouth hanging open.

How long he waited there numb and puzzled, he didn't know. But when Centurion Mystacis gripped his elbow and brought him out of the trance, the chamber was empty.

"The Proconsul wants to see you on the patio," Lartha whispered.

"I hope it's a job offer," Alerio whined.

"I don't understand," Lartha commented.

"Never mind, let's go see the Proconsul."

"I was sent to fetch you, sir," the cavalry officer said. "I don't believe the invitation included me."

"It does now," Alerio told him. "Come with me."

***

The garden and the meandering pathways had vanished. Now the view from the patio was of dirt ramps allowing access to an embankment built up against the wall. On the top were Legionaries with javelins and archers with bows. Spread among the infantrymen and bowmen, combat officers went about the business of directing the defense of Palermo. The rest of the garden had sprouted tents and stacks of supplies to support the men on the wall.

"Proconsul, you wanted to see me?" Alerio inquired.

"Sit down, Alerio," Florus directed. Seeing Lartha Mystacis, he said. "That will be all Centurion."

"Don't go too far, Mystacis," Alerio instructed. "We may have things to do."

"Yes, sir," Lartha exclaimed. "I'll go to the wall and throw a few javelins."

Lictor Sisera and Proconsul Florus watched the cavalry officer strut through the supply area.

"He's a good man," Alerio offered.

"He saved us all," Florus mumbled. Then he turned to Alerio. "I suppose being slighted by the Consul gave you an inkling of what this conversation is about."

"I gave him my political support. It reawakened an old wound with an enemy. And now I face a trial and exile for no other reason than I backed Lucius Metellus," Alerio remarked. "All that and I get snubbed by a man I guessed was a friend. I can presume, but please Proconsul, tell me what this conversation is about."

"Even with your support, Lucius Metellus never had the votes or the popularity to get elected as one of our Consuls," Florus informed Alerio. "He had to make a deal with Lucius Longus to get the position. In the negotiations, Longus steps aside this year. Next year, Metellus won't oppose Longus' run for the Consul seat."

"And what about me?" Alerio questioned.

"I don't know what happened during the Punic campaign," Florus confessed. "But Longus surely worships at the altar of Epiales when it comes to you."

Alerio blinked at the mention of the God of Nightmares. For a moment, he considered returning to Rome and stabbing Lucius Longus through the heart.

"At least, that would be worth the exile," Alerio hissed.

"Excuse me, what did you say?" Florus inquired.

"What about my senate seat?"

"I'm afraid there's no senate seat in your future," Florus informed Alerio. "Longus will block it every year. But I do owe you for the Punic chalice affair. Maybe in five years or so, I can help you with my supporters. I don't know what else to say."

Alerio hung his head for several heartbeats. Then, a pressure against his right shoulder pushed him forward and straightened his back. Sensing the Goddess Nenia's presence, he raised his head and studied the defenders on the wall.

Centurion Mystacis hefted a javelin, reared back, and snapped forward releasing the missile at a high angle. Bent over the wall, the cavalry officer watched the trajectory of his weapon. Then he jumped up and raised his arms in victory before running to get another shaft. After watching Lartha gleefully throw another two javelins, Alerio turned to the Proconsul.

"How important is your control of Philetus Smaltum?" he inquired.

"Between his farming, shipping, shops, and metalsmith facility, Master Smaltum has connections throughout Sicilia and the Republic," Florus answered. "His influence is quite valuable. Why?"

"I want to draw on the favor you owe me," Alerio answered.

"What can I do for you here in the middle of a city under siege?"

"Appoint me to the position of Senior Tribune in the Sicilia Legion," Alerio told him.

"I can do that easily," Florus replied. "For what reason, I can't fathom."

"In writing, please, sir," Alerio requested. "And I want Lartha Mystacis, and his thirty cavalrymen placed under my command."

"Consider it done," Floris said while he wrote Alerio's warrant of office on a piece of parchment.

After stamping it with his Proconsul seal, he handed the document to Alerio.

"And I want command of two Centuries of infantry and their skirmishers," Alerio added.

He tucked the parchment into a pouch and waited.

"Well, you see I've agreed to standdown my Legion here in the city so Lucius Metellus, you understand, can get the

212

honor of defending Palermo," the Proconsul explained. "It's just good politics on my part."

"Without a doubt," Alerio confirmed. "But I wasn't talking about your forces here in the city. I want command of the garrison at Poggio Ridente."

"And what would you do with them?" Florus questioned.

Alerio stood and put his hands over his head and waved at Lartha. When the Centurion noticed him, Alerio motioned him down off the wall.

"What we're going to do, Proconsul," Alerio stated, "is test a theory."

"What theory, Senior Tribune Sisera?"

"I'll let you know, sir, if it works out."

Lartha Mystacis jogged down from the wall and retraced his path to the patio.

"Proconsul Florus has been kind enough to appoint me Senior Tribune of the Sicilia Legion," Alerio told the young cavalry officer.

Larth saluted and inquired, "Why would he do that, sir?"

"Let's just say, it's the result of a hateful deal. Let's go, we have to get through the Qart Hadasht lines when they break for their noon meal."

"Do they really stop fighting at noon so they can eat?" Mystacis asked.

"No, but that's when we're breaking out," Alerio said.

The two marched off the patio, leaving Proconsul Aquillius Florus wondering what he had unleashed by hiring Alerio Sisera. And upon whom?

***

The walls of Palermo sat on a southwest to northeast axis as if aimed at the harbor. With the heaviest attacks coming from the river side, Lartha Mystacis walked his thirty cavalrymen through the city, heading for a less contested gate.

"Where do you think you're going?" a Senior Tribune from Legion North demanded.

Two squads of infantrymen rushed to block the road. With their spears leveled on top of their shields, they presented a fearsome barrier.

"Sir, we're leaving Palermo," Centurion Mystacis answered. "But truthfully, I have no idea where we're actually going."

"If you don't have a purpose," the staff officer pointed out, "your actions could be considered desertion."

"No sir, we have orders," Lartha assured him.

"Whose orders? I don't recall signing off on any mounted patrols."

A rider in the center column kneed his horse forward.

"What's the hold up?" Alerio asked. Then with a sweep of his arm, he directed. "Clear those men off the road."

"And who are you?" the Senior Tribune inquired.

"Senior Tribune Sisera of the Sicilia Legion," Alerio answered. "As I understand it, Consul Metellus has requested that the Legions remain separate so he can reap the honors of this campaign. Therefore, I don't require his or your permission to take my command out for a ride. If you have a problem with that, you should take it up with Proconsul Florus."

"I just don't know," the Senior Tribune stammered.

214

"Well, I do," Alerio boomed. "Clear this road and open the gate. Or I'll have my Legionaries take control."

"What's your name?"

"Be sure to get it right when you tell Consul Metellus," Alerio suggested. "I am Senior Tribune Alerio Carvilius Sisera."

"Clear the road," the senior staff officer ordered. "And Sisera, I'll remember you."

"I hope you will," Alerio said as he guided his horse back to the center of the columns. Once settled in the formation, he shouted. "Centurion Mystacis. Take us out of Palermo."

The columns started forward as the gates opened. Beyond the portal, a cheer went up from the Qart Hadasht mercenaries. They assumed the Legion had run out of the deadly javelins and were coming out to fight. But it wasn't infantry that appeared.

Centurion Mystacis walked his mount out of the gateway. Behind him, pairs of riders came through the portal. They spread out in a pyramid formation while holding their mounts to a slow walk. When the seventh pair of Legion riders passed through the gateway, Alerio Sisera whistled a shrill note.

Hearing the signal, Lartha Mystacis drew his sword, waved it over his head, and bellowed, "Charge!"

At their officer's command, the pyramid formation surged forward.

Chapter 21 – Crisis of Fighters

Alerio yanked his mount to the left, kicked the beast with his heels, and galloped to the farthest position on that side. Behind him, as if sucked from the gateway, the remaining fifteen cavalrymen burst onto the plain.

Mercenaries in the path of the wedge dropped behind battlements to avoid the flashing hoofs. Or, they died on the lances of the cavalrymen.

The initial charge punched a hole in the Qart Hadasht line. But while the middle collapsed, on the sides, soldiers raced to unseat Legionaries riding on the flanks of the formation.

On the far-left side, Alerio Sisera slashed at a soldier who attempted to grab his leg. Another threw a spear. Leaning into the horse's neck, Alerio let the shaft pass over his back. But then, two mercenaries jumped at his mount. One he sliced with the tip of his gladius and the other caught a hobnailed boot in the chest.

Off balance, but beyond the Qart Hadasht assault line, Alerio clung to the saddle while leaning out over the horse's side.

Behind the widest part of the wedge formation, the cavalrymen following remained in two columns. They rode fast and straight, avoiding the soldiers who closed in to retake the busted positions.

A horse appeared beside Alerio, and a hand cupped his head. With a shove, Lartha Mystacis pushed Alerio upright in the saddle.

"Are you injured, Senior Tribune?" the cavalry Centurion asked.

"Only my pride," Alerio responded. "How many did we lose?"

Mystacis circled an arm over his head and glanced at his three cavalry troop leaders. After repeating the signal to get confirmation, the cavalry officer smiled at Alerio.

"No riders are down," he reported. "We may have a few bleeding in the saddle but they made it through. Orders, sir?"

"We'll keep riding north," Alerio told him.

He stopped talking while adjusting his seat on the trotting horse.

"Sir, we want to fight," the Centurion protested. "North is away from the mercenaries."

"Once we're out of sight, we'll angle west," Alerio clarified. "Our goal is to collect the infantry from the garrison at Poggio Ridente. Then we'll test your elephant theory."

"It was you who pointed out the flaw in it, sir," Mystacis offered.

"Tell me Centurion, when aren't war elephants screened by infantry?"

"I don't know, Senior Tribune. When aren't elephants protected?"

"When they're with the army's baggage train," Alerio submitted.

***

Once through the siege line, they rode hard for a half mile. Off to their right, between warehouses and the residents of poor neighborhoods, they saw stretches of the bay. At a spot beyond the view of the Qart Hadasht army, Lartha Mystacis signaled a turn to the left while slowing to a trot.

"How far to the garrison?" Alerio asked.

"It's three miles west of Palermo," Lartha answered. "But we're taking the scenic route."

Alerio glanced around at the squalor of the fishing villages, the hovels of the dockworkers on the coast, and compared them to the cultivated farms and homes inland. He had seen cities and towns where people scrambled for scraps and eked out a living doing anything they could. Here in Palermo, the ocean was bountiful and the land productive. It was one of those places where the underclass didn't starve.

"No wonder the Empire wants the town," Alerio commented.

Beside him, Centurion Mystacis leaned over his horse and inquired, "Did you say something, Senior Tribune?"

"No," Alerio replied.

The thirty cavalrymen and their officers trotted by farms and through fields and grove of trees. Soon, as if they were approaching a sleeping giant, high ground appeared.

"Poggio Ridente is up there to our left," Lartha pointed out. "The garrison's job is to guard the mountain approach."

"Is that why the Qart Hadasht army came down the river?" Alerio questioned.

"The river has benefits and one drawback," Lartha explained. "They have to cross the river to attack the city, but it also provides a barrier to a counterattack. Plus traveling to Palermo along the flood plain is faster and easier for an army than taking the mountain route."

"A couple of centuries ago, Greek philosopher Heraclitus observed, out of every one-hundred soldiers, ten shouldn't even be there and eighty are just targets," Alerio stated. "Nine are the real fighters. And every army is lucky to have them, for they make the battle. But one, one is a warrior. And he will bring the others back."

"Sir, I don't understand," Lartha confessed.

"You said they came down the river because it's faster," Alerio responded. "It's also easier to retreat upstream. All we need is to convince their fighters that all is lost, and they'll flee."

"And how do we do that, sir?"

"We remove their elephants," Alerio proposed. "Without the wall of war beast waiting on the far bank, the Legion can come out from behind the walls, and attack across the river."

"And how do we convince the Legion to come out, sir?"

"That, Centurion Mystacis, I'm still working on," Alerio admitted.

***

The cavalry came to a stream. Clear water flowed from a rocky formation at the base of a hill. While they took turns filling waterskins and allowing their mounts to drink, Alerio peered up at the green, but rocky slope.

"It must be over three hundred feet to the top," he remarked.

"The foothill is over four hundred feet high, according to Legion engineers," Mystacis informed him. "It's why the road up twists and turns. And after our talk, I can see the disadvantage to an invader having to come down that measured trail."

"Let's get to the garrison," Alerio urged. After pulling himself into the saddle, he added. "I need to know who I'll have to fight to gain command."

"Sir, do you think it'll come to bloodshed?"

"Not all fights involve blades or fists," Alerio remarked.

The cavalrymen started up the serpentine trail, weaving their way back and forth towards the top. As they neared the pinnacle, Alerio could see the walls of Palermo on the flatland. They appeared small at that distance. In the other direction, he noted the higher peaks of the mountains behind the garrison.

But even from the highest elevation, he couldn't see the Oreto River to the south, or the Qart Hadasht army. Both were obscured by the thick forest growing along the riverbanks.

***

The Legion garrison might not be in direct contact with the Empire army, but the men were as prepared as the fort would allow.

"Who's that with you, Centurion Mystacis," an Optio asked from behind a low wall.

Unfortunately for the NCO and the Centuries, their defensive walls were only five feet tall.

"Who are those supposed to stop?" Alerio inquired. He nudged the mount to the wall, stepped off the horse, and onto the barrier. In four paces, he walked the top, until he looked over the Sergeant at the interior of the compound. "I'm Senior Tribune Sisera of the Sicilia Legion. Who are you?"

"Sir, I'm Optio Bengt of Palermo East," the Sergeant replied. "While the walls aren't much, we know how to defend ourselves."

He pointed over his shoulder. Twenty archers stood with war bows drawn and their arrows pointed at Alerio. On either side of the archers, an equal number of skirmishers stood with javelins resting in upraised palms. In front of the sixty ranged weapon experts, eighty Legionaries waited behind their shields. Another eighty stood at positions around the compound.

"I count two hundred and twenty men," Alerio bellowed. "Do I have twenty fighters?"

To his amazement, the twenty bowman immediately took three giant steps forward.

"Three paces?" Alerio questioned.

"Because when you get around to asking for the warriors," one explained. "We Cretan archers will have already identified ourselves."

"What's your name?"

"Zarek Mikolas, Senior Tribune," the archer responded. "We are your warriors. We know the wisdom of Heraclitus and we will bring the others home."

"Does he always brag like that?" Alerio asked Optio Bengt.

"All the archers do, sir," the NCO answered. He waved to men on the gate. "But they're dependable in a fight and are unnaturally good with their bows."

The gates swung open, and Centurion Mystacis led the cavalry into the compound. Alerio noticed a rider taking the reins of his horse. Figuring to make a grand entrance, he bent at the knees.

"Don't," Bengt shouted.

But Senior Tribune Sisera had already jumped into the compound.

Alerio braced for the landing, expecting to show his athleticism. The landing didn't come at ground level. Instead, he ripped through a layer of branches covered in dust. Breaking through, he landed hard at chest level to the dirt of the fort.

"We've dug traps, sir," the Optio pointed out.

The entire detachment stood silently. Even the cavalrymen reined in their mounts. Everyone sensed trouble and a hush fell over the garrison as the new Senior Tribune stood in the trench trap.

"Give me a hand?" Alerio asked while extending and arm.

Bengt gripped his wrist and yanked. To his amazement, the staff officer popped out of the trench, flying much higher than the strength of the pull warranted.

Alerio landed and squared his shoulders. Then he reached down and patted at his tunic.

"An excellent addition to the fort's defenses," he allowed while slapping at the fabric. His antics sent a cloud of dust into the air. Alerio coughed loudly and spit. "Excellent indeed. If the fall doesn't kill you, this nasty dust is sure to. Let's have the men who dug this trench step forward."

A young Centurion ran from the far side of the fort to stand beside Bengt.

"Centurion Bulbus Flictus, sir," he declared. "The men of Florus Century West dug that section. If there's to be punishment, I'll stand for it."

"A worthy confession," Alerio stated. "But I asked for the diggers, not the authority. Now, if you please."

The eighty men who manned stations around the fort began collecting into ranks. Alerio stood stone-faced while they straightened their lines. Once done, he squatted and scooped up a hand full of the dried silt.

"This is the worst tasting dirt, I've ever come across," he exclaimed.

Before he could say more, someone called from the back of the formation, "How much experience eating dirt does a senior staff officer have?"

Centurion Mystacis pushed off his saddle, landed on the ground, and headed for the loudmouth. At the same time, Centurion Flictus faced in the miscreant's direction and took a step.

"Stand down," Alerio ordered the officers. Then he added for the Legionaries. "That's a good question. I was an infantryman and a weapons' instructor before earning my place as a combat officer. And because I need the exercise and you asked, I'll be holding weapons drills after our mission. Any more comments?"

Until now, the Legionaries had not focused on their new commander. After the answer, they noticed the battle scars and the hard muscles of a swordsman. Most of them groaned at the thought of drilling under a Legion weapons specialist.

"You were saying the dirt tastes bad, sir?" someone inquired. Probably in hopes the Senior Tribune would forget about the training session.

"I said the dirt is foul and anyone digging it must still have the taste in his mouth," Alerio exclaimed. After more than a few murmurs of confirmation, Alerio announced. "After this mission, I will personally hand mugs of vino to sufferers of this travesty. You understand, purely medicinal, to get the taste out of our mouths."

Laughter rolled through the ranks. When it ended, Sergeant Bengt inquired, "That's twice you said after the mission, sir. What mission are we going on?"

Alerio looked over the heads of the Century until his eyes met Lartha Mystacis. Then he winked and the Centurion of Cavalry understood that sometimes you didn't need blades and fists to win a battle.

"We're going to help Metellus Legions North and South find what they lost," Alerio replied.

"What did they lose, Senior Tribune?" Bulbus Flictus asked.

"Their courage," Alerio answered.

The detachment roared Rah! And Alerio knew he had command of the garrison.

***

Moonlight reflected off the surface of the river. While the illumination brightened the landscape, along the riverbank, it only served to enhance the shadows. Concealed in the bushes, Senior Tribune Sisera, Centurion Mystacis, and Sergeant Zarek Mikolas of the Crete archers shivered as they observed the Qart Hadasht camp.

"The elephants are big," Mystacis whispered. "But they're just animals. And animals can be controlled."

"War elephants aren't sheep to be herded," Zarek muttered. "It would be easier to control them if we took their handlers."

"You want to include fifty animal handlers in our raid?" Alerio questioned.

"I counted over sixty elephants," the Centurion offered, "and just as many handlers."

"We can threaten, possibly injury a few handlers to get their attention," Zarek explained. "After that, they'll take the elephants anywhere you want, sir."

"I liked the plan when we were going to burn the wagons, stampede the beasts," Alerio whined, "and be gone before the rear guards could react."

"Sir, no one is suggesting that we rob the Empire General of his treasury," Centurion Mystacis remarked.

"Sir, why scatter the elephants when we can capture them?" Zarek inquired.

Alerio rubbed his forehead, took a last look at the camp, then slid down the embankment. The others followed. When all three were in the water, they swam to the far side of the Oreto River.

"I'll gather the infantry and give them instructions," Alerio said while he dried off and strapped on his hobnailed boots. "You two get the skirmishers, bowmen, and cavalrymen together and tell them. I'll be along later to answer questions."

"You could just issue orders and remain in the fort, Senior Tribune," the archer commented. "It'll be safer there."

"When this is over," Mystacis promised the Cretan bowman, "I'll tell you about Legion North of the Punic expedition. And the heroics of Battle Commander Sisera."

"What heroics?" Alerio growled. "Everyone died. Brief the men. I'll see you later."

Alerio took the reins from a cavalryman, mounted, and kicked the horse into motion. After weaving through the trees, he emerged on a wagon trail. Forgetting what he rode, he kicked the horse again and gave it extra rein. Rather than charge into the night like Phobos, the horse slowed and began picking its way along the dark trail.

"If you hadn't gotten too old," Alerio said as if speaking to Phobos, "I'd be halfway back to Poggio Ridente by now."

Then, the horse stepped down into a deep rut before walking up the far side.

Alerio contemplated the leg breaking channel, and added to his talk with Phobos, "Maybe you aren't the only one getting too old for this way of life."

Act 8

Chapter 22 – The Long Linen Scarf

Lieutenant Azmelqart of the General's elite guard started the morning at the changing of the guard. In tall helmets with blue capes, fresh guards replaced the overnight sentries at General Gisco's command tent. At the same instant, more of the blue cloaks emerged from their bivouac area and began patrolling the rear campsites. The patrols protected the teamsters, the craftsmen, and the wounded from robbery. Additionally, they gave the Captains and Majors confidence that their belongings would be secure while they were at the siege line.

However, before leaving the rear area, the commanders rode to the General's compound. While they shuffled into the big tent, Lieutenant Azmelqart began an inspection of the entire Qart Hadasht camp.

Inside the command tent, General Gisco greeted the Majors and Captains with enthusiasm.

"Today gentlemen, we will break through the gates, or force the Legions to come out from behind their walls. Today, we will have a proper battle."

"The reserves will be ready if the Latians circle around and cross the river," declared a Captain.

"We'll move up the war elephants when the Legionaries run out of javelins, and start fighting man-to-man," another Captain informed the General.

"Can't stand to see your brutes harpooned?" an infantry Major sneered at the Captain of the war elephants.

Sensing a challenge coming, General Gisco moved to stop the conflict before it escalated.

"We have thirty thousand infantrymen, slingers, bowmen, and cavalry," Hasdrubal pointed out. "Why do you insist on denigrating the elephant unit?"

"Because they're only good in open field fighting, General," the Major answered. "While they stay with the baggage train, chew leaves, and fertilize the land, my infantrymen have to stand under a rain of arrows and javelins."

"Every component of my army has to work together," Hasdrubal explained. "When the Legions come out, I expect the elephants to rush forward, and cross over with the reserves."

"We'll cross over and destroy the Republic's army," the reserve Captain guaranteed. "And you'll soon be able to claim Palermo for the Empire."

"We'll be there, as well," the elephant commander assured the General.

After going over the battle plan for the day, General Hasdrubal Gisco and his commanders left the tent. Once mounted, they rode for a crossing spot on the Oreto. From there, they'd ford the river and ride to the siege lines at Palermo.

In the absence of the army's leadership and their bodyguards, units of the veteran guard patrolled the rear area. When their paths crossed, the blue capes saluted their officer and Azmelqart returned the courtesy.

The Lieutenant strutted around the camp making his own rounds of the supply depots, the wagon parks, and the animal pens. Yet even as he strolled through the camps, the Officer of the Guard kept his eyes turned in the direction of the General's compound. Those tents contained Hasdrubal Gisco's personal possessions and more importantly, the treasury of the army.

Azmelqart wasn't the only one who understood the compound was the prime area of his responsibilities. His blue capes and their NCOs were also aware. As well, entities outside of General Gisco's chain-of-command understood the significance of the command tents.

***

Under cut brushes and branches, Cretan bowmen hid beside Legion skirmishers. They watched the patrols and the Qart Hadasht officer vanish behind wagons and tents then reappear on the far side of the campsites.

"They are pretty, aren't they?" Zarek Mikolas muttered.

"I'd like to have one of those blue cloaks," a young archer whispered.

"If an elite guard gets that close, he'll run his spearhead through your heart," Zarek warned. "If one comes at you, use your arrows, and keep him at a distance. It'll save your family the mourning period."

"I hear you, Lochias," the archer said, acknowledging Mikolas' rank as an NCO.

Long moments later, a bush wiggled as if a breeze blew up from the river.

"Senior Tribune Sisera, if you're ready to launch the attack," Zarek Mikolas uttered, "just give the word. You don't have to announce it by waving a branch in the air."

"I figured with all the chatter, you decided the cavalry was taking too long," Alerio shot back, "and wanted to invite the blue capes over for breakfast."

"A fair trade of insults, sir," Zarek allowed. "By your moving around, I take it you're also worried about the appearance of the cavalry."

Alerio didn't respond. He looked north into the thick forest. Then he scanned the Qart Hadasht camp for a moment before tapping the young bowman.

"I've fought the blue capes on the pitching deck of a warship," he cautioned. "They are tough, well trained, and work together as a unit. In other words, if they get close, they will put a spear through your heart."

"I'll be sure to keep them at a distance with my arrows," the young archer promised.

Alerio and the fifty-four men of his assault unit waited nervously under the bushes and limbs. Off to the east, the sun climbed into the sky. Far to the north, Lartha Mystacis used his reins to whip his horse.

***

"Cut him off," Centurion Mystacis screamed to the riders keeping up with him.

The last of the Qart Hadasht soldiers from the roadblock gripped the horse's mane and kicked until he almost fell off the mount's back. Clamping his legs closed, he screamed and used his body to mimic a fast gallop. Despite his antics, the Legion cavalry closed the distance. As the horses raced southward along the wagon road following the river, the soldier wanted to scream at his Sergeant. But the Empire NCO lay dead along with the rest of the soldier's troop.

"I tell you boys, down at Palermo, they're raking in honors and getting rich," his Sergeant whined. "But here we sit staring at wagon ruts and watching for oxen carts of supplies to creep by."

The five mounted soldiers of the blockade had heard the grouching so often, they put their heads down to avoid making eye contact. If by accident, the Sergeant caught one of them looking, he would begin the tirade all over again. It's why they didn't see the columns of riders until they were close.

Javelins flew from the columns, striking the NCO and four of the soldiers. The lone survivor of the volley reached the horses, untied one, and leaped on bareback.

"Cut him off," Centurion Mystacis bellowed again.

In answer to the officer's goading, Troop Leader Magnus Cotta raced ahead of his column. With hoofs flashing and cavalry sword in hand, the nobleman reached forward and slashed the escapee in the back. The Qart Hadasht soldier tumbled to the ground. Five paces later, the panicked horse slowed, then stopped and stood breathing hard while quivering.

"Excellent riding, Cotta," Mystacis complimented the cavalryman.

"Thank you, sir," Magnus said. "I claim the honor of first blood spilled during this operation."

"If we do our job right, it'll be the last drop shed," Lartha Mystacis remarked. "Gather your troop and fall into the back of the columns."

The twenty-eight Legion horsemen regrouped on the wagon road and headed south towards the rear area of the Empire army.

***

Unlike the evenings when the cries of the wounded ripped through the air, and men bellowed tales of bravery to drown out the injured, early in the day, the rear area of the Empire army was almost hushed. Part of the reason being any disturbance or disagreement would draw a collection of blue capes. And none of the tradesmen, merchants, or teamsters wanted to suffer justice on the spears of the General's guards.

"All is peaceful, sir," a Qart Hadasht NCO reported.

Lieutenant Azmelqart peered around at the campsites. Men chopped wood for fires that crackled, animals munched on hay, and craftsmen hammered, cut, or scraped on the material of their trade.

"No doubt, the Goddess Tanit is before the walls of Palermo with our allies," Azmelqart proposed. "Pray the Goddess of War remains there."

"Yes, sir," the Sergeant acknowledged.

He dipped his head and spear in salute and marched away. The officer was as good as any and better than...

The calm of the camp erupted in shouts of panic. At first the blue capes ran towards the disturbances. But in moments the small patrols were overwhelmed with calls of distress. Then a rider, then another, plus lightly armored men came from around wagons and appeared from between tents.

"Protect the General's compound," Azmelqart ordered. "If they're bandits, we'll retaliate once the treasury is secured."

"Yes, sir," the Sergeant of the guard replied. With his command voice, he instructed. "Fall back to the compound. Fall back and group into your Companies."

The sounds of hoofs came from behind Azmelqart.

"Orders, Lieutenant?" a courier inquired.

"Hold for now," the officer informed him. "But stay close. Let's see what develops."

When a string of Legion riders appeared on the road, Azmelqart grabbed the courier's reins.

"We're under attack from the Latian Republic," the officer described. "I'm ordering the reserve force back to camp. Now, go."

The messenger jerked the reins and yanked his horse around in a half turn. For a moment, the horse reared up. In that instant, the Qart Hadasht courier sat upright with his shoulders squared, his back forming a perfect target.

***

"I can drop the messenger," offered a young archer.

With an arrow notched, he drew his bowstring back to his ear.

"You do that, and I'll break the bow over your head," Zarek Mikolas threatened.

"What about the officer? I can put him down."

"Leave him," Zarek answered. "We've got elephant handlers to wrangle. Come on."

Now that they had shown themselves, the fifteen bowman and forty skirmishers stepped back and away from the tents and wagons. Once out of sight of the blue capes, they sprinted for the elephant holding area.

Left standing beside a wagon, Senior Tribune Sisera watched the blue capes race to defend the compound. As if to hasten them, one of his cavalry troops braved the spears to ride close by the collection of ornate tents. The maneuver caused the guards streaming from their sleeping area to join their comrades in protecting the General's compound.

"I need to find out who led that charge and get him a medal," Alerio commented.

After a final look at the response of the blue capes, he saluted in the direction of the cavalrymen. Then he ducked behind the wagon, turned, and sprinted towards the river.

***

Alerio crawled out of the water on the far side of the Oreto and waved five archers from their hiding places.

"The action's started," he informed them. "You might as well get set."

While the bowmen selected locations and uncapped bags of arrows, Alerio ran to the trees above the riverbank. A pair of cavalrymen with a spare horse, and a servant with his war gear waited in the forest.

"How's it going over there, sir?" a cavalryman inquired.

Alerio stripped off his wet tunic and accepted a dry one.

"So far we have the blessing of Averruncus," Alerio answered while taking his battle armor from the servant. "We've avoided calamity, thanks to the God."

Once dressed, Senior Tribune Sisera pulled himself into the saddle, kicked the horse, and rode away from the river. One of the cavalryman trotted beside him.

"I would have rather stayed on the riverbank, sir," the mounted Legionary stated. Then he caught himself and added. "Only to see the crossing."

"As would I," Alerio agreed.

They broke out of the woods, crossed a field of wild grass, and turned south on a main road. Not far from where they started on the road, they took a wagon track back towards the river. A little over a mile farther on, a squad of Legionaries intercepted them.

"Compliments of Centurion Flictus, sir," a Legion Corporal greeted Alerio. "The Centuries are staged inside the tree line."

Alerio nodded his understanding but remained mounted.

Clouds drifted across the blue sky and birds flew from the woods to the fields. Alerio watched the birds in flight but didn't follow them to the ground. His eyes remained elevated, searching the heavens to the north.

***

The river water churned, creating waves. Almost lost in the artificial breakers, several bowman and the Legion skirmishes struggled to swim next to the giant beasts. High above the torrent and splashing, animal handlers rode on the necks of the war elephants. In the confusion, one or more might have reversed direction and returned to the Qart Hadasht camp.

They would have except, on the far bank, five archers waited with notched arrows. Whenever a handler looked back, an arrow shifted, targeting the errant rider with a potential arrow in his chest. The threat kept all sixty elephants moving in the proper direction.

Sergeant Zarek Mikolas and six archers remained on the Empire side. But they didn't watch the crossing. Their attention remained on the campsites and the charges of the cavalry.

"The animals are ours," a bowman observed. "What are we waiting for?"

"The cavalry," Zarek replied.

"They're just riding around in circles," the archer noted. "What are they waiting for?"

"Taking the elephants was to save Legionaries' lives during the coming battle," Zarek explained. "Pulling the reserves away from Palermo will draw the Legions out to fight."

"Oh, the cavalry is waiting for the reserves," the bowman offered.

"Not anymore. Gentlemen relax your bows and pack them away," Zarek instructed while bending his bow to remove the string.

On either side of him, the Cretan archers shoved their bows into leather holsters. Next, they folded the ends and tied them tightly. When the first riders splashed into the river, the archers waded out and began to swim.

***

Centurion Mystacis reined in on the riverbank. Blowing hard and sweating, his steed wanted to plunge into the cool water. But the officer held the beast while he counted his command.

"Centurion, we are all accounted for," Magnus Cotta reported. A smile showed on the young noblemen's face. "And on our heels are every reserve unit in the Qart Hadasht army."

"In that case Troop Leader, we should go," Mystacis declared.

He released the reins and his stallion charged down the bank and ran into the river. Cotta's horse was right beside him.

***

Zarek Mikolas came to his feet in waist high water and high stepped to shore. At the line of archers, he snatched the holster off his back and unpacked his war bow.

"What do we have?" he asked.

"A line of light infantry is making their way through the trees," an archer answered. "Do we let them reach the water?"

"How far ahead are the elephants?"

"They are long gone, Lochias."

"Then hit the infantry at the tree line," Zarek informed his archers. "Nobody reaches the water unless they're decorated with one of our shafts."

In response, the line of Cretan archers notched arrows but rested the bows on their thighs. Zarek put a knee in the center of his bow, flexed the weapon, and fixed the string to each end.

"What's our status, Centurion," he asked Mystacis as the cavalry officer and his horse emerged from the river.

"We didn't get a count," the Centurion answered, "but I'd say most of their reserves are coming to save the General's gold."

Zarek Mikolas pulled a yellow scarf from the bow holster and tied an end to a shaft. With the linen dangling like a pennant, he notched the arrow.

"With your permission, sir?" he inquired.

"Send it, Sergeant," Mystacis responded.

While arrows loosed from powerful war bows streaked across the river, a single arrow with a long linen scarf soared high into the sky. And while Qart Hadasht light infantrymen died at the tree line from arrow wounds, over a mile away,

Senior Tribune Sisera saw the scarf, dismounted, and charged into the forest.

Chapter 23 – Behind the Shields

The scuta of the Legion heavy infantry was unwieldly. Even in an open field, only drills and skills allowed the men to use the tool effectively. In a forest, the big shields proved a major hinderance to movement. As a result, Alerio and the Corporal raced ahead while the squad members became strung out. The mad rush around tree trunks and thorn bushes ended at a clearing.

Centurion Bulbus Flictus, his Optio Tabeferi, and Optio Bengt of Palermo East squatted around a bare patch of dirt. They studied markings drawn in the soil.

"Give me a report," Alerio requested as he stepped from between a pair of trees.

"The river and reserves are here, sir," Tabeferi described. His hand passed over multiple lines representing the mercenaries staged across the Oreto.

"To the west are the siege embankments with the Qart Hadasht army behind them," Bengt illustrated by tracing wavy lines in the dirt. "If we march on the siege lines, we'll be fine. But any deeper into their ranks, and we'll be fighting on two fronts."

"They'll have to ford the river and cover a good distance. But then, the reserves will become a problem," Tabeferi projected. "We'll do damage to their siege line before having to withdraw."

"What if the reserves weren't there?" Alerio questioned.

"If we crossed from the trees to their flank quickly enough," Bengt replied, "we could crash into the main force and cripple them."

"But once the mercenaries regroup, sir, we either retreat to the forest," Tabeferi stated, "or we break for the protection of the javelin canopy from the walls of Palermo."

"I've just received a signal that the reserves have gone," Alerio informed them. "We're going to march our assault line into their main force and break this siege. Go prepare your squads."

Tabeferi and Bengt stood and paused as if they were going to say something. Rather than voice an opinion, they jogged into the woods.

"Senior Tribune, I'm not contradicting you," Flictus cautioned. "But we're just two Centuries. And most of my garrison Legionaries were auxiliary before infantry training."

"You have good Latin NCOs. I trust they'll keep the lines together," Alerio responded. "Plus, the men have good combat officers in command."

"Combat officers, sir?" Flictus inquired.

"That's right, I'm taking control of Palermo East," Alerio told him. Seeing the nervousness on the young Centurion's face, he asked. "Where are you from?"

"Sicilia, Senior Tribune. My family was one of the first to claim land on the island," Flictus explained. "I've an uncle who's a Senator, but my father didn't care about politics. He wanted a big farm. I'm the first Republic citizen from Sicilia to become an officer."

Alerio glanced at the squad who accompanied him from the road as they collected around the clearing. They were a mixture of Latin, Umbria, Etruscan, Sicilian, and Greek.

Rather than an anomaly and a departure from the 'only Republic citizen Legion', they were the citizen Legionaries from a new land.

"Someday soon, Proconsul Aquillius Florus will be out of a job," Alerio projected.

"Excuse me, sir?" Flictus said inhaling sharply. "Sorry, Senior Tribune, I get anxious when I hear men of authority talk about removing others from power."

Alerio's head spun as a realization came to him. How often had Senator Maximus openly discussed political warfare against notables? In every case, Alerio wanted to run from the discomfort of hearing disrespectful comments, or what he assumed were treasonous ideas. Now he was one of those powerful men. He would have to learn to watch his words.

"I meant, the Proconsul will be replaced by a Governor for the Province of Sicilia," Alerio clarified. "However, before that happens, we need to remove the Qart Hadasht forces from Palermo."

"With just one hundred and sixty infantrymen, four NCOs, and two officers," Flictus listed, "against an Empire army?"

"We have an advantage, Centurion Flictus."

"What's that, Senior Tribune?"

"While the Qart Hadasht General is invading," Alerio responded, "you and your Legionaries are fighting for your homeland."

***

At the edge of the forest, Alerio scanned the siege embankments and the mercenaries crouching behind the mounds of earth. Although beyond javelin range, they could still be reached by arrows and projectiles from slingers. So, they stooped to make smaller targets while their officers and NCOs remained farther to the rear. Behind the commanders of the forward forces, soldiers sat around fires drinking and waiting.

"They should attack the gates any moment now," Alerio observed.

"How can you tell, sir?" Bengt asked.

"Drink is a mighty potion for foolhardy bravery," he answered. "Those soldiers are sucking down liquid courage as fast as the officers can pass out the wineskins and tap the beer barrels."

"I thought they were having a party, sir," Bengt offered.

The Legionaries nearby heard the remarks. They laughed and shared the dialogue between the Senior Tribune and their Sergeant. Alerio allowed the words to spread down the assault lines.

"They're hyped and intoxicated," he exclaimed. "Let's go see how drunk. Century, Palermo East, forward."

At his command, the eighty Legionaries stepped off. Farther down the line, Centurion Flictus issued the same order. In a few steps, one hundred and sixty heavy infantrymen of the Sicilia Legion approached the edge of the forest. Most caught a glimpse of the battlefield through the trees. Stomachs turned and a few vomited.

**

Ten thousand mercenaries of the Empire sprawled across the grassland. Most were drunk and all were confused. The orders to attack the walls and gates of Palermo had not come. Instead of commanding the assault, General Hasdrubal

Gisco and his staff rode to the river. They crossed the Oreto then raced upstream, leaving their army perplexed.

Alerio noted the flight of the Qart Hadasht command staff.

"Hold," he directed.

The order raced down the lines, the Legionaries halted, and breathed a sigh of relief. Maybe the Senior Tribune had come to his senses and wanted to call off the attack.

"Optio Bengt, gossip has been the poison of armies since the first war party," Alerio informed the NCO. Because Bengt stood ten paces away, the three ranks of the assault line heard the staff officer clearly. "One hundred and eighty years ago, the Greek philosopher Socrates told a tale of gossip."

"Yes, sir," the Optio replied. Although, he had no idea where the Senior Tribune was going with the lecture.

"A man ran up to the philosopher and asked if Socrates had heard the news about one of his students. Socrates said before you continue, answer three questions. The man agreed. First, is the news about my student true? I don't know, the gossip replied, I overheard it. Next Socrates asked, is what you're going to tell me about my student good? No, the man answered. Socrates nodded wisely and asked a final question. Is the information useful? Not really, the gossip replied. Well, Socrates said, if what you want to tell me is neither true, nor good, nor useful, why tell it to me at all?"

"Sir, I don't understand," Bengt admitted.

Mumbling of agreement came from the maniple lines.

"We are waiting for the gossip about their General to race through the army," Alerio answered. "I'm sure based on their responses, none of the mercenaries are familiar with the teachings of Socrates."

"How can you know that, sir?" Bengt asked.

"Because half the army is looking at the river and a goodly portion are pointing upstream," Alerio told him. "I think the rumor of their General running away has put an edge on their nerves. Let's help them follow their commanders. Forward, double time."

With knees pumping, the Legionaries move swiftly out of the forest. Once unencumbered by the trees, their scuta snapped together creating a moving wall of shields.

***

The two Centuries plowed Empire mercenaries into a pile before their charge stalled. Mired down at the stack of wounded, the Legionaries braced as soldiers ran to the Legion formation and attacked. Much like a child who steals a jug of honey, the Centuries had more success than they could handle.

"NCOs, we need space to work," Centurion Flictus ordered. "Stand by to advance and step back."

Tabeferi and Bengt, and the Tesserarii of their Centuries relayed the information to the three lines. The squad leaders repeated the orders, and the pivot men recited the instructions. In three blinks of an eye, every man in the three lines knew what was coming

Centurion Flictus called the maneuvers, "Advance, step back, step back!"

For a heartbeat, the shields on the front rank pulled back and paused. Then in a brutal surge, the wooden scuta hammered forward. Swords and spears were deflected, out of position hands and arms twisted painfully on the propelled shields, and chest and heads absorbed impacts. Stunned, the mercenaries at the front wobbled.

A half step into the massed bodies was all the Maniples could manage. But they concluded the pace with naked steel coming from between their shields. With falling mercenaries filling the space, the Centuries took two steps back and reset their lines.

"Second rank, standby to rotate forward," Flictus alerted the Legionaries. When his words had flashed through the rows, he exclaimed. "Second rank, rotate forward."

Shields, angled sideways, shoved between the exhausted Legionaries at the front. Hooked by the edges of the scuta, the front row was pulled back, and the second line moved to the front.

"Brace," the Centurion called out.

The three lines solidified so the Legionaries could catch their breath and get orientated to the change. Only then did Bulbus Flictus take his eyes off the front and check again on the left flank of the formation.

***

When the Centuries came out of the woods, combat officer Flictus, and staff officer Sisera were delighted with the progress. Their infantrymen had performed perfectly, almost too perfectly. They hit the flank of an unprepared enemy and as if they were a sharp spearhead, the assault line plunged deeply into the Qart Hadasht army.

When they saw Legionaries taking the fight to the siege forces, bowmen on the walls of Palermo doubled the number of arrows they shot. Also motivated by the assault line, the slingers tripled the number of lead pellets tossed down from the walls. And, although out of range, Legionaries threw javelins. The standoff weapons filled the sky with a storm of steel, lead, and iron.

Enough metal sleet fell that the mercenaries behind the siege embankments were forced out of position. Farther down the siege line, they had a clear path to escape the deluge. Closer to the forest, the hundreds of men deserting the Empire line fled directly into the left flank of the assaulting Centuries.

"Optio Bengt, you have command of Palermo East," Alerio informed the NCO while drawing his gladius.

The Sergeant had his eyes to the front. Looking at the fighting along the face of the shields, he estimated the number of soldiers heading for his section of the formation.

"Are you going somewhere, sir?" he inquired.

"I'm going to stop us from getting rolled up like a cheap Anatolian rug."

At the reference, Bengt's head snapped to the left. Hundreds of mercenaries were fleeing the siege line. Unfortunately, those between the Legion formation and the walls of Palermo had only one breakout route.

"Good luck, sir. I have command of Palermo East," Bengt acknowledged.

Flictus heard the exchange and glanced quickly to see how badly Alerio Sisera was hurt. Then, for a moment, he wished the Senior Tribune had relinquished his command due to injuries. Instead, Sisera faced left with a few Legionaries to guard the flank against a torrent.

Centurion Flictus ignored the stampeding warriors heading for them and alerted his staff, "NCOs, we need space to work. Stand by to advance and step back."

***

Alerio pulled three Legionaries off the Maniples and placed them with the five men he had on the left flank. A single line of eight shields backed up by a solo officer was hardly optimal. But it was all Senior Tribune Sisera dared to pull off the assault line.

"Don't get overwhelmed," he instructed his flank defense. "Before you go down and break our wall, dump the barbarians."

"But that'll put them behind us," noted one of his men.

"You leave them to me, Legionary," Alerio answered. "I need the exercise."

The rush of tribesmen drew closer. Several split from the mass and angled to circle around the Legionaries. If this was a coordinated attack, Alerio would worry about being enveloped by the enemy. But the panicked mercenaries were more like water flowing around a rock. They would continue to flow downstream.

However, as if the Legion formation was a boulder in a flood plain, a lot of the flow would wash over the Legionaries. The danger of being inadvertently overrun did worry Alerio.

"Standby javelins," he ordered. "Throw two."

A flight of eight javelins flew across the short distance. The long iron shafts punched through shields, armor, and flesh. In every case, the barbed heads halted the headlong rush of the front row. Those following tripped, slowing the pack. A second flight of javelins took down eight more mercenaries. Skipping and stumbling over sixteen wounded comrades, slowed the crowd to a fast walk.

"Draw," Alerio shouted, "and brace."

Frightened men, like a mob, had no leader, conscience, or logic. As such, those grouped in the center remained compacted by those on the sides. Without the freedom to dodge away from hazards, they came directly at the eight Legionaries.

Steel blades knifed from between infantry shields, killing and maiming them as they ran. But even as fleeing men died, warriors in the cluster decided to take a few Legionaries with them. Stepping on the bodies of their fellow mercenaries, the soldiers threw themselves onto the wall of shields.

Early in their training, Legion infantrymen participated in grueling drills with their scuta. Driven to their knees in soft dirt or mud, the Legionaries were expected to hold and maintain the wall no matter the weight thrown against them.

Alerio prowled behind the eight men watching for the breaking point. Before any of his Legionaries were driven to their knees, he bellowed, "Dump them. Dump them, now."

In answer to his order, the eight Legionaries widened their stance, and squatted while tilting their shields backwards. To keep from being assaulted under the raised shield, they slashed with their gladii blades. Then the empty shields snapped down and the wall was reset.

***

Behind the Legionaries, ten slightly confused mercenaries sprawled on the ground. Had they pushed through? Did they break the Legion wall? Did…"

Alerio jumped over the warrior on the end, stabbing him in the back as he passed over the body. He landed beside the next one. After delivering a kick with the toe of his hobnailed boot, Alerio hopped to the next downed mercenary.

Eyeing a short sword held by another barbarian, Alerio stopped to chop off the fighter's hand. While the man gripped his stump and watched his life's blood spurt out,

Senior Tribune Sisera tested the balance of his gladius and the new sword.

Whirling the blades, he stalked towards the remaining six. Two hopped up and rushed him. One was a professional and charged with the shaft of his spear held level. But one of Alerio's blades smacked the spearhead aside while the second blade sliced away a section of the spearman's face. The man stumbled away with a slab of flesh hanging from his lower cheek and nose. Using two hands, he tried to push the skin back onto his face.

The second spearman, paused to gawk at the plight of his partner. His unprofessionalism cost him when the gladius slipped between his ribs and punctured his heart. Alerio pulled the blade free and ran at the final four.

Two screamed, dropped their weapons and placed their hands over the severed tendons in their legs. They quivered on the grass and their cries of pain drew the attention of the final two from the shield dump. For a moment, they lost focus. Alerio waded in and the warrior's lack of attention cost them their lives.

Optio Bengt walked between the two with ruined legs, shaking his head.

"They never learn to look behind them," the NCO observed. "Sir, Centurion Flictus thinks we should form a defensive square and make for the trees."

"Are we done in?" Alerio asked while scanning the attack formation. "How many did we lose?"

"Our job is done, Senior Tribune," Bengt told him. "The marching Legions are coming out. Unless you want to continue the fight."

For the first time, Alerio looked at the gates to Palermo. From each portal, columns of skirmishers ran onto the battlefield. Then Legion heavy infantrymen jogged out followed by cavalry, slingers, and bowmen.

In response to the emergence of Consul Metellus' Legions, those Empire mercenaries still fighting, turned, and ran for the river.

"We are mostly done for the day, Optio," Alerio told him. "At least, the military operation is over."

"Is there another kind of operation that we should be aware of?" Bengt asked.

"Not you, your Centurion, or your Legionaries," Alerio responded. "What's next is up to me."

Chapter 24 – Forcing Awards

The garrison appeared just as it did before the mission. Normally that would be acceptable, but Poggio Ridente should be crowded with giant beasts.

"Centurion Mystacis, isn't something missing?" Alerio questioned as he dismounted.

"All is well, Senior Tribune," the Centurion of Cavalry reported. Then after saluting, he mentioned. "Oh, you're referring to the elephants."

"The question and the absence of a bunch of overly large animals should be obvious," Alerio stated.

"We started to feed them the horses' hay," Mystacis explained. "But then we learned elephants eat the leaves of trees, the branches, and tall grasses. They're up in the hills feeding. I've posted guards to watch them."

"How many did we take?"

"Sixty elephants," Mystacis bragged. "Earlier, we learned that several other groups of elephants got away when the army retreated."

"How did you hear about that?" Alerio questioned.

"A cavalry patrol from Metellus Legion North swung by. Of course, by then we learned the elephants ate leaves, branches, and tall grasses."

"Just how did you learn that?"

"When I hid them in the hills before the cavalry patrol reached the top."

"You are a clever and resourceful officer," Alerio complimented him. "In the morning, I'm going into Palermo and make my report to Proconsul Florus. I want to include the name of the troop leader who harassed the blue capes at the command tents."

"Those were the tents of General Hasdrubal Gisco," Mystacis informed Alerio, "the Empire's supreme military commander for all of Sicilia."

"You learned that from the patrol?"

"No, sir. The elephant handlers told me," Mystacis said. "Come to the office and I'll send for troop leader Cotta."

***

The sequence of actions from the last several days rolled around in Alerio's head. He took a gulp of water then realized he was parched. Half a waterskin later, he capped and rested the container on the desk. Just as he retracted his hand from the skin, the door flew open. A heartbeat later, a youthful cavalryman swaggered into the office.

"What can I do for you, Senior Tribune?" the man asked.

The statement presupposed that Alerio had a situation that only the horseman could resolve. Alerio understood where an infantry officer or an NCO of heavy infantry got their self-assurance. What he couldn't puzzle out was the source of the horsemen's arrogance. It could be the speed of traveling on a fast-moving horse putting too much air into their lungs. Or maybe the constant bouncing in the saddle scrambled their brains.

Shrugging off the analysis, Alerio inquired, "Cotta. Why do I know that name?"

"My father is Senator Aurelius Cotta," the troop leaders suggested. "Perhaps you know him."

"I don't but I'm sure my father did," Alerio responded. "Your troop's charges at the blue capes helped sell the attack this morning. I wanted to get your name and to thank you."

"Magnus Cotta, sir," the cavalryman said. "If you put my name in the report to the Senate, it will make my father very happy."

"I'm afraid the report will come from the Proconsul," Alerio told him. Then a flash of insight came to Alerio, and he change his mind. "You know what? I'm going to do my best to have your name read in the Senate chamber. That should please your father."

"It will, sir," Magnus assured Alerio. "If there's nothing else?"

"Dismissed," Alerio instructed with a wave of his hand.

But his mind wasn't on the departure of the young cavalryman. Alerio was back to analyzing things. Things that needed to be clear in his head before he met with Proconsul Florus.

***

Every town under siege sported one feature. Along every block, down the alleyways, and side streets, piles of ash and charred wood marked the place of a cookfire. The city's defenders were careful to haul in firewood to make their posting as comfortable as possible. But they weren't efficient in cleaning up after the battle. Eventually, wind and rain would wash away the debris.

Alerio and his four-man escort walked their horses around the spots of cold campfires.

"You can go see your people at the garrison," Alerio offered. "I can make my way from here."

"We can't do that, sir," one cavalryman advised. "Centurion Mystacis said to stay with you until you returned to Poggio Ridente or left Palermo."

"Why would I ever go back to Poggio Ridente?"

"We don't know, Senior Tribune. It's one option," another rider answered for the group. "We are your First Century until you leave."

"Do I need bodyguards?" Alerio questioned.

"Centurion Mystacis said with the way you left Palermo you might."

"But I'm a Senior Tribune."

"Yes, sir. That's why you have a First Century."

"You might be only four Legionaries, but you seem dedicated," Alerio remarked. "Let's go."

They rode down the main street, dodging the rubble of old campfires. On the far side of the city, the party turned right onto Via Roma. At the villa, an Optio and six infantrymen blocked their way.

"The Consul and Proconsul are meeting," the NCO exclaimed. "No visitors."

"I'm Senior Tribune Sisera of the Sicilia Legion," Alerio told him. "I need…"

252

"Spears," the Optio ordered. The six shafts dropped, and the steel heads targeted Alerio. "Sir, I've orders to take you into custody."

Cavalry horses were trained to respond to handsfree commands. When the spears lowered, the four horsemen applied pressure with their knees. By the time the NCO finished the word 'custody', the six infantrymen were on their backsides after being knocked over by the horses. And the dismounted cavalrymen held naked blades in their hands.

"You go in, sir," one of his escorts advised. "We've got this under control."

"I'm not sure you'll be safe," Alerio worried. "I don't want to be responsible for bloodshed between Legions."

Behind him, the gate creaked and Alerio whirled around to face the new threat. But no threat appeared. Instead, Optio Tatiana and Tesserarius Fidenas saluted. Behind them a squad of Sicilia Legion infantrymen waited inside the gateway.

"Can you tell me what this is about?" Alerio asked his former bodyguard and valet.

"We don't know, Senior Tribune," Tatiana replied. "The Consul said for safety reasons, his Legion would have security outside the villa. We have the inside. So please sir, you and your personal guards come in."

"And these guys," a cavalryman inquired. He pointed his blade at the infantrymen.

"They were assigned to guard the street," Fidenas observed while opening the gate to accommodate the horses. "We'll leave them to it."

Alerio marched through the portal wondering if the Consul really feared an attack from inside Palermo. Or, if the infantrymen were there to detain a specific Senior Tribune.

***

Consul Lucius Metellus occupied one side of the table and Proconsul Aquillius Florus the other. As if a barrier intentionally placed between them, they had stacked pieces of parchment in the center. At forty-two years old, Metellus had just reached the age requirement for a Consul. Florus, at sixty-two, had served as a Consul nine years earlier.

Also separating the two, Lucius Metellus represented the slick politicians who grew in power from the expansion of the Republic. On the backs of the Legions, they bent the rules of treaties and pushed enemies, almost daring them to resist. Most foreign governments and tribes didn't, out of fear of the Legions.

A foil to the brash new breed, Aquillius Florus embodied the diplomats who worked for years to hold the fledgling Republic together. Before the conflict with Qart Hadasht, the highland and lowland tribes required encouragement to remain part of the Republic. When a tribe broke a treaty, a Legion marched on a portion of the rebellious territory. Thus, the troubles remained localized, leaving room from diplomatic solutions.

"…and so, you can see the reasoning, Florus. It's better for everyone if the Consul's Legions take credit for routing the Empire army," Metellus articulated his argument in an overly smooth manner. "Besides, this is not a fight you can win, should you report otherwise."

Alerio stood at the doorframe listening to the words and seething. After a deep breath to calm his anger, he strutted into the room.

"Proconsul Florus, good morning," Alerio greeted the older man. He added a salute before continuing. "I have two officers from the Sicilia Legion who deserve medals."

"Sisera, we're way beyond that sort of thing," Metellus scolded. "The Consul's Legions will take credit and the Proconsul will receive compensation through other channels."

"Sir, these two men risked their lives and limbs to serve you," Alerio protested. "Surely, their deeds can't be ignored."

"What deeds could they have performed?" Metellus mocked. "My marching Legions carried the battle. Isn't that right, Florus?"

A tremor ran down Aquillius Florus' hand. It didn't stop until the Proconsul made a fist.

"What deeds?" he inquired while pressing the clenched fingers into his chin.

"Magnus Cotta rode his cavalry troop into the spears of General Gisco's elite guards, numerous times," Alerio answered. "Because of his bravery, the reserves left their position on the riverbank to defend the army's treasury. You can't award him a medal and get a commendation from the Senate unless you acknowledge his acts."

"What act?" Metellus growled. "If he wasn't there."

"Troop Leader Cotta drew the reserves away from Palermo, allowing the Consul's Legions to enter the battlefield against even odds," Alerio responded. He pulled a letter from a pouch and placed it in front of the Proconsul. "I've written up the certificate of endorsement."

A noise rose in Consul Metellus' throat. Before it fully voiced his disapproval of the proceedings, Aquillius Florus shot out his arm and extended a finger as if it was a dagger.

"Hush, I'm reading," the Proconsul ordered.

With a huff, Lucius Metellus crossed his arms and waited.

After reading the certificate twice, the Proconsul rested it on the table.

"I noticed that you signed it Lictor Sisera, a witness," Florus commented to Alerio. "And not as Senior Tribune Sisera, the commanding officer."

Metellus slapped his hand on the tabletop and almost came out of his chair.

"Fine, I acknowledge the accomplishments of young Cotta," the Consul asserted. "I know his father and the old man will love hearing his son's name read before the Senate. And he'll brag for a year about pinning a medal for bravery on the chest of his progeny."

"I'm glad we're not going to argue about this," Florus remarked.

"Although, I do have one stipulation," Consul Metellus warned. "I will co-sign the warrant, but the name Alerio Carvilius Sisera must be stricken from the document. Do that, and I'll present the certificate of bravery to the Senate myself."

Slowly, Aquillius Florus elevated his eyes to Alerio's face. He expected to see anger, or at least the tension of a building rant. Instead, a smile crossed the Lictor's face.

"That's agreeable to me," Alerio offered. He grabbed another letter from the pouch and laid it beside the first.

"And I have a letter of commendation for Centurion Bulbus Flictus for leadership above and beyond his station."

***

"No, no, I've already given away too much," Metellus complained.

His words were that of a merchant in a trade negotiation and not those of a leader of the Republic. This time, it was the Proconsul's hand that smacked the tabletop.

"Are these bushels of grain we're discussing? Carts of radishes or a crop of olives?" Florus chastised the Consul. "No. No you said. Well let me say no, no to your indignation. We, Consul, are discussing honor. We are judging the bravest of our sons. Men of our Legions who deserve a fair hearing for their deeds. Now shut the Hades up, while I read."

Lucius Metellus was a man of many faces. Alerio knew him as a false friend. He had seen the cruelty and selfishness when the Consul had the upper hand. And now Alerio recognized him as a coward, fearful that he couldn't keep all the honor for himself.

"Surrounded by the mercenary army, Bulbus Flictus held his small detachment together in the face of overwhelming odds," Florus read. "As the only combat officer of the Legion on the field of battle, he was instrumental in holding the enemy at bay until relieved by the marching Legions. In recognition of his leadership, Centurion Flictus has earned the gratitude of the Republic and should be honored accordingly. Again, signed Lictor Alerio Sisera, witness."

"He's an officer doing his job," Metellus griped. "Why are we even entertaining this certificate?"

"Well, as I read..." the Proconsul began.

"Sir, if I might have a say?" Alerio asked.

"I do have your letter," Florus reminded Alerio. Then he pondered the written words for a moment before saying. "You have something to add, Lictor Sisera?"

"Centurion Flictus is the nephew of a sitting Senator," Alerio informed the two senior politicians. "That alone is good for you both. On top of his affiliation, Bulbus Flictus is a citizen of the Republic and a son of Sicilia. Among those beaming at his medal ceremony will be his uncle's faction, and members of the greens supporting the building of infrastructure and roads in Sicilia. Plus, the whites for the trade our settlers on Sicilia bring to Rome. And finally, the reds will cheer because they believe Sicilia was always fated to become part of the Republic. For those reasons gentlemen, Centurion Flictus must be rewarded." Metellus and Florus had a brief staring contest before the Consul spoke, "You know my condition. Delete Alerio Carvilius Sisera's name from the certificate, and I'll support it."

With a pained expression on his face, Aquillius Florus looked at Alerio.

"Nothing that I didn't see coming, Proconsul," Alerio acknowledged.

"You know Sisera, I expected that our talks had helped you," Florus remarked. "But your political gamesmanship is lacking. Maybe I should amend that to say, it's totally absent."

"Sir, if I might suggest, you'll want to get the Consul's signature in writing and his seal for the awards and commendations," Alerio proposed. "You see, sir, I did learn something."

Aquillius Florus waved over his secretary and one of the Consul's aids. After receiving instructions, the assistants took the letters and moved to another room.

***

"That will be all, Lictor Sisera," Metellus said, dismissing him.

"Consul, I acquiesced to your demands to assure the awards went to the Senate," Alerio argued. "The least you can do is allow me to witness the signing of the certificates."

"In duplicate," Proconsul Florus added. "This is hard negotiations, Sisera. Go stand in the corner and watch. You might learn something."

With the permission of both the Consul and Proconsul, Alerio marched to a table with glasses and a pitcher of wine. He poured a glass and listened to the Co-Consul of the Republic and the Proconsul of Sicilia as he sipped. Both men carried the seal of the Roman Senate and the proxy authority of the legislative body.

"I've already sent the partition for a triumph to the Senate," Metellus informed the Proconsul. "I expect your report, with two exceptions, will support my request."

"There's nothing preventing me from giving my wholehearted support to your parade," Florus told him. "As long as you don't expect me to attend. I hate the spectacle of watching a thousand defeated mercenaries marched through the streets of the Capital."

"The citizens love the display of might by our Legionaries," Metellus gushed. "And I enjoy the parties at the grand villas for the weeks that follow."

They talked about the logistics of feeding the marching Legions while they chased the Qart Hadasht army to the sea.

At a point in the discussion, the secretaries returned with the documents.

Florus and Metellus read a set then scratched their names and stamped the pages. Then they exchanged the sheets for review and signing by the other party.

"And that is that," Metellus announced. With squinting eyes, the Consul leered at Alerio and ordered. "You can leave now, Lictor Sisera."

Alerio marched across the room and stood close to the Proconsul.

"Proconsul Florus, do I have your word that the awards will be presented for Cotta and Flictus?"

"You do. I have legally binding documents to that affect," Florus assured him.

"And, has the title Lictor and my name, Alerio Carvilius Sisera been removed from all documents?"

"Unfortunately, they have been, Alerio," the Proconsul told him. "For the sake of your deceased father, I am sick about it."

"You have what you wanted, Sisera," Metellus exclaimed. "And I have what I wanted. Now get out while real men do business."

"Yes, sir," Alerio said acknowledging the order.

He marched three step towards the door before turning around.

"Proconsul Florus, I almost forgot. What do you want me to do with your share of the spoils of war?"

Consul Lucius Metellus jerked when he realized he had missed something during the negotiations.

Jumping to his feet, he screamed, "What spoils of war?"

Act 9

Chapter 25 – To the Victor

Aquillius Florus canted his head to one side, then tilted it to the other. Almost as if he was trying to bring Alerio Sisera into focus. After several rotations, he addressed Alerio directly.

"Enlighten me, Lictor Sisera," he requested. "What enemy property have you seized, and, by all means, what is my share?"

"Sir, the Sicilia Legion captured sixty elephants during our mission to draw off the reserves," Alerio informed him. "I claim fifteen as my domatium from you as payment for my services. You, of course, are free to distribute the remaining war elephants as you see fit."

A silence fell over the room. Both Metellus and Florus weighed the social benefits of possessing elephants. Finally, Metellus interrupted the quiet.

"As the Consul/General, I'll take twenty-five for my Triumph parade," Metellus announced. "You can do whatever you want with the rest, Proconsul."

Aquillius Florus had already underestimated Alerio once. Having his title and name removed from the warrants for commendations took him out of the chain of command for the Sicilia Legion and the marching Legions. This left Alerio Carvilius Sisera as an unassigned Colonel from the Southern Legion. His participation in the battle actions were as a free senior staff officer with the right to claim his own compensation.

"What, Colonel Sisera, are you going to do with fifteen war elephants?" Florus inquired.

Lucius Metellus' mind filled with visions of crowds cheering him as he led a procession of war elephants through the streets of Rome. Slumped in his chair, the Consul's disinterest was evident in his posture.

"I plan to march them to the forum in Rome and stake them out at Temples," Alerio responded. "Fifteen elephants will draw a nice crowd for a few days. I'll take advantage of the curiosity and plead my case to the public."

"That'll get you populist support," Metellus acknowledged with a casual wave of one hand. "But you'll still lack senatorial backing. In the end, you'll be right back to being nothing."

While the Consul belittled Alerio's plan, the Proconsul held up both hands as if asking to be given something.

"After your public display," he questioned, "what will you do with the beasts?"

"Why, what every battlefield Commander does," Alerio said, "I'll walk them to the government building. There, I'll distribute them as donativa to selected Senators."

Metellus sat upright as if someone had shoved a hot poker up his cūlus.

"Just when do you plan to bribe the Senators?" he demanded.

"It'll take me eight days to transport the elephants to Ostia. Another few days to walk them to Rome," Alerio checked off the steps by extending his fingers. "Three days on display. And finally, one day to hand over the prizes to the Senators. Let's call it fifteen days to complete the objective."

"But my Legions are still in the field," Metellus protested. "I can't be ready in fifteen days. Your parade of war elephants will make mine appear as if I'm copying you. Following in your footsteps will undermine my victory at Palermo."

Alerio's face remained stony and only a flutter of his eyelids transmitted any expression.

"I hadn't considered that," he lied.

"So, you won't take your elephants to Rome," Metellus proposed.

"I didn't say that, sir," Alerio responded by smiling.

"I'll have you arrested, and the elephants seized."

"My warrant for Colonel is from the Senate," Alerio reminded the Consul. "It'll be an interesting trial because my first witness will be Proconsul Florus and both of your Battle Commanders."

The Consul didn't want his report on the battle for Palermo contradicted in front of the Senate. Backed into a corner, Lucius Metellus offered in a small voice.

"I'll seize the elephants."

"Yes, sir, that is your right," Alerio allowed. "But you'll have to find them first."

Metellus deflated as if he was a wineskin squeezed dry. As the Consul shrunk, Alerio put on his blank expression. The Proconsul appreciated that Sisera didn't gloat over his political win.

"Gentlemen, we seem to be at an impasse," Florus observed. "You both want something. Sisera, what does the Consul want?"

"Lucius Metellus wants a parade with forty war elephants, two Legions, and the recognition of his leadership at the battle of Palermo by the citizens of Rome."

"I believe that sums it up," Florus agreed. "Metellus, what does the Colonel want?"

"Alerio Sisera wants to be a Senator of Rome. A named legislator recognized by all citizens, friends, and foes of the Republic."

"It's been summed up and spoken aloud," Florus proclaimed. "Shall we commit the details to parchment?"

The Proconsul made a fist to keep his hands from shaking. This time, rather than the nervous gesture of pressing it against his chin, Aquillius Florus placed the closed hand over his heart.

"If Sisera will present the elephants to the Senators in both our names, I'll bring his nomination up in the Senate," Metellus countered.

Alerio saluted and said, "Consul, I'll see you in Rome."

His turn-about was crisp and his steps rapid as he marched to the doorway. Florus' fist came off his chest and extended like a punch towards Metellus.

"You dare to disrespect the negotiations," the Proconsul boomed. "Colonel Sisera come back here."

"Proconsul?"

"As you know a Consul cannot be removed from office," Florus explained. "But after his year as a Consul, he can be brought up on charges. I'm appointing you as my Lictor to investigate Lucius Metellus for dereliction of duty and mismanagement during the attack on Palermo."

"Florus, you can't be serious," Metellus gasped. "Even if the investigation proves nothing, it'll ruin my last months in office. Is there nothing I can do to prevent this?"

"My Lictor for the case is efficient and effective," Florus warned. "I might add, Alerio is also tenacious. If you think about it, Consul, there is really only one way to stop him."

Lucius Metellus blinked several times. As a sitting Consul, he could appoint a Senator. If he was later brought to trial and found guilty of a civil or criminal charge, his appointees could be removed. It dawned on him, Florus would be forced to drop the investigation to protect Alerio Sisera, if…

"By the power vested in me by the God Jupiter and the citizens of the Republic, I, Lucius Caecilius Metellus, Consul of Rome, appoint you, Alerio Carvilius Sisera to fill your father's seat as a Senator of the Republic."

"I will support the Senate and the people of Rome," Alerio answered.

He looked at the Proconsul.

"Let's have a drink while the papers are drawn up," Florus offered.

"In triplicate, if you please, sir," Alerio added.

"Of course, Senator Sisera."

***

The weather was pleasant during the first week of September. Dressed in his ceremonial armor, Alerio Sisera rode a stallion down the middle of the boulevard. As the lead rider in the Triumph, he received little applause.

Behind him, a crier announced, "Make way for the war elephants. These are war beasts from the Punic Coast. Imagine facing one of these brutes in combat. All cheer

General Lucius Metellus for bravely standing against these huge monsters. Make way for the war elephants. These are war beasts..."

Behind the crier, forty massive elephants lumbered through Rome. The elephants got collective gasps of astonishment from the crowd.

Alerio chuckled because trailing the elephants came the Sterculius worshipers. Men with carts and shovels, scooping up the offerings dropped by the beast to honor the God of Manure. No loud roars marked the passing of the poo carts.

Farther back, Legionaries marched in formation, their armor gleaming, their shields newly painted, and the iron bands around their scuta buffed and rust free. Calls of 'Rah' from veterans and 'Euge' marked the parade of Legionaries.

At the rear and traveling through the loudest cheering and screaming rode General/Consul Lucius Metellus, the hero of Palermo. And the man responsible for supplying the free bread that was being handed out to the population.

At the front, Alerio spotted a young man in a washed-out woolen shirt and pants. He wouldn't have given the youth a second look except for the gladius on his hip, the old sandals on his feet, and the look of wonder in his eyes. The Capital had that effect on people when they first came to Rome.

Chapter 26 – Abuse or Is It Use?

Tarquin came through the office door beside his sister. Once over the threshold, the five-year-old twins ducked down and separated. In a pincher action that would make any Legion proud, they circled Alerio's desk. Coming in from either side, they attacked their father.

"Barbarians," Alerio cried as he lifted them from the floor. "Barbarians have breached my shield wall."

The twins squealed as he lifted and lowered them rapidly. With each up and down, they laughed and screamed, "Rah!"

Gabriella eased part way into the room. She stopped and rested her back on the doorframe.

"I don't want you gone for a good long time, husband of mine," she instructed. "That Legion cheer your children are using is because they spend too much time with the household guards."

"I'll speak with Mancini about that."

"You misunderstand me, husband. He and the other guards protect the children," she explained. "But what they need is their father's influence and guidance."

"I plan to be around to provide both."

"That's good, because there's a Centurion Efrem here to see you," she told him. "I was afraid he brought news of another expedition."

"My days of running off to war are over, wife of mine."

Gabriella had to wrestle the children away from Alerio. With one under each arm, she left and a few moments later, the old combat officer marched in.

"Good morning, sir," he stated while saluting. "I wanted to report in before traveling to the training area. Mostly, because I have a question."

"Out with it," Alerio urged.

"You're building two triremes to defend your merchant fleet, I understand that," Efrem began. "But is it legal to staff them with Marines trained in Legion tactics."

"That's an interesting quandary," Alerio replied. "Socrates did say *we should care about what is actually just, not what seems just to most people.*"

"I think I liked you better when you were a little boy trying to hold up a gladius," Efrem complained. "I don't understand what Socrates has to do with my question."

"He was under a sentence of death when he said that," Alerio explained. "He meant that he considered himself guilty. As do I."

"Then why build and crew the warships, if it's wrong?"

"Because the alternative is to allow Illyrian pirates to steal from my family," Alerio told him. "I have the means to construct the ships and I have you to train the swords and shields. But is it right to abuse my authority?"

"It seems like you're using your authority to protect what's yours."

"Am I?" Alerio pondered. "Or have I become like the men who employ their power simply for the pleasure of exercising it?"

"I wouldn't know, sir."

"Unfortunately, Centurion Efrem, neither do I."

The End of Abject Authority

***

A Legion Archer is a new series from author J. Clifton Slater

With Hannibal raging through the heart of the Roman Republic in 218 B.C., the Senate decided on a daring strategy. They would attack the Punic cities of Iberia in hopes of drawing Hannibal back across the Alps. However, with so many Legionaries dead at the hands of the Carthaginian General, the Legions were short of manpower. For the daring campaign, they looked to auxiliary troops from client states and foreign mercenaries to fill out the ranks of the invading Legions. One unit proved itself invaluable during the fighting – a Band of archers from the island of Crete.

Famous in ancient eras and through medieval times, the bowman from Crete were renowned as expert marksmen. Due to their loyalty and toughness, Companies of archers from the island nation were valued as mercenaries by leaders such as General Xenophon and his 10,000 Hoplites, and Alexander the Great.

It wasn't by accident the men from the island developed expertise with the bow and arrow. Boys from Crete were schooled from an early age on how to pull the powerful bow, hit their targets, and to survive the hardships of war. According to unidentified ancient sources, "Give a Cretan enough arrows, and he will conquer the world."

Here's a sample from book #1, *Journey from Exile*

***

The mountain stream gurgled as it cascaded down the rocks before collecting into a deep pool. In summer, its waters refreshed and soothed. Hunters and hikers, fortunate enough to locate the pond, discovered the water to be a wonderful solution to a parched throat.

But in winter, ice needed to be chipped away from the edges in order to fill a waterskin. And, the cold water was sure to bring shivers to the hands that held the container. For the boy submerged in the frigid water, his tremors far exceeded simple shivers.

"Jace, stay with me," Zarek Mikolas urged in a soothing voice. "Still your breath so your hands are steady. Calm your heart so your eyes are clear. Now tell me of General Xenophon's archers."

The blue lips were shades of gray in the moonlight. While the sixteen-year-old had no color in the dark, if someone held a torch close to him, they'd see he had no color in his cheeks anyway. Beyond the almost deathly pale, the quiver of his voice and the clattering of his teeth were obvious signs of partial hypothermia.

"On the left bank of the Euphrates River, two great armies fought," Jace stammered. Pausing, he inhaled rapidly three times as if he had run sprints. "When the day ended, Cyrus the Younger was dead, his mercenary army fled, and..."

A fit of shaking sent out waves that washed back and splashed Jace's face. He jerked his head away from the dampness. As the only part of his body not submerged in the freezing pond, he attempted to keep his head dry.

"Focus, breathe," Zarek instructed. He looked to the east and searched the sky for signs of the morning. But there was nothing in the black heavens. So, he continued to offer what help he could. "Fled, and?"

"And to their dread, the Persian army sought and caught the Hoplites," the boy got out in fits and spurts. "Supplies were naught, but for the flights of arrows from Persian bowman. Plucking the spent arrows from the wounded and the ground, Cretan archers returned the gifts.

With accuracy and sacrifice, the archers held back the Persians with their own shafts. The Cretans died with honor so the ten thousand could flee to the sea."

"A fine rendition," Zarek complimented. "Stay awake boy. Don't let your body betray you."

Jace opened his mouth to yawn but his jaw rested too close to the waterline. In mid shiver, his chin dipped, and water flooded his mouth. Coughing and spitting, he threw his head back and screamed into the night.

"Enough. I've had enough," he bellowed in rage.

Despite his cries, Jace Kasia remained in the water. With only his head showing above the surface, his body convulsed while gratefully, the feeling left his feet, shoulders, and hands.

Earlier in the day, a run took him around the mountain. It lasted from midday to dusk. By the end, his legs wobbled, and he hobbled. Before then, he shots two hundred arrows with a self-bow. More than enough to cramp his left hand. With so many pulls of the bowstring, the skin on the fingers of his right hand shredded and bled. And due to the repetition of pulls and releases, the muscles of his shoulders burned as if on fire.

But now, there were no cramps in his legs, or pain in his hands, or fire in his shoulders. The bitter cold had overridden all other sensations.

Yet, Jace Kasia did not attempt to crawl out of the water. He remained in the pond at the foot of the mountain stream.

***

The winter sun offered light to the surface of the pond and the boy's stiff, cold face. And while it didn't offer warmth, its appearance offered relief.

Zarek kicked away the ice from the edge, waded out, and lifted Jace from the water. Dragging his limp form to the shore, he sat him on a fur wrap and vigorously rubbed the boy's arms, chest, and legs.

"Wait, what are you doing?" Jace questioned.

"Open your eyes and you'll see," Zarek suggested.

Slowly, Jace lifted his eyelids and peered at the sun.

"I did it?" he asked before falling back on the animal fur.

"Almost," Zarek told him. "Now it's a simple hike to the cabin."

"That's easy for you to say," Jace mumbled.

With help, he got to his feet. But then he tilted dangerously to his left.

Before he toppled over, Zarek said, "Still your breath so your hands are steady. Calm your heart so your eyes are clear. Focus your mind on the task."

Jace managed to pull the wrap around his shoulders then took a cautious step. In several unsteady paces, he moved to the trail and stumbled down the path in the direction of the cabin.

Zarek's old injury cause him to limp, but he stayed behind the boy. With a wide grin on his face and his chest expanded, the archer hobbled with pride. And despite his age and handicap, he managed to stay close in case Jace stumbled.

***

By midmorning, they reached the rise above Zarek's three room cabin. Down in the yard, a donkey sensed their presence and peered upward.

"Look, Master Mikolas, Tansy's here," Jace observed. Still groggy from the overnight ordeal, he lifted his eyes following a line of smoke drifting from the chimney. "Do you suppose Neysa is here, as well?"

"I don't think the old donkey came up here on her own," Zarek offered. "And if it's not my sister burning my firewood, the stranger better have coins."

With a renewed sense of urgency, Jace shuffled down the path. Even in his exhausted state, he outpaced the old archer. At the bottom, Tansy greeted Jace. Almost as if the donkey knew he was hurting, she walked beside him letting Jace lean on her back. At the doorway, Jace and the donkey strolled into the cabin.

"Out, get out," Neysa Kasia shouted. With an apron, she shooed the intruders back.

Jace and Tansy retreated from the fierce woman.

"No, not you, Jace. Get yourself in here and have a seat," she instructed. "I was talking to that stubborn donkey."

Jace shuffled to a rustic chair and slowly lowered himself down. Moments later, Zarek appeared in the doorframe.

"Look at the boy," Neysa growled. "He's done in and looks like death. It's a wonder you didn't kill him. Going hunting in the dark. And coming back empty handed."

Silently, Zarek limped to a storage box, untied the leather bindings, and lifted the lid.

"Are you hungry?" Neysa inquired. "You must have gone out early. You both look hungry. Come brother, sit and I'll dish out a big bowl of my pork and celery stew."

Zarek didn't address his sister. After a few more moments with his hands in the crate, he lifted out an object and turned to face the table.

"You've been tested in the ways and thrived in the adversity," Zarek exclaimed. He extended a Cretan war bow at shoulder height. Seeing the weapon and realizing the meaning of the words, Neysa Kasia brought her fists to her mouth to stifle an emotional outburst. "Today, you are no longer a boy. No longer a fieldhand or a fisherman. Today, Jace Kasia, you are a Cretan archer. To signify your right to the title, I present to you your first war bow. May it keep you safe, fed, and employed."

Jace's mouth hung open and he stared at the beautiful bow. Composed of wood, bone, and sinew, the deadly weapon could be mistaken for a polished work of art.

From behind her hands, Neysa coached, "Jace, you should take the bow. Yes, now."

With tears in his eyes, Jace stood and accepted the weapon.

"When you came to me," Neysa cried between the words, "You were a squalling little Latian child. Still wet from the sea and exhausted from the shipwreck. Now you are a Cretan man, an archer."

"But I haven't been to the Skopós," Jace protested. "Don't you have be Cretan to attend an academy? To become an archer?"

"It's true you must be born of Crete to be accepted in the Skopós," Zarek admitted. "But the 'Aim' is no more than a place for group learning. You, Jace, have passed the tests alone, and without companions to comfort you."

"Yes, yes," Neysa exclaimed while drying her eyes. "Now sit, both of you while I dish out some stew for my men."

Jace collapsed into the chair, leaned back against the cabin wall, and closed his eyes. In a heartbeat, he fell asleep. But even in slumber, he didn't release the war bow he hugged to his chest.

"Should I wake him?" Zarek asked.

"Let him rest for a while," his sister replied. "I'll warm him a bowl later."

She dished out bowls of stew and they sat at the table and ate. And as Zarek Mikolas and Neysa Kasia had done for the last twelve years, they watched over the Latian boy who washed up from the sea.

End of Sample

Journey from Exile, the first book in *A Legion Archer* series.

***

A note from J. Clifton Slater

Thank you for reading *Abject Authority*. Together we have journeyed through nineteen books with Alerio Sisera. We've participated in the major land battles of the 1st Punic War and many of the sea engagements between Carthage and Rome. And we've explored technology, the Gods, mythology, and lifestyles of cultures in the mid-Republic and several societies around the Mediterranean. With Alerio claiming a seat in the Senate, we've come to the end of his saga as I originally planned it.

Will there be more Clay Warrior Stories books? *Nescio*? In Latin, *Nescio* translates to "*I do not know the name.*" For me it means, I can't imagine the next title or another story for Alerio.

Below are some historical notes from *Abject Authority*.

Roman Republic Social Wars

160 years after the events in *Abject Authority*, the tribes of Samnites and Marsi revolted in what was called The Italian Social Wars. The conflict lasted from 91 B.C. thru 89 B.C. I used the Sabine in place of the Marsi tribe for this book to show the unrest, although only the Marsi joined in the revolt.

Both tribes had disputes with Rome over citizenship, voting rights, land distribution, and a lake drained to stop malaria and create farmland. For the Marsi, it was Lake Fucine. Fucine flooded yearly, and a number of canals were dug over the centuries to drain and control the water. While the engineering made interesting reading, the Sabine history won me over. Plus, when Roman General Dentatus drained the Sabine lake near the Rieti Valley, he created Marmore Falls.

Marmore Falls, Italy

At 541 feet, Marmore Falls is reported to be the second tallest man-made waterfall in the world. Although re-engineered to cascade over three cataracts in 1787, the waterfall remains impressive today.

The falls were created to solve the problem of disease from a stagnant swamp. Consul/General Manius Dentatus ordered his Legion engineers to dry up the swamp. Their solution was to dig a high land canal. Once completed in 271 B.C., the canal diverted the Velino River and dropped its water into the Nera River. Without the input of water, the wetland in the Rieti Valley dried up, creating farmland. Today, the combined flow of the two rivers powers hydroelectric plants on the Nera River.

Mythical Highwayman

My inspiration for the Bronze Man came from historian Cassius Dio. He described a bandit who actively satirized the Roman judicial system. Dio wrote, "Bulla Felix is never really seen when seen, never found when found, never caught when caught." The Latin name Bulla Felix translates to Lucky Charm, meaning the highwayman was probably a fictitious character.

In the best antihero tradition, Bulla never killed, but released his victims unharmed after taking their valuables. Then he distributed the wealth among the needy. As with all good myths, the Robin Hood tale goes back much farther than the 15th century.

The Bronze Man, as Lictor Alerio Sisera discovered, was not a generous thief but a gang set on rebellion. I felt compelled to use some elements of the myth in *Abject Authority*.

The Coin

The description of the coin in the story is a combination of two coins minted in 89 B.C. Both heads are of Sabine King Titus Tatius. But on one coin, his beard resembled bunches of grapes. I described that head and matched the reverse with the imprint of men carrying off women. This was one of the few times in the Clay Warrior Stories series that I've reached forward and used an object from before the year in which the book was set.

The Abduction of the Sabine Women

Whether mythology or history of the founding of Rome, or a little of each, the story of the kidnapping of the Sabine Women is fascinating. The tale gives us a glimpse into the world at the time of Rome's founding. In it are lessons about survival, betrayal, greed, justice, and the willingness to sacrifice for a greater good. I hope you enjoyed my rendition of the story of the Abduction of the Sabine Women.

Spartans and Sabines

Dionysius of Halicarnassus, in book II section 49 of the Roman Antiquities, wrote of a group of Lacedaemonians who left Sparta and settled near the Sabines. His proof for their intermingling was stated as... *"they say that many of the habits of the Sabines are Spartan, particularly their fondness for war and their frugality and a severity in all the actions of their lives."*

I don't know if the Spartans intermarried with Sabines. But you may have noted in reading the Clay Warrior Stories, whenever I find Spartans in history, they get included in the story.

Alerio's Hometown

For the Sisera farm, I picked an area around the town of Cintolese, Italy. Cintolese rests 32 miles by winding roads NW from Fiesole. An ancient Etruscan settlement, Fiesole was the trading town where Alerio got into trouble in book #1, *Clay Legionary.*

Roman Consul/General Sulla destroyed part of Fiesole in 80 B.C. as retaliation for the citizens' support of a rebellion by the Plebeian class. It was rebuilt some years later.

Fiesole continued as the center of trade in the region until 59 B.C. In that year, Julius Caesar built a settlement for his veterans next to the Arno River. Located less than three miles from Fiesole, he named the new town Fluentia. Today, Caesar's settlement is the larger of the two cities and is known internationally as Florence, Italy.

Tiberius Coruncanius

While the gulf between Plebeians/commoners and the Patrician/noblemen had closed by 251 B.C., many social restrictions still existed. One person who challenged the norm was Tiberius Coruncanius. He came from a wealthy family, became a Senator and in 280 B.C. a Consul of Rome.

Tiberius Coruncanius was a commoner who became the first Plebeian to hold the office of Pontifex Maximus, the head of all temples in Rome. As well, in a period without organized training for lawyers, Tiberius lectured to anyone who wanted to learn the Law of the Twelve Tables.

Trials at the time were handled by a law scholar called a Jurist and an Orator, a speaker who eloquently presented the case to a Magistrate. Through his teachings, Tiberius Coruncanius created a new class of Plebeian advocates for people accused of crimes.

Chariot Racing Colors

Blue, Green, White, and Red were the colors of ancient Roman chariot racing teams. Important people, including Senators of the Republic, picked their favorite color to show support and clustered under the banner of that color. I found nowhere in my readings an association between racing colors and political ideology. The connections in *Abject Authority* are purely my invention to simplify the division between characters and their politics.

Palermo / Panormus

If you look for writings on The Battle of Palermo, you'll find reports from 1676 during the Franco-Dutch War. For details on the engagement in 250 B.C. you'll need to look up the Battle of Panormus. While Panormus was an older name for the Sicilian city and more historically accurate, I used Palermo in the story for clarity.

In truth there is confusion on the reported number of war elephants commanded by General Gisco. We do know that many were captured during the battle and sent to Rome. The elephants were paraded through the streets as part of Consul Lucius Metellus' Triumph procession.

The Punic Graveyard

The Punic Necropolis of Palermo was lost to memory until 1746 A.D. during the construction of a hotel. Dating back to the 7th Century B.C., the Carthaginian graveyard accepted interred bodies and cremated remains. Individual resting places range from burial in simple pits to sarcophagi, carved in limestone and covered with terracotta tiles, and chamber tombs with steps carved in the rock for access. If you visit Palermo, the Punic Necropolis has a building built over a section and the curators offer walking tours.

Sundials/Shadow Clock

Early Egyptian sundials divided a sunlit day into 10 parts. They used five in the morning and five in the afternoon, plus a sunrise period at dawn and a sunset section at dusk. Makers of ancient shadow clocks many times inscribed a humorous or a serious motto on the base of the sundial. The motto Alerio read in the courtyard of the Proconsul's building was my creation.

Triple Filter Test

Greek Philosopher Socrates, 470–399 B.C., is credited with creating the Triple Filter Test. It's taught as a lesson to curtail gossip and rumors. Using the measure of Truth, Good, and Usefulness, a student of the filter test can better judge errant information. In its most basic form, passing the test requires the data to be either Good or Useful with Truth being the baseline.

Consuls

During the Roman Republic, the Senate elected two Consuls yearly to run the government and be the Generals of marching Legions. During their term as Rome's Chief Magistrates, they had a lot of authority. Among them, they possessed the power to appoint a Senator.

***

I appreciate emails and reading your comments. If you enjoyed *Abject Authority*, consider leaving a written review on Amazon. Every review helps other readers find the stories.

If you have comments e-mail me.

E-mail: GalacticCouncilRealm@gmail.com

To get the latest information about my books, visit my website. There you can sign up for the newsletter and read blogs about ancient history.

Website: www.JCliftonSlater.com

Facebook: Galactic Council Realm and Clay Warrior Stories

I am J. Clifton Slater and I write military adventure both future and ancient.

***

Other books by J. Clifton Slater:

Novels of the 2nd Punic War - *A Legion Archer series*
#1 Journey from Exile   #2 Pity the Rebellious
#3 Heritage of Threat   #4 A Legion Legacy

Historical Adventure - *Clay Warrior Stories series*

#1 Clay Legionary
#2 Spilled Blood
#3 Bloody Water
#4 Reluctant Siege
#5 Brutal Diplomacy
#6 Fortune Reigns
#7 Fatal Obligation
#8 Infinite Courage
#9 Deceptive Valor
#10 Neptune's Fury
#11 Unjust Sacrifice
#12 Muted Implications
#13 Death Caller
#14 Rome's Tribune
#15 Deranged Sovereignty
#16 Uncertain Honor
#17 Tribune's Oath
#18 Savage Birthright
#19 Abject Authority

Fantasy – *'Terror & Talons'* series
#1 Hawks of the Sorcerer Queen
#2 Magic and the Rage of Intent

Military Science Fiction - *'Call Sign Warlock'* series
#1 Op File Revenge
#2 Op File Treason
#3 Op File Sanction

Military Science Fiction – *'Galactic Council Realm'* series
#1 On Station

#2 On Duty
#3 On Guard
#4 On Point

Printed in Great Britain
by Amazon